A DARK
WHIMSY

DS LaLonde

ISBN: 979-8-218-84302-1

DEDICATION

For WCL

BOOKS BY DS LALONDE

A Dark Whimsy

The Savage Panacea Series

A Bleak Remedy

A Multitude of Menaces

The Fiends and Paragons Series

The Entangled Dragon

An Infernal Bugbear

1 FAIRIES

"Fairies," growled the unwashed man leaning against the bar, his voice raised so it would carry over the classic rock music. A few heads turned his way, but the speaker kept staring ahead, draft beer to his lips. Next to him, a friend snickered.

Spoken aloud as it was, instead of spelled, the word might have referred to ferries, the marine vessels that carry cars and trucks across a body of water. Or perhaps to the magical beings from folklore.

But, being honest, he didn't seem like a folklore buff who might be interested in pixies, elves, or sprites. Perhaps the watercraft might have intrigued him, although why he would so pointedly announce that in the tavern was unclear.

The conversations around him lulled for a moment, a collective holding of breath, expectant of more. He continued drinking, giving his mesh trucker hat a tug, as if for luck. It was cocked off to the side, held on by naught but grease, wood chips, and pomade. The hat displayed the name of the company he worked for, Cayuga Logging and Reforestation. Beyond the hat, he wore a flannel shirt, faded jeans, and leather boots, all of which he'd worn to work that day, out in the trees.

Those in his group were all dressed similarly, and they were of two general body types—either lean or potbellied. The speaker was of the lean sort, wiry and hard from years in the logging industry, sawing down trees and loading them on trucks to be carted away to the mill.

After a moment, he repeated himself, removing all doubt as to his meaning. "Fairies," he snorted, the slurred word laden with derision. He craned his head to look into a darkened corner, peering over the heads of his drinking buddies. "Damn fairies," he elaborated, with a curt nod.

In the corner sat two men at a table. They'd been holding

hands, whispering to one another, bothering no one. Sensing the attention, one of them removed his hand from his partner's and instead wrapped it around his beer, a move that clearly irritated his companion. Suddenly mum, they kept their eyes down, pleasant conversation now over. The one who had pulled his hand away blushed, seeming to draw into himself, shrinking before their very eyes. The other man fumed, lips pinched shut, brow furrowed in anger.

Upset as he might have been, he said nothing, since he and his partner were drastically outnumbered. He'd fought losing battles before and was willing to take the bumps and bruises but didn't want the same for his partner.

The logging crew was the dominant force within the tavern, drinking away their Friday night. There were several of them, hardened from long days working with axes, feller bunchers, and chainsaws. Some of the loggers laughed and grinned at their friend's pronouncement, even as another looked irritated, and yet another became suddenly uneasy. Another looked embarrassed, or perhaps even mortified, and winced in the direction of the couple in the corner as he pulled back from the rest of the crew, distancing himself but saying nothing.

Nervous shifting about ensued from the other patrons, those who weren't part of the logging crew.

Among them were an older couple drinking wine.

Also, a lean person in a dark-blue baseball hat at the far end of the bar from the gay couple.

And a trio of middle-aged women, who had been happily whispering amongst themselves but were now shaking their heads and tsk-ing.

The only ones oblivious to the drama playing out were the teens at the dartboard. In their defense, they were too young to legally be at the bar, so they could be excused for lacking familiarity with the resident social cues. They were so taken with being served drinks that the roof could have come crashing down and they wouldn't have noticed until it was too late to escape.

The bartender, an aging Black man, frowned but said nothing, instead continuing to resolutely stare at the television, perhaps wishing he was somewhere else.

There was a scrape of chairs as a man and woman in their late twenties hurriedly left, leaving half-finished drinks. They had decided to continue their date elsewhere. Someplace without inebriated louts, if possible.

The only other people present were Jeff and Owen. Jeff was an entirely nondescript guy in his early twenties—tanned skin, brown hair, brown eyes, of average height and weight, neither handsome nor notably not so. His best friend Owen was taller, wider of shoulder, and far more handsome. Owen's eyes were blue and his shoulder-length hair was blond. He looked like nothing so much as a "handsome surfer dude" delivered from central casting. If Jeff were provided by central casting, he would have probably played "background guy number three."

Jeff shuffled his feet, sipped his beer, and cringed. There was a lot of cringing going on. The situation was tense. He knew the men at the bar. The loudmouth's name was Murray. Hopefully Murray would settle down and shut up. Jeff really hoped so. So far, his taunts had been reasonably harmless, or at least harmless enough to not risk getting beaten up over. Ideally it wouldn't come to that, but if there was violence Jeff knew he'd be dragged into it. He really, really hoped that didn't happen.

He thought about stepping in and pulling rank on Murray and his pals. In a way, Jeff was their supervisor. Sort of. But just barely, since he was more of a go-between, carrying messages and directions from the real bosses.

Across the beer-sloshed table from Jeff, Owen leaned

forward, watching Murray, ready to leap in and do something. He wasn't likely to sit still much longer. Once it became certain Murray was angling to start trouble, Owen would intercede.

Jeff readied himself, since he'd back Owen in whatever he did. That's what best friends do.

"Fairies," Murray muttered again, as though he were contemplating the word, letting it roll around in his mouth to get the flavor of it. Whatever the flavor was, he enjoyed it, for he seemed intent on repeating it over and over, as many times as it would take to reach whatever action his inebriated mind sought.

In the darkened corner, the more apprehensive, or perhaps wiser, target of Murray's taunting urged his friend to leave. But his friend refused.

Murray downed a shot and kept sporadically glancing at the couple, mumbling evilly as he did so. A few of his cronies did the same. They were followers, while Murray was their boozy leader.

"Fairies make me sick," Murray announced. But not so sick as to stop drinking, Jeff noted.

It was too much. Jeff had just resigned himself to stepping in when someone else spoke up, relieving he and Owen of the moral burden for a moment.

"You leave them boys alone," hissed one of the trio of women. She wore big dangly earrings and heavy makeup, although not enough to hide the infuriated red glow on her cheeks.

"I's just kidding," slurred Murray. Craning his head back, he examined the woman carefully, then gave her an ornery squint that lacked so much as a hint of repentance.

With a carefree belch, Murray turned his attention back to the bar, only to find that the lean person in the dark-blue baseball hat was now standing next to him.

4

Jeff thought the person was vaguely familiar but wasn't sure from where. It was a small town though, so everyone was at least a bit familiar.

The stranger was tall, looming over the loggers. And very attractive. Either handsome or beautiful in Jeff's lexicon, depending on if they were a man or woman, which wasn't immediately clear. Jeff assumed they were a woman since he found them attractive, but on further consideration decided on man.

He had sharp features, including a pointy chin and high cheekbones. Long light-brown hair the hue of tree bark kissed by the first sunrays of dawn spilled from under his baseball cap and flowed down into his jacket.

He or she, probably he, asked, "And fairies are bad, are they?" His voice was soothing, oddly reminiscent of the tinkling of bells. He smelled of springtime, blooming wildflowers, and fresh rain.

"Well sure," Murray responded with the belligerent confused certainty of someone either truly drunk or notably dimwitted. As it happened, Murray was both.

The bar quieted. Except for the teenagers, who kept on giggling as they flung their darts and drank their drinks. Also, the music was unaffected, continuing in all its 80s rock glory.

"How so?" the stranger asked, with such sincere inquisitiveness that he might have been seeking the answer to life's greatest mystery. He leaned forward, encroaching on Murray's personal space. It wasn't particularly threatening, but then again it was.

"Just saying it's wrong, is all." Murray shifted uncomfortably under the stranger's intense scrutiny. He leaned back, his withdrawal halted by the wooden bar behind him.

"Wrong? What do you know about fairies?" The stranger cocked his head, inspecting Murray like a featured display in a

5

museum of archaic oddities.

"Not much," Murray snorted, elbowing his nearest crony. That man kept his head down, not liking the vibe rolling off this tall stranger.

The stranger leaned forward as if to whisper in Murray's ear, although he spoke even louder than he had thus far. "I see. Well, I applaud you for admitting your overwhelming ignorance. But still, I must insist you stay quiet on this topic."

After, the stranger giggled, a happy enough noise, although unconstrained and either menacing or jolly, Jeff couldn't decide which.

"I can say what I want. What are you, one of them? You look like you could be." Murray's gaze probed his drinking buddies, seeking support but finding only downturned eyes and shuffling feet.

The stranger paused, an unnaturally wide grin playing across his pink lips, stretching from ear to ear. It was a feral smile, bereft of goodwill, stacked high with warning and perfect teeth.

After an uncomfortably long span of time, seconds dragging on into eternity, during which Murray squirmed and sipped his beer, the stranger said, "Let me remind you that your time on this earth is frightfully short. What's more, life is full of repercussions."

Murray turned away, setting both elbows on the bar. It was a retreat, as certain as if he'd blown a bugle and waved a white flag. "Whatever," he muttered.

The stranger reached out and gave Murray's shoulder a friendly squeeze. "Anyway, enjoy your drink. I wish you pleasant journeys." With that, he returned to the far end of the bar and ordered a bourbon.

Minutes passed, the bar's atmosphere returning to relatively normal, if somewhat reserved. Except the teens, one of whom staggered outside to vomit, unaccustomed as he was to anything stronger than the occasional stolen sip of wine from his mom's glass. His friends laughed. The bartender scowled but continued to serve them.

Eventually Murray, after downing a shot of something cheap and brown, went to the bathroom. It was an uneasy odyssey, full of staggers, burps, and bumped chairs.

While Murray was in the bathroom, the couple he'd been harassing exited the bar. They nodded to the stranger while walking out, receiving nothing but a quizzical look in return.

When Murray came back, his fly was only partially zipped, a flap of faded blue flannel poking out, sopping wet. After peering slowly around and registering the absence of his taunting targets, he walked out the door, not sparing a glance at the tall stranger. "Y'all wait here," he announced, which was unnecessary, since no one was inclined to follow him.

Jeff fidgeted, uncertain what Murray had in mind. He imagined the couple were far enough away that the drunk bastard wouldn't find them, if that was his plan. But then again, perhaps not. "Maybe we should head outside," he cautiously offered, hoping Owen wouldn't want to.

Owen nodded, gulped the remainder of his draft beer, and said, "Probably a good idea, just to check on stuff."

Yet, before they'd stood, the tall stranger set his drink down and walked out the door.

Jeff and Owen exchanged contemplative looks, communing with their eyes as only best friends can. Reaching an unspoken mutual decision, they sat back down and opened their phones to pour their respective attentions into them. Whatever the stranger intended, he seemed capable of doing it without them, and if Murray learned a lesson, it was all the better.

Murray didn't come back. Neither did the stranger.

The trio of women left, chatting about where their kids

would be attending college.

Their departure shook Jeff loose from the hypnotic trance of social media. "We might as well go," he said.

"Yup." Owen stood up, stretching languidly.

They'd only made it a few steps before the shrill screams began outside. Jeff and Owen joined the rush to the exit, finding one of the trio of women, she of the big dangly earrings, pointing up with one hand while her other was melodramatically clamped over her mouth. The clamp was ineffective though, as another garbled shriek came pouring out of her.

Following her pointing finger, Jeff's gaze went up, up, up.

Next door to the bar, wedged between it and a coffee shop, was a dog park. In the middle of that dog park was a huge tree. It was thick-trunked and bendy, sending a myriad of branches sprawling hither and yon, casting the park in shade through most of the day.

The first thing Jeff saw in the streetlight's illumination was a dangling pair of work boots amongst the leafy branches, at least twenty feet off the ground. They were Murray's boots, which he knew since Murray was still wearing them.

Murray was clutched in the tree's wooden embrace, entwined in the branches as if they'd grown there over decades. Vines and boughs held him tight, twigs decorating his body. One branch, as thick as Jeff's wrist, was curled around Murray's neck, holding it bent at a sharp angle. Above his newly crooked neck, his dead eyes were open and bulging, his tongue poking from his mouth, which was thrown wide as if gasping for enough air to scream.

2 WINTERBOTTOM'S COFFEE SHOP

All things considered, it hadn't been the best weekend. Nor had it been relaxing. Jeff had spent most of Saturday and part of Sunday dealing with Murray's death, recounting his recollections to the police, again and again. And then to his bosses. And then to the other workers. Then there'd been the matter of shuffling the work crews to account for Murray's loss, which he'd been forced to participate in, even though he didn't know enough to be very helpful, having only been on the job a few months.

Although Murray's death was officially being labeled as a suicide, Jeff had sincere doubts about that. If it was a suicide, it was an awfully strange one. More likely, it was an inebriated escapade gone horribly wrong.

The way Jeff saw it, Murray had climbed up into the tree in some drunken crackpot scheme. Then, through an improbable twist of fate, he must have gotten a limb wrapped around his neck, a thick unbending limb, that had somehow formed just right to cradle his throat. And then he'd slipped, breaking his neck and slowly choking to death as he dangled above the dog park. It was unlikely and awful, yet Jeff couldn't deny the karma involved, even if it was a particularly lopsided version of karma. Of course, he didn't share that karma thought with anyone except Owen. They'd conversationally beat that topic to death Saturday night over beers and *Halo*.

But despite the dearth of weekend rest or fun, Monday morning arrived. The sun was over the horizon and beating down unmercifully, amping up the humidity and setting the bugs to buzz.

On his way to Winterbottom's Coffee Shop, Jeff's attention was caught by the droopy police tape encircling the dog park. The yellow tape was already being ignored, as life had moved on. Within its cautionary perimeter, a man was staring at his phone while his beagle relieved itself by the tree Murray had swung from.

Despite being mesmerized by the beagle's obsessive scratching of the soil after it finished its business, Jeff continued his quest for coffee. Yet, he was preoccupied, having just got off the phone with his Uncle Chet, who was also his boss. Nothing Chet said was particularly interesting, but it did put Jeff in a mind to think about life in general.

Uncle Chet was a nice, jovial sort of guy, unlike his brother, Jeff's dad.

Jeff's dad was a noncommissioned officer in the Army. He was an unpleasant man, completely shorn of any vestiges of good humor when his wife, Jeff's mother, died several years ago. Cancer had swept in like a tornado, upending their relatively happy lives, leaving Jeff and his dad with no one but each other, which wasn't enough for either of them.

Jeff had been thrilled to leave home and start college, desperate to escape the oppressive gloom his dad generated. He'd never looked back. Lonely and in desperate need of a friend, he'd met Owen the first afternoon of the first day of his freshman year. They'd been best of friends ever since.

He'd chosen psychology as a major, mostly since he didn't know what else to do with himself. Owen majored in computer and information sciences. In hindsight, that was a much better choice than psychology. Knowledge of computers was the kind of thing that helped one actually become gainfully employed.

After graduating, Jeff faced the unforgiving fact that he didn't know what to do and had no particular prospects. That wasn't unusual, most of his friends were in the same boat.

Mercifully, Uncle Chet had offered him a job, so he'd taken it. He'd balked at first, since mowing down trees felt wrong. But he relented once Chet convinced him their extensive reforestation efforts were well ahead of industry standard, though current industry standards were a mystery to Jeff, so he had to trust Chet on that one. And Chet's company, Cayuga Logging and Reforestation, tried to stay carbon neutral, even if that was difficult. Okay, totally impossible.

So began Jeff's illustrious logging career, right there in the small town of Cayuga. Luckily Owen had come along, since he could work from anywhere in his new job doing something computer-y that Jeff didn't understand.

One hurdle to Jeff's success was that he didn't know anything about the logging industry. Or about trees in general. But he knew a few things. Birches, oaks, and maples, those were your hardwoods. That's because they weren't pines. And pine trees had needles. Both hardwoods and pines were important, and the surrounding area was a mixed forestry region, meaning there were patches of both leafy trees and piney trees. That pretty much covered his body of knowledge. Beyond that, he listened to what Chet said into his earpiece, then conveyed that to the actual workers, which earned him the title of supervisor, providing him with a completely undeserved position of mild authority, wholly derived from nepotism.

He often wondered if he should go back to school. But for what? Computer something? Maybe forestry? In his most private and fanciful version of the world, Jeff wanted to go to medical school. Unfortunately for that plan, he hadn't been gifted with a vast intellect, nor the boundless curiosity or inherent drive required to overcome that lack of genius. Also, his grades had been only middling. And there was the stumbling block that he wasn't that interested in medicine, but rather just in being a doctor, mostly to make money and rub it in his dad's face.

Jeff was broken from his existential occupational reverie by

11

Ivy, who was just leaving the coffee shop. She was a consummate distraction, the enemy of focused reasoning.

Ivy had sparkly glitter on her face and her flowery sundress. The sparkles seemed to move and sway if you stared long enough. He was convinced they floated in the air around her as well, sparkles and shimmers dancing through her personal atmosphere. However, it was difficult to say, since Jeff didn't look at her for too long, for fear of being caught ogling.

She was immensely beautiful, with tinkling laughter, a tangled mane of long red hair, and huge green eyes. Her skin was pale, bordering on stark white even though she always seemed to be outside. Ivy was light on her feet and full of energy, barely engaging the ground as she moved, always giggling as though life was her own insider joke. She came and she went, appearing and disappearing seemingly at random, leaving a faint trail of a pleasant smell Jeff couldn't identify. Something flowery and natural, not generated by stodgy scientists in a lab.

She drifted to Jeff's side, sundress swirling and drifting as if gravity didn't apply. "I love these frappes," she gushed, as though continuing a conversation.

Ivy sipped from the reusable straw thrust into her huge tumbler. Her eyes, which up close seemed unbelievably large and impossibly bright green, burrowed into Jeff's mind, spreading confusion.

Not entirely sure if she really knew his name, Jeff was immediately tongue-tied. She had that effect on people, disorienting like one of those tricky pictures you had to look at just right to see the image hidden within. He blushed and managed to awkwardly mutter, "Yeah, me too. Frappes are … my favorite."

She giggled, which felt like it was at him, not with him. "What kinds have you tried?"

"Um, the … uh." Racking his brain for flavors, Jeff came up dry. What was a frappe again? A fog rolled in whenever she talked to him.

Green eyes glistening, Ivy giggled some more. It had a jocular malevolence to it. She said, "I used the last of my money on this. Can I have some of yours?"

After a short infinity of his attention wandering down confused highways, Jeff realized his wallet was in his hands, being proffered up to her. She took what he had, then laughed at him. With a sweet smile, she gently touched his cheek, cradling it lovingly, before giving it a slap that rocked his head back on his neck.

Ivy turned away, coming face to face with an old woman in a straw sun hat.

"Nice lid," she said, plucking the hat off the older woman's head. The woman didn't seem to notice beyond a confused, slack-jawed smile.

Donning her new hat, which she had to force down over her crown of red tresses, Ivy floated off, leaving the ground behind as if it were a burden for others, but not her.

Feeling a befuddled disconnection, Jeff returned to his coffee house trek.

Mental fugue clearing a second later, he spun back to get another look at Ivy. She was gone, although she hadn't actually floated away, obviously. He knew that. People didn't float, except in water.

Anyway, Ivy was special. She'd been in town a few months, just a bit less than Jeff had been. Yet, within days, she'd known everyone. People flocked to her like mosquitoes to campers, even if no one knew much about her.

This is perhaps a good time for a few words about Jeff's love life, or lack thereof.

Before he headed off to college, his family had moved with

great regularity, as his father's military service shuttled them from one base to another. Not being particularly outgoing—and lacking sufficient charisma, athleticism, or attractiveness to overcome that shortcoming—had rendered Jeff girlfriend-less, spending his high school years looking on from the dating sidelines.

Matters improved in college, where he'd had an arbitrary, standard-issue girlfriend throughout the entire four years. Her name had been Diana, and she'd been a mathematics major, very buttoned down, very uptight.

And, most importantly, very religious. The sort of religious that took celibacy seriously, to the point where she and Jeff had kissed on many occasions, although without much fervor, as though they were accountants sealing a strange deal. But it had never gone further than that, which had been difficult, and … frustrating. Jeff would have been entirely exuberant to advance their relationship into the realm of sex without the slightest reservation and he'd always assumed she would come around to his way of thinking, but Diana was a brick wall of chastity.

Months ago, at the end of their senior year, Diana informed him they had broken up. She had decided, she told him, that they had no future since he wasn't serious enough about the Lord, nor his profound teachings. She'd noticed he only went to church when she made him, and she had sincere doubts as to his devotion to the Christian way of life she planned for herself and her future children.

In fairness, all that was true. Jeff had no particular feelings on religion or church beyond the obvious, such as agreeing that you should be kind to others. That one went without saying. Other than that, he disagreed with a lot of the church's stances, which caused endless friction with Diana through the years. Upon reflection, he was surprised she kept him as long as she did.

After the breakup, Jeff had initially been upset but quickly came to realize he'd dodged a bullet. He was sad, but not too sad, mostly simply regretting the years spent trying to convince himself he loved her, which in hindsight he didn't, if he understood love correctly. His time with Diana had been occasionally fun, frequently onerous, but always better than being alone. And thus, his college years had passed in chaste dating servitude.

Regretfully, as it played out, he'd never been intimate with Diana. Or with anyone. Ever. Owen was the only person he'd ever confessed his virginity to. That's the way it was, Owen knew everything about him and he knew everything about Owen.

Anyway, Ivy was Diana's polar opposite, a carefree wild child. Perhaps that was why he found her so fascinating.

And that was part of the problem, in that he suspected he was too boring for Ivy's tastes. Most of his weeknights were spent with Owen in front of the TV, playing video games or streaming shows. Then Friday and Saturday nights were for the bar. So, five out of seven nights would probably bore her silly, since Ivy didn't seem like a hang-around-the-house type. It was easier to imagine her dancing naked around a fire deep in the woods or rampaging through a rave at five in the morning.

Rationally, Jeff needed someone who was more his speed, which was, he felt, a rather adult admission to have confronted.

He entered Winterbottom's Coffee Shop, his cheek still stinging from Ivy's robust slap.

The coffee shop was family owned and operated. The Winterbottoms, a married couple, were an English guy and Asian woman in their fifties, give or take. Hard to say how they'd ended up in the middle of nowhere, USA, since they were decidedly more urbane than most of the townsfolk.

Speaking of someone more his speed, Carla was behind the

counter, just as she always was. Jeff was fairly certain she was a Winterbottom, probably the daughter of the owners, but he hadn't asked. It felt as though asking would require a level of familiarity they didn't yet have.

Unlike Ivy, Carla was an entirely reasonable prospect for dating.

Carla was always reading, always sipping mochas. Her black hair held a few subtle artificial white streaks, just enough to make her mysterious and angsty. A single simple piercing decorated her left eyebrow and thick, black-framed glasses swallowed half her face. He liked the glasses. Moreover, he liked her. Or, he thought so, even if beyond polite conversation and ill-informed guesswork, he didn't really know much about her. Being honest, she was one of the few women around his age—that being early twenties—whom he saw regularly, so that might have been part of her appeal. Proximity breeds attraction, he recalled from a psych class.

Approaching the counter, Jeff attempted to concoct a witty opener but came up dry. He almost said, "How about that crazy suicide, eh?" It was perhaps better than nothing, but probably worse, so he kept it to himself.

She looked up from her book, a dog-eared, creased paperback where vampires and young women fall madly in love and run off together into the sunset. Or, really, after the sun sets, since, you know, vampires. Recognition dawning, she smiled and said, "Hey there, you shaved your mustache."

That was a fact, he had done that a few days ago. The mustache hadn't been working, looking more like the stubble generated by a three-day shaving embargo rather than the razor-less month he'd given it to flourish. Annoyingly, Owen could have grown half a Viking's beard in that same time. "Yeah, it wasn't really working for me."

Squinting her eyes and cocking her head, Carla gave him a

look of great consideration, suggestive of a judge pondering a potential death sentence. Finally, she said, "Shaving was a good move."

Was that a sincere compliment or was she simply being nice? Assuming the former, Jeff reflexively raced to return it.

"I like your glasses," he blurted, second-guessing the words as they fled his lips.

"Thanks," came her automatic response, barely registering the compliment. "What will you have?"

She tucked a bookmark into her paperback and set it down.

Rummaging through his repertoire of interesting comments and finding nothing there covering romantic vampire novels, he said, "Dark roast, please."

An expectant look bloomed on Carla's face, eyebrows up, a little smile as she gazed at him intently. She made no move to get coffee. So … she wanted to talk more? He was unprepared with a topic. Perhaps the weather? He imagined she was searching for something to say as well.

An awkward two seconds later, Carla asked, "What size?" She was, seemingly, vaguely annoyed.

"Oh!" he gasped, his ego deflating. "Uh, large please."

Grabbing a cup, she turned away to pour. "Where's Owen?" she asked.

That deflated him even more, such that if his ego were a helium balloon it would be a sagging latex heap unable to rise off the carpet.

But it was no surprise. As Owen's friend, Jeff felt perennially overlooked. If one were of a mind to categorize people into archetypes, Jeff was a sidekick, whereas Owen was a handsome hero. That was part of why Owen was such a great friend, since what value was there to a sidekick if he had no hero to stand beside? A lonely sidekick is just sad and meager. Without doubt, if there were any pulling swords from stones to be accomplished, it would be done by Owen.

"He's working," Jeff said.

"Well tell him to come by. We're stocking that passion fruit green tea he likes," Carla said. Reading between the lines, the vibe was quite clear that Carla hoped to see more of Owen.

"Will do," Jeff replied. Her interest in Owen wasn't the surprise of the century. Jeff had witnessed it time and again. But she was destined for disappointment, like so many others before her.

Owen wasn't attracted to girls or boys or anyone anywhere along the gender spectrum. In college, he'd dated a girl for a month or so to try it out, and because that's just what people did. They'd had sex twice, but he hadn't cared for it. Another time, Owen had dated a guy for a few weeks, but that hadn't been right either. Romantically and sexually indifferent, that was Owen's inclination. Sadly, his disinterest had left a string of politely rebuffed people, such as Carla would doubtless become, in his wake.

Leaving Winterbottom's moments later, large coffee clutched in his hand, Jeff felt bad for Carla. Owen would feel bad about it too, if he ever realized she liked him. Actually, even beyond feeling bad, Owen would be embarrassed and distressed, just as he was every time this situation arose. But his romantic elusiveness was perhaps the only way Owen would ever intentionally disappoint anyone. Letting people down horrified him.

Owen's inherent nature was entirely compassionate and valorous, with heroism hardwired into his persona. He'd simply been born that way.

All his life, he'd been the best and brightest. Everyone's friend. An altruistic, self-effacing leading man who would carry groceries for little old ladies without a second thought while always doing the right thing and putting others before himself. In other words, the sort of person everyone loved, but also found mildly annoying at times.

But Jeff theorized that Owen's propensity for heroism had to go beyond his inborn character traits. Experience must play a role as well, perhaps in the form of a childhood incident of the sort that often fuels the origins of gloomy superheroes who stalk the night looking to rebalance the scales of their lives. Somewhere in Owen's secret backstory must reside a tragic twist of fate that augmented his inherent propensity for valor, intensifying his need to help others. A fire, a murder, an abduction, something he had failed to prevent and needed karmic retribution for.

He'd once proffered that theory to Owen, hoping for an admission that would give him a peek behind the curtain of his best friend's psyche. But Owen denied it with an unassuming smile and good-natured chuckle. Even if such an event were to exist, he would take it to his grave, carrying the burden alone, never once sharing it. His problems were his own, not someone else's. Such was the way of heroes, their stoicism both a strength and a flaw.

3 MECHANIZED MURDER MACHINES

By the time Jeff got to the worksite, the day's labors were well underway. His absence had done nothing to slow them down, which was generally indicative of his average impact. His daily contributions mostly involved ghosting around the site, relaying messages from management while trying to stay out of the way.

In his few months here, he'd learned that logging was well-orchestrated chaos. There were different guys running around doing different things, most of them terrifying and deadly. The things, that is, were mostly terrifying and deadly, while only some of the guys were.

Within two hundred yards of him, the assorted crews were cutting, chopping, chainsawing, and delimbing trees that were then dragged or cabled over to the landing, where they were stacked and hauled away on trucks.

They harvested particular trees based on criteria Jeff couldn't yet fathom. Then, some areas were marked for managed enrichment planting to ensure optimal restoration and sustainment of a long-term healthy forest. Jeff didn't understand the enrichment part any more than he did the harvesting part, but hoped he'd figure it out sooner or later.

Without a doubt, Jeff preferred the reforestation parts of the business, which featured less falling arboreal giants to crush you and fewer spinning blades to decapitate you.

The worksite could get so loud. The growl of the chainsaws. The throaty snarls of the feller buncher. Ear protection was required, although some of the old guys didn't use it. The mostly deaf older guys, which was perhaps a chicken-and-egg scenario.

Worst were the mechanized murder machines. The delimber and the aforementioned feller buncher, each completely terrifying.

A structural cousin to an excavator, the feller buncher was a tracked vehicle, yellow for safety and visibility, that replaced the excavator's digger bucket with a contraption that grabbed trees in a cozy steel hug before slicing them through with a spinning blade the size of a trash can cover.

The delimber, another tracked vehicle, was a contraption from nightmares that held entire felled trees while running blades along the sides to shear the branches away.

But the danger wasn't entirely of the automated variety. There were plenty of blades being swung and levered with nothing but muscle and bone to drive them on their way.

The chatting men swinging axes were on autopilot, seemingly barely paying attention, having done this so long that their confidence made them appear careless. Their cavalier attitudes, earned through experience, nevertheless made Jeff uneasy.

It was like watching someone distractedly juggle machetes and torches. You presumed they knew what they were doing and hadn't taken up the hobby on a whim. But for those in the audience who had rarely seen the act previously, it was pure horror.

A reprieve from the noisy mayhem came in the form of a task. According to the all-knowing voice issuing from his headset, Jeff was to head towards Sector G12. The whole operation would be moving there soon, so Uncle Chet wanted him to scout the territory and make sure all was well.

There were larger roads for the logging trucks to enter through, but Jeff took the shortcut, driving the company Jeep along backwoods rutted roads. It was bouncy and tight, but silent and solitary, so a good break from his usual activity of relatively superfluous supervising.

Eventually, the map and GPS agreed he had arrived at

Sector G12.

It was distinctly different than the surrounding forest. The first thing he discerned was that it was a mostly deciduous area, as opposed to coniferous. He went to jot that down and saw it was already clearly marked in the notes he'd been provided. It was disheartening, for it would be his major observation of lumber interest.

Sector G12 was densely packed with towering trees that blocked the sun, the resulting darkness laying a gloomy pall along the sector's border. In fact, the trees saturated the boundary of the area so tightly that he was surprised there was enough room for the root systems. Even the branches were completely intertwined between neighboring trees, armoring the area from the sun, layering it in shades of darkness. The shadows within were deep, shifting and impenetrable, protecting G12's secrets from outsiders.

Stepping into the denser tree cover, it felt as if twilight had stealthily slunk in, even though it was only midmorning. Lush vibrant greens were replaced by understated dingy greenish hues, while the browns amplified, hitting every tone from a light peanuty hue to a deep chocolate one.

Cell coverage dropped precipitously. That wasn't unusual, but it was irritating since navigation was difficult without his phone reliably telling him where he was.

The diminished noise in G12 struck him almost immediately. The branches still swayed in the breeze, rustling and crackling along to the arboreal rhythms of nature. Yet, the soft scurrying of small animals and singing of birds ended sharply at the border. G12 had a distinct soundtrack all its own, restricted for its use and no other, devoid of wildlife but replete with the lazy songs of oaks, maples, and birches.

There was a clear path forged into the woods, so he took it. That was a good thing, since within a few minutes, he'd have been lost if not for the trail. It didn't fork or otherwise branch, so there was little chance of losing his way. Still, every few minutes he stopped and looked back just to be sure he knew where he was.

He'd been briefed on what to look for in these walk-aheads. However, he'd forgotten most of the specifics and hated to ask again, since it seemed so simple. Anyway, management already had detailed maps of the terrain and tree types. They simply liked to have a walkthrough before rolling in to start working, just to ensure nothing untoward was afoot. Since he didn't know a spruce from a maple from a birch, Jeff mostly just looked for campers, bears, hikers, funky fungal growths, or anything generally weird. Lacking any of those, he always reported everything was fine, which had worked so far.

Tromping the trail, he was uneasy but found nothing outright alarming that would inspire him to report back that the area wasn't ready for cutting.

Just off the path, the dead leaf cover formed a dense carpet, as if it had been building up for centuries. Curious, Jeff stepped from the trail onto one of the denser spots, just to test the feel. The footing was spongy, as if untold inches separated him from the soil below.

The sound of running water dribbled to him through the trees. That matched up with the map, which showed a stream cutting along one side of the sector. Finding the water should help if he got lost. You went up the stream or possibly down it. Probably one way was better than the other but he wasn't sure which. Maybe up.

The stream's babble faded quickly, muted before he'd gone ten yards farther up the trail.

As Jeff was preparing to turn back, a noise passed through the trees, one of purposeful movement. Having become accustomed to the lack of wildlife sounds, the movement was jarring, like a fire alarm in the dead of the night. A powerful aroma invaded his nostrils, sweet and pungent, the smell of rot.

Whatever it was crashed through the brush. It was something large, too burly to slide seamlessly between branches. The blundering advance marked it as a creature not of these woods, unable to blend in. Or, if it belonged there, it was an apex beast, a predator that had no need to move cautiously to maintain secrecy and safety, for there was nothing for it to hide from. Its boisterous passage felt out of place, insulting the forest, its very presence an affront.

Picturing a hairy beast with nasty claws, Jeff froze, straining his ears for more information. Grunts, growls, directionality, anything. Black bears were common, but mostly harmless. And their scarier cousins, brown bears, weren't found in this part of the country.

The sounds of breaking branches and fluttering leaves persisted, moving in some direction, Jeff knew not which. It might have been getting closer or farther, but the densely packed trees baffled and misdirected the noises such that it was impossible to tell.

Gradually the scuffling noises diminished, meaning whatever it was had passed. Or stopped, perhaps listening and sniffing, licking inch-long fangs in anticipation.

Turning ever so carefully, Jeff retreated back up the path, retracing his steps. This reconnaissance was over.

Boots stirring dead leaves, he struggled to maintain his bearings, focusing on the path ahead.

Flattened grass. Bent branches. Mud scuffed away to reveal the close-packed roots, a knotted embrace between one tree and the next. Those were his guideposts to escape. The path would lead him to safety, he just had to stay on it.

Yet, he couldn't shake an eerie feeling nibbling the back of his neck, raising the hairs on his forearms. That creepy feeling said he was being watched. Paranoia was in full effect. Sometimes the forest did that to him.

Shadows pressed all around, somehow overpowering the scant bits of sunshine, blotting them away. Yet, sometimes the sun spilled through in a glorious golden crescendo, the contrast to the shadows making their dark holdfasts even deeper, blacker.

A nagging uneasiness froze his feet, drawing his eyes to focus between a pair of trees just off the trail. He thought they were perhaps maples.

He'd been staring at the spot for two seconds, or perhaps two minutes, when he realized a person was there. Or at least a face. Jeff had to incline his head back to see it well, for the eyes were several inches above his.

It was a somber face, dropping in and out of sight with the swaying of the branches that blocked the sun's pallid rays. The face was there, then engulfed by the woodland gloom. It reappeared, now with prominent serrated triangular teeth, like miniature arrowheads, displayed in a horrid grimace. Overlarge eyes glinted like diamonds in a field of coal. The swaying branches and shadows worked to hide the face once again. When it was visible once more, it appeared normal.

The steady countenance was full of some emotion. Not rage exactly, but something close to it. Rage was an entity Jeff was intimately familiar with and could recognize instantly. He'd seen it on his dad's face time and again when drunk, ranting about border security, the economy, or foreigners.

No, this face held an emotion cut from the same cloth as rage, but distinctly different. This face held malevolence. It was malicious, a cold hostility infusing its every curve and line.

"Hello?" Jeff ventured.

The grave face did not respond.

"Thought I heard something moving around. I guess that

25

was you." Jeff craned his neck to get a different angle on the stony face. It looked sort of familiar.

"Thought it might be a bear, so …" Jeff shrugged.

No response from the person, if person it was, not simply some happenstance trick of the light.

"Well, guess I'll be on my way," Jeff mumbled nervously. Suspecting he might be hallucinating, he backed away from the cold visage.

Moving out of the darkened tree cover, the face revealed it had a body, proving it was no figment of his imagination. Or if it was a hallucination, it was one Jeff's mind was thoroughly committed to.

The person that emerged was entirely reminiscent of the stranger in the bar the night of Murray's supposed suicide. Tall and lean, well built, and very attractive. As with the other stranger, gender was a coin flip but Jeff was thinking male, mostly due to height and width considerations. This forest dweller had dark skin that tended towards bluish indigo, although such a hue seemed impossible. Perhaps it was a trick of the light. His hair, white as bone, fell to chin level. The eyes peering at Jeff were black of both pupil and iris, lively yet dead, like an evil animatronic bear.

His otherwise unblemished skin was marred by a network of scars, puckered rivers of lighter flesh. A quartet of them ran parallel to one another, starting at his neck and veering down to disappear beneath his shirt, the clear consequence of what Jeff assumed to be a bear attack. The majority of the scars, however, formed intricate symbols, purposefully carved into the canvas of his flesh.

The similarities between this man and the stranger in the bar made their association immediately obvious. They were both odd, somehow entirely different than the average person on the street, yet entirely different in an identical way to one another.

They belonged together, a matched set, that fact was immutable.

This strange woodsman wore dark clothes that were nondescript, homemade but tailored with the greatest skill and care.

Something about him was wrong, menacing. Jeff turned to run but didn't, since he was a grown man, and grown men didn't flee from strangers for no reason. It would be silly. Or would it?

A black bunny emerged from the trees and settled beside the stranger. It was very large for a rabbit, but not chubby and fluffy and adorable like a Flemish Giant one might see at county fairs. No, this bunny was long limbed and rangy, almost like a midsize dog. Its black fur was wiry and its ears long and pointy, leaning back off its skull. Several tufts of its sable fur were spiky, almost like quills. The only relief from the bunny's relentless blackness was its eyes, which glistened a lime green. Overall, the beast looked mangy and possibly inbred, the sort of creature you'd be hesitant to turn your back on.

"You shouldn't be here," said the dark stranger. Such a phrase could be a threat or a warning, but Jeff was leaning towards the threat interpretation.

"Well, uh," Jeff retorted. The dark stranger made leaving the area sound like an excellent notion.

"You could be seriously hurt here," the stranger declared. "Or gravely wounded. Most likely killed." Malice enfolded the words, which were otherwise riddled with indifference towards Jeff's possible wounding or death.

"I'm scouting ahead for Cayuga Logging and Reforestation. We have harvesting rights to this area," Jeff said, the words feeling woefully inadequate.

The stranger's mouth hung open as he listened, triangular teeth glistening, their sawtooth edges undulating as the shadows shifted. His huge black eyes rarely blinked, holding Jeff in place like a specimen pinned to a board in high school biology class.

"You should cut trees elsewhere," the stranger said in silky, yet icy, tones. It came across as a command, not a suggestion. This was an individual accustomed to being listened to and followed. Jeff's dad had once taken him to an assembly on base where an Army general had spoken. This stranger's mannerisms were reminiscent of that general.

"That's not really my call." Jeff realized he sounded apologetic, like the lowest enlisted man trying to explain away some horrid error to the general.

"That's a pity," the dark stranger stated, although it felt unlikely that pity was an emotion he partook in.

"Yeah," Jeff commiserated.

The black bunny cocked its head, examining Jeff as if sizing him up for a meal.

"Is this your bunny?" asked Jeff, gesturing at the odd beast. There was no better way to make friends than to show interest in someone's pet, no matter how scruffy and off-putting it might be.

"I suppose," answered the dark stranger.

"Cute," said Jeff, although it definitely wasn't. It was a soapy bath and two camera filters away from cute. "What's his name? Or her name?"

"Its name is Jellybiscuits." He said the name as one word, although the emphasis was mildly off and the pronunciation subtly awkward, making it sound not completely like the words jelly and biscuits fused together. Regardless, Jellybiscuits was the shape Jeff's brain hammered the name into.

"Huh," said Jeff.

"It would be best if you left now," the stranger said. He breathed deeply, bracing himself. "I won't be responsible for

28

whatever tragedy otherwise happens. You've been warned."

Leaving was a good idea. Quickly casting about and seeing dozens of trees, each identical to the other, Jeff had a panicky realization that he'd forgotten which direction he was traveling on the path. He gazed at the map he'd been clutching throughout the conversation, but it gave him no information he could readily decipher and act upon.

In a blink, the dark stranger was closer, within easy reach, those ripsaw teeth looming. He smelled of raw leather, burnt wood, and salty tears, but also flowers, possibly roses.

"Well, I was pretty much done," Jeff said, taking a few steps away, his boots sinking into the spongy leafy undergrowth. He frantically looked up and down the path, which was difficult, for it was nearly invisible once you were off it.

Jellybiscuits stared at Jeff, not moving so much as a hair. When it didn't move, the bunny looked like a poorly executed example of taxidermy.

The stranger huffed. "That way," he said, extending a spidery finger up the path to the right.

Gambling that he was being told the truth, Jeff scurried off in that direction.

A pervasive feeling of being watched was his companion as he fled up the path, imagining the bloodthirsty gazes of a backwoods hillbilly murderer and his carnivorous bunny upon him.

Finally seeing the Jeep through the trees, he sprinted, even as tinges of rationality came roaring back, wiping the fear from his mind. To be honest, the stranger in the woods didn't fit the backwoods hillbilly murderer stereotype. Yet, that didn't prove his innocence of ill intent.

His shaking hands struggled to jam the key in the lock, as he wished the Jeep was new enough to have a fob instead. Once inside with the doors locked and engine on, he drew a shaky breath and settled himself.

What had really happened, after all? Some nut in the woods had said it was dangerous out there, which it probably was. And then he'd asked them to cut trees elsewhere, which wasn't terribly unusual. People got used to their hiking trails and didn't want the inconvenience of loggers in their way for a few weeks.

It was brighter now that he was out of G12. In that clearer light of day, Jeff decided he was just being silly. Although, it did strike him that the light was weaker than it should be.

Checking his phone, which had reception again, Jeff saw most of the day had burned away. It was late afternoon. Feeling immensely drained, he went straight home.

4 THE WRONG WAY

The next morning, Jeff was a little late arriving at the worksite since he'd been on a call with Uncle Chet. After much deliberation, he'd elected not to go into detail on the stranger in G12, instead saying he thought he'd seen a hiker, which wasn't a big deal. He'd told Owen, of course, but even then he'd left out how creeped out he'd been.

He parked along the dirt road, at the end of a long train of pickup trucks. Walking past the trucks, he passed several old men chain-smoking cigarettes and pipes.

On nice days, some townspeople with time on their hands would watch the logging operation. Mostly codgers ranting about how they did it better in their day, before all these mechanical thingies and make-work-easy doodads.

Wading through the cloud of exhaled nicotine, Jeff saw the gear had been moved, as planned. However, it had been shifted in the wrong direction. The heavy equipment rigs were a hundred yards to the west, the exact opposite direction from where they were supposed to have been moved, which was towards Sector G12.

Jeff found the site boss, a thick fireplug of a Black man nicknamed Pinkie. It was an ironic nickname, since he'd lost the pinkie from his left hand. He was also missing part of the neighboring ring finger from the same accident, but that loss hadn't been interesting enough to impact the nicknaming process.

Pinkie was studying a felled, delimbed tree, pondering it as if he were about to dismantle it further and assemble a house from its sundered remains.

As Jeff approached, Pinkie's gaze rose to take him in, but immediately bounced away again in disinterest. Pinkie viewed Jeff as the worksite's bodily equivalent of an appendix, a vestigial piece of ornamentation largely superfluous to proper functioning. The exceptions being either when Jeff was relaying orders from Chet or when Pinkie was explaining something to him. It wasn't that Pinkie was unkind, he was just busy.

"What's going on Pinkie?"

"Whatcha mean?" Pinkie asked, attention returning to his tattered clipboard. It was old school, just a metal clip holding papers to a brown board, a cheap pen hanging on a string tied to the hole in the clip. It had no cover, which left it vulnerable to constant soakings whenever it rained. Yet he carried it everywhere, keeping track of whatsoever he felt the need to, writing constant notes.

"Why'd stuff get moved that way?" Jeff gestured towards the feller buncher, only visible on the horizon as a yellow metal dinosaur peeking between the trees. "We're supposed to be heading to Sector G12. You're going the wrong way."

Confused, Pinkie stared at the clipboard, his personal roadmap to what the day was supposed to hold. "Oh yeah, we were supposed to go to G12, but then we were told to go that way instead." He poked a callused finger towards the distant machinery.

"By who? Did Chet call?" A surge of panic shimmied through Jeff's spine. If Chet called in instructions straight to Pinkie, it would cut out the middleman. And he was that middleman, so he'd either be unemployed or working a chainsaw, either of which was bad, bad, bad.

"Uhh," Pinkie muttered, his brows furrowing as if battling the world's sharpest migraine. Squinting, he helplessly scanned around before jabbing his finger again, this time towards one of the trucks waiting to be loaded with felled trees. "Those guys told me."

Following Pinkie's pointing, Jeff saw the tall stranger

who'd confronted Murray the night of his alleged suicide. And standing by him was the ominous shadowy man from Sector G12, whose skin was now less of an indigo shade, but instead rather black or even a charcoal gray of sorts. It was hard to judge colors at a distance.

They both wore orange vests, yellow hard hats, dark slacks, and light blue button-up shirts with the sleeves rolled up to their elbows. In Jeff's experience, those outfits marked them as engineers, investigating a worksite while pretending they might perform manual labor. They each carried what looked like a rolled-up blueprint, an item that had no place at a logging site. It was hard to put your finger on the specifics, but they looked out of place, as if they'd been superimposed onto an image where they didn't belong. The overall effect was that of a goofy cartoon rabbit disguising itself to mess with its uptight human nemesis.

Jeff's first instinct was avoidance, having no wish to see the man from the woods again. Yet, curiosity and a sense of duty propelled him onward, waving his hand to get their attention.

Seeing Jeff, the lighter stranger smiled and waved the rolled blueprint in the air in a sort of salute. With his other hand, he pointed behind a tree. He then strode towards it purposefully, as though his pointing index finger were dragging him along. The darker stranger followed, flinging a casually belligerent look at Jeff.

They marched behind the tree—Jeff thought it might be a sycamore—and never came out the other side. It was a lone tree, and not that wide, with no place to shelter the tall pair. By some odd trick of the light, they had disappeared.

After circling the tree a few times while growing increasingly more puzzled, Jeff paced back to Pinkie. He made a mental note to contact the office to see if there'd been engineers on site or something else that might explain the odd strangers.

Moving to the wrong sector was a setback but not exactly a big deal. Accidents happened, and there were plenty of trees to be thinned out over this vast stretch of forest. However, it did make him look bad, as if he couldn't properly relay instructions from one person to the next, which was ninety percent of what his job actually entailed.

Jeff struggled to contain his irritation, since Pinkie must have thought he was doing the right thing. Helping to stifle that sharp flash of ire was the fact that he didn't actually feel like he had much authority over Pinkie when it came right down to it.

Back at Pinkie's side, Jeff asked, "What were their names?"

Rubbing the back of his neck, Pinkie replied, "Don't know."

"Why'd you do what they asked?"

"I'm not sure," Pinkie said, as though stating a dawning revelation.

Seeing that Pinkie was embarrassed and eager to move on, Jeff said, "Fine, but just to clarify, random guys from the woods don't direct where we cut next."

"Well, in hindsight I can see that," said Pinkie. As they spoke he continuously monitored what the work crew was doing, making meticulous notes. He moved slowly through the site, Jeff at his heels.

Several crows buzzed by overhead, cawing vigorously. After they passed, Pinkie shook his head vigorously, almost dislodging his hard hat. "I didn't question it, because I thought you all had come to your senses."

"What do you mean?" Jeff asked, yelling to be heard over the roar of a chainsaw.

"It's spooky over around G12. Everybody knows that."

Based on yesterday, Jeff agreed with the assessment of spookiness, but didn't know that was something other people thought as well. After all, he was still relatively new in town, having just learned where the best pizza was. It was Jabroni's, for the record. "How so?"

"Just dark and quiet and sketchy, stuff like that. People say it's haunted." Pinkie found a million different places to look, with none of them including Jeff.

"Haunted?" Jeff tried to inject fearless incredulity into his response, but it came out as a timid rasp, barely more than a squeak.

"Yeah, or something like that. Indian burial ground maybe. Who knows?"

"Well, we'll see about lining up an exorcism," Jeff said, thinking it might actually be a good idea. "But from here on out, I pass orders down, not anyone else, okay?"

"Yup, hundred percent," Pinkie replied. He was distracted, jotting furiously on the fifth sheet of paper down on his clipboard. When the work of tree cutting was underway and the chainsaws were singing, Jeff was not amongst Pinkie's priorities.

Realizing he was losing Pinkie's interest, Jeff gathered all the authority he could and infused his voice with it. "Okay, but for now, stuff is already moved to, umm …" His eyes roamed the landscape, trying and failing to summon up the sector designation for where the equipment was mistakenly being moved. He really should know that.

"Sector B3," Pinkie offered.

"Uh, yeah, we'll be there a few days and then move to G12."

"Yup, sure," Pinkie said, watching a felled tree being cabled away.

With that settled, Jeff pivoted his attention to getting some work done. He strode through the worksite, pretending he knew what he was doing.

Almost instantly, he noticed Jellybiscuits atop a recently cut stump, its green eyes brazenly following him. The bunny showed no concern for the men and machines around it. Rather, its attention was firmly affixed to Jeff.

Jeff waved his hands and whistled at the bunny. "Get," he hollered.

It didn't move, so he took a tentative step towards it, assuming it would flee. It did not. Rather, it hopped from the stump, covering several of the yards between them in a single bound. Again, it settled on its haunches, watching him. Its mouth hung open, revealing blackened teeth.

A battle of the wills ensued, as bunny and man stared one another down. Within seconds, Jeff lost, backing away, watching the bunny but not meeting its gaze. It was probably rabid. Best not to mess around with it.

He walked to the lone tree where the pair of hypothetical engineers had vanished. They still weren't there. Over the next hour, he drifted around the worksite, avoiding Jellybiscuits while getting different angles on the lone tree, unable to comprehend where they'd vanished to.

Their disappearance had been weird, as if they'd been mirages of a cool pond in the midst of a scorching desert, shimmering into nonexistence as he'd approached.

Ivy had done something similar the other day in front of the coffee shop. Taken together, there was a pattern. A pattern that made him anxious. The obvious answer was an amalgamation of random chance and optical illusions. Or perhaps something more disturbing, such as a problem with his eyesight. Or his attention span. Or stress. Just so long as it wasn't his sanity, it would be fine. Anything other than that, he could deal with.

5 UNLIKELY HURDLES

Three weeks passed. The company's work continued at multiple locations. Trees were felled at a few sites. Seedlings were planted somewhere else altogether. Lumber was processed back at the mill. Yet no work occurred in Sector G12, none of its arboreal titans collapsing to the soil before being ferried away to their dismemberment and subsequent eternal rest.

That lack of progress was unfortunate, since Uncle Chet insisted G12 be processed. Not that he considered there to be anything unusually special about that section of woods. But harvesting a subset of its trees was part of the plan, and Chet was a man who liked a plan. That was how business worked for Chet. First A, then B, then C, pounding through tasks in a precise order, deviations not to be tolerated. Thus, he urged Jeff to steer the work crews towards G12.

And Jeff steadfastly conveyed those urgings to the crews. Trees were trees, after all, even if some parts of the forest were a little darker and danker than others.

Yet, circumstances conspired to block their earnest advance towards Sector G12, as a host of unlikely hurdles were continually thrust into their path, waylaying them at every step.

Some of the setbacks were minor, barely more than nuisances. Such as those provided by the wildlife.

Sudden swarms of wasps.

A trio of aggressively hangry bears, no Goldilocks required.

Other hindrances were more significant, usually centered around machinery.

Large pieces of equipment failed, slowing down progress as sweat and muscle were substituted for diesel-powered leviathans.

Smaller pieces of equipment were misplaced, there one

second and gone the next.

One morning they found several chainsaws on a cable forty feet in the air, strung between towering spruces. That one was clearly intentional, although the cameras monitoring the worksite overnight caught nothing.

Although these hazards and nuisances were of a miscellaneous nature, they were consistent in a single respect, in that they only befell Jeff's crew when they were moving towards Sector G12. If they went in any other direction, the sun would shine and all was right with the world. However, if anyone advanced towards G12 with so much as a hatchet in hand, a swarm of wasps would descend or a tree would fall in their path.

Through it all, the two strangers, and their bunny, often lurked at the periphery of the worksite.

Not yet knowing the strangers' names, Jeff thought of them as the darker one, whom he'd met in the woods, and the lighter one, who'd been at the bar the night Murray killed himself. Sometimes they were together, and sometimes not. Jeff and Owen glimpsed one or the other in town several times, casting about as if looking for something. But whatever it was seemed to continuously elude them.

6 OLD EYES

The fox huddled against the rough bark of a pine tree, giving its most sincere impression of a fox that wasn't there. It didn't move at all, beyond fearful trembling and panting.

It had set out that night with humbles hopes of catching a nice juicy rabbit. Those were its favorite. But lacking that delicacy, a tasty mouse or chubby chipmunk would do.

But it had hunted too close to the road, that vast hard dark trail with stripes down the middle that the scary metal monsters roared past on. It feared those monsters, for one had claimed its brother last winter.

Yet, it wasn't the metal monsters that concerned the fox right then. Nor their accompanying humans, who were always inside the metal monsters, perhaps being slowly digested.

No, there were other predators afoot. A pair of them. Sharp and nasty. Fast. Impossible to escape. The fox's survival hinged on being invisible.

But the fox needn't have worried. The predators saw it and didn't care, having eyes for another quarry that night. An unsuspecting one.

Even amongst those that prowled the night, the eyes of these two predators were distinctive. Gleaming, wide, and hungry.

That distinctiveness was absolute, since each of the two sets were notably distinct from the other. One set shimmered colors, like a muted rainbow, heavy on the green. The other was dark and blank, like coal flecked with obsidian.

They were old eyes. Not ancient, but very old. Centuries, certainly.

The predators were crouched along the road in one of the side trenches that humans loved to dig. It made the coal-eyed predator uneasy, being so close to the border of the section of the deep dark woods where it lived. It was loath to stray far from home. The consequences were significant.

Huddled together, the two predators were watching a hitchhiker. Plodding along, boots clapping against the blacktop, making no attempt at stealth. Innocent of the evils surrounding it. Delicious. Perfect. Someone who wouldn't be immediately missed.

And they were inhaling the human's odors. Nylon, leather, and sweat, with body spray layered over the top.

He was foolhardy, jamming his thumb out in search of a ride even though he was nearly invisible to the passing vehicles until they were atop him. But he wasn't invisible to the old eyes. They saw everything.

The coal-eyed predator heard its soulmate titter, a hungry noise that it knew well. Remembered well. They'd been apart but were often back together now, reveling in one another's company. In their shared interests.

Hopefully they would soon always be together. Until then, every moment stolen together was a treasure.

With unbridled glee, the coal-eyed one fell upon the hitchhiker, an avalanche of nightmares. It swept him into the woods, reeling him in like a fish on a hook.

Like an empty-headed fish, your average human was ignorant of the fact they were hunted by higher beings. They didn't remain watchful enough, but instead idly meandered through their environs, oblivious to the various dangers. This one paid the price for that inattentiveness.

The predators slowly disassembled the hitchhiker, while being careful not to shred his jacket. The one with lighter, rainbow eyes fancied the garment. It was expensive and entirely waterproof.

The rainbow-eyed one giggled, enjoying the wet splatters, meaty rips, and vigorous screams.

It was music to the coal-eyed one's ears. The giggles, not

the screams, although they were nice as well.

The violence excited them, fueling their passions, serving as kindling for the blazing inferno that was their relationship.

Monsters strode these woods.

7 A BRITTLE FRAMEWORK OF WHITE STICKS

It was a lovely day, although windy, when Jeff had his next conversation with one of the strangers.

Emerging from a porta-potty, Jeff scrubbed his hands together to work in the foamy sanitizer he'd slathered them in.

He was certain he was the only one using the hand sanitizer. Time and again, he'd tested that, twisting the nozzle and leaving it at a precise angle. But it never moved, its alignment unwavering. If anyone else used it, the care they took not to move the nozzle stretched credulity.

The door had just slapped closed behind him when he was startled by a voice, smooth as honey.

"Hello, worker bee," said the brunette stranger from the bar, whom Jeff thought of as the lighter one. As opposed to the other, who he thought of as the darker one. It wasn't the best naming system.

The stranger smiled, although it was not an expression of joy. His face, though flawlessly attractive, had a default state of merry resignation, with a pinch of sorrow, leaving just enough room for a smidgen of what might be lunacy.

He stood in the liminal area between the forest and the worksite, toffee hair twisting in the wind, hands in the pockets of roughcut green pants. His matching vest was unbuttoned, displaying a lean musculature, built for optimum functionality and bereft of moles, hair, or even nipples, the surface smooth and hard as a marble countertop.

Up close, when the wind blew his hair just right, one could see that his ears were oddly proportioned, with long pointed tips, although Jeff got but a fleeting glance and might well have been wrong.

"Hey there," Jeff replied, flicking his hands to clear them of sanitizer. He'd used way too much. "So, I never caught your name. I'm Jeff." He skipped thrusting his hand out for a shake, because he'd just left the bathroom and it felt weird. Plus, his palms were still sanitizer-sticky.

Failing to share his own name, the stranger said, "The fates are conspiring to keep you away from a certain area. I believe you call it G12." As he spoke, he commenced walking along the edge of the clearing, which held a tangled nest of felled sticks and rough branches.

Jeff joined him on the deadfall, eyes down to avoid tripping in the chaos of jagged pointy limbs and shorn logs. He barely kept his balance, even as the stranger walked naturally, his bare feet gliding from one safe haven to another with no apparent effort.

"Uh yeah, it seems so," Jeff stammered, his focus on staying on his feet instead of on snappy comebacks. His boots cracked and clumped through the wooden debris.

Jellybiscuits was there as well. It scuttled along close to them, traveling on a parallel path along the edge of the fallen limbs. The black bunny moved awkwardly, almost limping, although not exactly. Rather, it was as if it had just woken from a long nap and all its limbs were still asleep. Bad vibes rolled off the ugly bunny, crashing into Jeff like ocean waves at midnight.

"You should listen to the fates, they're arbiters of each man's destiny. Poverty, success, health, or death, all are guided by fate."

Jeff mused on the stranger's words. "That sounds sorta like a threat."

"Not so, merely an observation." The stranger laughed abruptly, a tumultuous braying, far less pleasant than his speaking voice. The merriment was fleeting, chased away by a pensive scowl. "We need not threaten one another. The world is threatening enough. Anyway, people are fragile, nothing

43

more than sugar water and stringy meat draped over a brittle framework of white sticks."

That still sounded pretty threat-y. Perhaps a change of subject was in order. "I notice that you hang around here a lot. Are you interested in logging?"

The stranger waved a long-fingered hand, swatting Jeff's question aside. "I savor the wilds, careening through the oaks, inhaling the gusts along the leafy canopy, communing with the animals, feeling the moist soil between my toes, stomping the earth in a gleefully wild dance when the moon shines brightest."

Jeff's boot slipped, shearing bark from a rotten log, nearly spilling him into the knee-deep carpet of discarded tree limbs. The stranger didn't stumble, seeming as one with the tangled wood underfoot, the trees surrounding them, the songbirds above, all of it.

"Yeah, I do that too," Jeff said. That was entirely untrue. His comfort zone was the couch, playing video games with Owen while they ate pizza and brainstormed schemes to pay off their student loans.

"No, you don't," replied the stranger in a singsong voice. "You're an idle creature of video games and lazy afternoons, a vanquisher of pixel-based enemies, content to look up and see nothing but artificial lighting and plaster, while the stars in the night sky remain an utterly unfamiliar canopy." As he spoke, the stranger casually steered them over an especially aggressive heap of upturned pointy branches, similar to what might have been used as fortifications from intruders thousands of years ago.

Jellybiscuits assailed the barricade, unperturbed by its spiky nature.

"That's not entirely true," Jeff said. While nervously eyeing the sharp sticks below, he realized they looked as if they'd been whittled into crude spears, each lusting to quench themselves on his spurting blood. How had Pinkie and the guys let such a hazard pile up?

Vaguely intense gaze roaming the trees, the stranger said, "It is entirely and completely true, beyond a shadow of a doubt. You shouldn't be here amidst these glorious glades. None of you should. You're nothing but filthy pilgrims besmirching a pristine land, thoughtlessly despoiling its miracles. You should leave immediately, for your own good."

Okay, that was a threat. Probably. But it was still pretty ambiguous. If he could get the guy to say something more concrete, they could call in the cops. Then it would be someone else's problem, which was the absolute best kind of problem. "What the heck are you talking about? It feels like you're threatening us."

Even as his companion effortlessly glided over the piled branches, Jeff clumsily floundered across them, maintaining intense focus but still teetering like an amateur on a highwire. It seemed he'd been led there not for conversation, but rather to see if he would slip and puncture himself on this impossibly deep snarl of jagged oak javelins.

"Am I threatening you?" A maniacal smirk took root on the stranger's long face. He hesitated, giving the question due consideration. Shaking his head, he said, "No, I'm simply warning you." Sorrow and mockery were laced together in those few words, making their sincerity murky and unclear.

"Someone's been trying to slow us down, and it seems like it's you." Jeff wanted to point accusingly at the tall stranger but needed both hands to keep his balance. "Like, some chainsaws were hung way up in the air from the tops of some spruces several days ago. Did you do that?" He'd meant the allegation to be forceful, but it departed his lips sounding nervous and frustratingly whiny. It was hard to concentrate on flinging stinging accusations while picking his way over the pointy stakes, dodging impalement after impalement.

The tall stranger scoffed. "You sound silly. How would a person even do that?"

"I'm not exactly sure," Jeff said, before being distracted by a flap of umber fur. It lay just ahead of them, amongst the tumble of cleaved wood. A small mammal had been skewered on a twisted branch. It might have been a raccoon, but whatever it had been no longer mattered, for it was dead and rotting. The odor was pungent, sour, and wrong, surfacing abruptly and displacing all other scents, leaving nothing but death in his nostrils.

Scurrying over the discarded tree limbs, Jellybiscuits raced ahead in its lopsided gait to examine the dead body.

With what little breath he could gather through the reek of the decaying corpse, Jeff continued, "And you and your buddy were marching around here in hard hats and vests a few weeks back. You pointed our crew the wrong way."

A trio of songbirds erupted from the brush, flying inches over Jeff's head. He ducked, clutching his helmet, nearly spilling himself into the veritable tiger trap they were walking through, thereby joining the unfortunate raccoon. Straightening, he saw he was alone, talking to nothing but the wind, trees, and stinking, deceased critter.

8 GO FOR A SPIN

With a grandiose flourish, a hefty man offered Ivy his hand. "Would you care to go for a spin, little lady?" he inquired, his breath awash in the competing stenches of alcohol and cigarettes. He was in his late fifties and almost entirely unimpressive, beyond the gray beard that reached past his chest, its tangled length smeared with a prodigious coating of pizza grease, tomato sauce, and cheese.

"A spin, what is that?" asked Ivy, her huge green eyes eagerly drinking him in as her lavish eyelashes fluttered the air. She was intrigued but also amused by the proposal.

"A dance, my dear," he replied, the slur in his words announcing his complete inebriation. His right hand remained out, the offer still open, his grasping at his lost youth still underway.

"Sounds fun," she purred, placing her much smaller hand into his burly mitt and letting herself be led away from the table.

"We'll go for a spin," the bearded man drunkenly announced, at the top of his lungs. It seemed he didn't want anyone to miss his time in the limelight, dancing with a young beauty.

Ivy moved with a fluid grace, while the man drunkenly strutted. His left hand eagerly cradled her backside as he led her to a modest space cleared out amid the tables. The space had never been intended to serve as a dance floor but was nevertheless pressed into occasional service as such by the intoxicated or overexuberant.

They were in the dining room of Jabroni's Pizza, which was, first and foremost, meant as a place to eat pizza, exactly as one might expect. However, Jabroni's also served beer, wine, and a limited assortment of liquors, which led to many villagers viewing it as a bar that secondarily served pizza.

Watching the duo begin their awkward dance, Jeff was a little envious of Snakebite's bravado. That was the bearded man's nickname, Snakebite. Jeff was uncertain of the name's origins but had heard hints it came from his biker gang past. Whatever he'd once been, he was now one of Jeff's truckers, carting felled trees away to be processed.

When Snakebite started enthusiastically grinding his pelvis against Ivy, Jeff looked away. It was awkward and weird watching the old man's boozy flirtations. He returned his attention to his last slice of pizza. It was nearly gone, unlike Ivy's. Hers was arranged in a shredded pile on her plate. She hadn't eaten any, just ripped it up and moved it around, assembling elaborate cheesy pepperoni and crust piles, held together by the oily cement of grease.

"She's wild," remarked Carla, staring icily at Ivy. From what Jeff could gather, Carla was envious of Ivy's looks and general vibe, especially her propensity to always be the center of attention. That became extra clear when Carla was drinking, and right then Carla was drunk, although not as much as Snakebite was. That was sort of a pattern, Carla was almost always drinking when Jeff and Owen happened upon her after hours.

"Very lively," agreed Owen, watching the dancing duo as if they were the featured act on center stage. After swigging his beer, he added, "Wow, look at old Snakebite go."

Snakebite was spinning like a hulking, clumsy ballerina, his index finger pointing down onto his head, as if serving as the axle for his rotation.

Faster, faster, faster, he spun, a confused look on his face. Panicky, even.

In his wobbling revolutions, he rebounded from adjacent tables, sending drinks flying and stirring up irritated noises from the diners. Yet he continued spinning.

Hopping in place and merrily clapping, Ivy giggled like a lunatic. She'd donned Snakebite's green John Deere hat. It sat at a jaunty angle over her thick red curls, complementing the daisies also strung through her mane. Her bright sundress mildly swayed in a nonexistent breeze that didn't conform with her gleeful bounding as she applauded, urging Snakebite on.

"Well, he is pretty drunk," Jeff mused.

"It's still super weird though," Owen said.

That was true, Snakebite didn't normally imitate ballerinas, so far as Jeff knew.

"Speaking of weird, you were saying weird stuff was happening at work," Carla said. She tore her gaze from Snakebite, resistant to feeding Ivy's quest for attention.

Owen also looked away from the duo, refocusing on the pizza. He nodded, "It all sounds weird."

Before Snakebite's untimely interruption, Jeff had been describing the location of Sector G12 and detailing his creeping suspicions that someone was trying to keep them away from there, with that someone very possibly being those weird, tall strangers. It had all been news to Carla, while Ivy had nodded along knowingly. Owen, of course, had heard it all before.

"Yeah," Jeff replied, happy to return to one of his favorite topics. "You're from around here. You ever heard of anything strange about that area? Some guys at work said it was known to be a weird place, like haunted, or something. Obviously that's crazy." Jeff didn't think it was crazy at all, he sort of believed in ghosts. "You ever heard anything like that?"

Swishing the foamy dregs around her bottle, Carla gestured towards him with it. She was an occasional beer drinker, preferring brews that were domestic and cheap, no microbreweries for her. "Yeah, that's what people say about that area. Maybe haunted or maybe a monster, bigfoot, chupacabra, something."

She leaned forward, making her glasses slide down her nose. Pushing them back into place, she whispered, "Some hikers disappeared out there last year. They were just walking around, innocent and harmless as you please. Supposedly they weren't too adventurous, like they were the types that wouldn't stray much from the trail. Didn't matter though, disappeared, all gone. Search parties never found any trace of them."

Owen and Jeff nodded as one. Jeff said, "Yup," as Owen simultaneously said, "Saw that." The internet had informed them of the lost hikers.

"Could be bigfoot, I suppose," Carla said, working at peeling the label from her bottle with her thumbnail.

"Let's call that Plan B. I feel like it's those two random dudes that hang out in the woods," Jeff said.

His mouth full of chicken wings, Owen didn't say anything, but instead nodded, pointed at Jeff, and gave a thumbs-up. Behind him, a trio of college-aged women were ogling him and whispering. Owen had many such admirers, none of whom intrigued him.

Ivy slid back into her chair, pushing her plate of pizza detritus aside. At times, a person's face can assemble itself just so, into an indefinable combination of micro-adjusted mouth, cheeks, eyebrows and so on, such that it is obvious they have something to say and have been eagerly awaiting a chance to say it. This was exactly such an instance.

Across the room, Snakebite was staggering, his head turning in rapid circles, up left down right, as if passionately working a crick out of his neck. His eyes were spinning in their sockets, unfocused, like he'd just gotten off a horrific roller coaster.

He staggered about and crashed headfirst into a table,

sending drinks and food flying. Blood oozing from his forehead and nose, he thrashed about, moaning awkwardly.

"What the heck happened?" Owen asked. He would have run to the rescue, but several people were already crowded around Snakebite.

"I spun him," Ivy replied, her tone indicating the matter was closed and to please not ask questions with obvious answers. She was eager to say something else. "Anyway, I heard you talking. Those guys in the woods are complete jerks. Absolute monsters. It's totally them causing your problems, Jeff. It's just what they do."

The music had stopped. The people crowded around Snakebite were trying to help, asking what had happened. None of them mentioned Ivy. The waiter offered to call 911.

Distracted by the drama playing out across the dining room and bewildered by Ivy's indifference to it, Jeff said, "Uh … so you seem to know who I'm talking about."

She sneered, her usual carefree manner vanishing, replaced by venom. "Yeah, I do. Tall, handsome, athletic, one dark and the other light. They hang around in the woods." Ivy twirled her hand in the universal motion indicating they should move the conversation along without wasting time on nonessentials.

This topic clearly riled her, striking a nerve in a way nothing else did.

"Who are they?" asked Jeff.

"Troublemakers, that's who," Ivy roared, poking an angry finger in Jeff's face. She was working herself up into a frenzy. "And you're letting them push you around? Letting them keep you away from doing your job? From going where you're supposed to be?"

"Um … well," Jeff replied, barely avoiding the graceful finger jabbing at his nose. He was fumbling for words, withering under her intense scrutiny and shriveling from her accusatory tone.

"Take it easy," said Owen, although much of his attention was still on Snakebite. There was something about a person in pain that called out to him, as if he were convinced he was option number one to deal with any problem that arose.

Ivy continued, "And they're dangerous, with a long history of hurting people." There was a slight pause before the word people, as if she were searching for the proper term. Her brows were furrowed, her face a mask of indignant hostility.

"Sounds like they suck," stated Carla, even as she signaled for another beer.

"Yeah, them and their scroungy black bunny," said Jeff.

Ivy looked puzzled, and mildly troubled by that puzzlement. "I don't know anything about a bunny."

On the far side of the room Snakebite puked. It splattered on the tile, an aggressively malodorous tide of acidic froth and partially digested pizza chunks. People scrambled to escape.

"How are they dangerous?" Jeff asked. He was no coward but knew enough to avoid dangerous things. If you could be near either hazardous people or happy people, you chose the latter, that was just common sense. Anyway, he suspected Ivy was simply being melodramatic. That was her nature.

In a flash, the righteous fury dropped away as Ivy reconfigured herself to full-blown damsel in distress mode.

Her eyes grew even larger and were moistened by nascent tears. She nibbled her lower lip, pearly whites sinking deep into the plump pink flesh as she emoted angsty energy like lava from an active volcano. Jeff thought it was a bit much, but one glance at Owen told him that his best friend was eating this up.

With a nervous look around the pizza place, Ivy whispered, "I shouldn't say. But you can't let them boss you around." The tiniest of sobs escaped her lips. "I'm afraid of them."

Hugging herself, Ivy suddenly looked very small, helpless,

and alone. She gazed back and forth between Jeff and Owen, her green eyes unnaturally wide and bright, redirecting the cold overhead lights into a warm glimmering sparkle.

Carla was squinting at the cowering beauty, her own eyes half closed, drunkenly trying to decipher what kind of drama they'd found themselves mired in.

"Have those two hurt you?" asked Owen. He kept his voice low, perhaps not to embarrass her if the answer was an affirmative.

"They've chased me through the woods before." Ivy shivered, her gaze drifting away, into the wispy recesses of the past. "I got away, or I'm not sure what they would have done to me. The dark one has a big blade he likes to swing around. I thought they might kill me, or molest me, or both."

"Those bastards," muttered Owen. He was slow to anger, but once he'd reached that point he tended to stay that way until the matter was resolved to his personal satisfaction. Jeff had seen it time and again.

Ivy visibly gathered herself, as if mustering her strength for what she said next. "Also," she whispered, "I suspect they're cooking meth out there."

Jeff had the distinct sense that Ivy was now simply throwing conversational darts at the board, seeing what would stick, hoping for a bullseye, something that would rile them up, since she thrived on attention. And he was only partly buying her story, sensing traces of lies amongst the background of truth, or perhaps it was the reverse. Owen, however, was fully invested, nodding along to every word she uttered, her damsel in distress act stimulating his hero propensities. And once Owen's valiant urges were activated there was no going back. Heroism was in his blood, knit into his genome, probably reaching back many generations, taking roots in the knights of yore.

The notion that the strangers were out in the woods cooking meth seemed implausible. They were awfully clean and fit and handsome, not matching Jeff's preconceived mental picture for that particular type of scoundrel. But he could certainly be wrong, having nothing but television and movies to go by.

Although, Jellybiscuits did seem like it could be a meth cooker's rabbit. Raised amongst nasty chemicals, mutated into some perversion of a standard rabbit.

Anyway, he wasn't sure what all was involved in cooking meth, but it seemed as though there'd be a big sketchy house or dilapidated shed, or something like that, maybe with lots of those big blue barrels outside and black smoke churning out through a crumbling brick chimney. Fortuitously, his company was sending a surveyor across a swath of the woods tomorrow, with Sector G12 being included. If there was anything to see, the surveyor would find it. He had drones and everything.

"Easy answer to the meth cooking possibilities," Jeff said. "We're sending someone out to do some surveying of that area tomorrow. If there are any weird buildings or … meth stuff, he'll find it." Truth be told, he was quite content to let someone else go out there. If he never entered that spooky section of forest again it wouldn't break his heart.

"Perfect! We'll go along and check things out. I want to see these woods weirdos," Owen said. Once he'd said that, there was no question of whether they would go. Owen didn't back down, ever. It was one of the few traits Jeff would change about his friend if he could.

Wrestling to keep his cringes internal, Jeff mustered a modicum of enthusiasm and said, "Oh, great. Good plan, we'll do that." Spending the day tromping through the forest was not his idea of a good time, especially when it involved Sector G12 and its odd denizens.

That's the way it was though, being a sidekick, you did stuff that seemed stupid. Reading Owen's mind in the way that several years of being best friends allowed, Jeff knew Owen was picturing a citizen's arrest of the strange forest duo. And probably a gentlemanly thrashing, which was an awful idea. People in the meth industry probably didn't fight fairly, but rather were the types to bring machetes and broken bottles to a thumb wrestling match.

Ivy beamed, letting the full force of her delight wash over them. "You'll go out and take a look? You boys are the sweetest things. It's too bad I have a boyfriend, or I'd snap one of you up. Maybe both of you."

Across the room, Snakebite was in a booth, head tilted back and a towel held to his bleeding nose. A waiter pushed a mop bucket over to attend to the vomit.

The mention of a boyfriend piqued Carla's interest. Jeff's as well. Owen didn't care, with visions of valiantly smiting villains occupying his full attention.

"Boyfriend? What's the deal with that? Haven't ever seen you with anyone," Carla said. As she'd gotten drunker, she'd slid her chair closer to Owen. She now tentatively placed her hand on his forearm with the air of someone hoping to pet a feral cat but terrified of scaring it away. He didn't notice her light touch.

Ivy's damsel in distress act dropped away, replaced by agitation. "I have a boyfriend, yes. He's fun and handsome and perfect. A free spirit like me, a real sweetie. He was having some fun and got a little out of control, so he's locked away for a little bit. I'm waiting for him, but the whole thing is just so unfair."

As she spoke, Ivy's countenance grew darker, a ferocious scowl finding its way onto her delicate face, rearranging it into a beautifully malevolent facade.

The revelation of Ivy having a boyfriend in jail didn't

surprise Jeff in the slightest. Bad boys seemed more to her taste than someone like him, who'd never knowingly done anything wrong in his life.

Ivy continued before anyone else could speak. "You know, it was evil bullies, just like those two jerks in the woods, that picked on my sweetie, causing trouble and getting him locked up. They're what's wrong with this world, nosy people pushing other people around, imposing their will on them, on people like my sweetie, who're just trying to have fun and enjoy their time on this earth."

Under the weak lights of the dining room, Ivy snarled, her lips peeling back to reveal perfectly white pearly teeth, even though her canines struck Jeff as unusually long and imposingly serrated. Quivering with fury, Ivy's lithe body blurred for a split second, but that was but a trick of optics and lighting, no doubt. That was happening a lot these days. He should probably get his eyes checked.

Thrusting herself away from the table and to her feet, Ivy stomped off, her dainty feet pounding the floor in anger. Irritated sounds flew from her mouth. It seemed they must be words but were unrecognizable as such, bringing to mind a grawlix, one of those strings of symbols used to indicate swearing by cute little critters in comics.

As she stalked out, an EMT walked in, asking for Snakebite and a large pepperoni and mushroom to go.

9 A BAD TURN

They met the surveyor first thing in the morning, even before the sun had peeked its blinding head over the distant horizon. Jeff felt bedraggled and barely awake. Conversely, Owen was entirely bright-eyed and bushy-tailed.

The surveyor was a grumpy curmudgeon named Mr. Simpkins. That's what he was to be called—Mr. Simpkins—which was absolutely positively not up for debate. His skin was dark as molasses and his teeth were the color of over-ripe kernels of corn. A smile lit up his prematurely wrinkled face exactly once, that momentous occasion being when Jeff slipped in mud and tumbled down a hill coated with sticky pine needles.

Jeff and Owen's presence annoyed Mr. Simpkins. He made that clear. But as the day wore on he warmed up to them a bit, eventually even sharing his homemade jerky, which he was quite proud of. He never specified its origins, which might have been cow or deer or bison or something else altogether. Neither of them dared to ask. It felt unwise to question, so they simply smiled and chewed.

Despite his grumbly nature, Mr. Simpkins loved talking about his drones. He would roll his eyes at any question about the flying technological marvels but then hold forth with great passion, providing in-depth answers far beyond what he'd been asked. He would sermonize all day on quadcopters if given the chance. And don't even get him started on geofencing.

Beyond the drones and the jerky, the first portion of the day passed with little excitement. Jeff and Owen dutifully followed Mr. Simpkins, trudging through the forest like baby duckies after their momma.

He stayed well ahead of them, diligently toiling away at whatever it was he was doing, even as they dragged their feet, poking around the bushes and looking for anything unpleasant involving tall, attractive, mildly genderless men or squalid meth shacks. But if the forest had any macabre secrets, it refused to give them up. Jeff was relieved, happy to spend the day ensconced in boredom. Owen, however, was disappointed, his taste for adventure unrequited.

The day took a bad turn when they entered the pervasive shade of Sector G12. Jeff felt the gloom settle over them like a funeral pall, chill and dark, cordoning off the sun behind a curtain of leaves and needles. Normally fearless Owen tensed up as well, although he wouldn't admit to feeling any unease within the tightly packed trees.

As they hiked through the ominous terrain, Jeff and Owen talked. Their conversation was fifty percent unsaid, thriving on unspoken context while creeping through innuendo and surviving on shared experiences and assumptions.

"Remember that thing? With Tom? When it rained?"

A chuckle. "Yeah, this is totally like that. More trees though."

"Totally."

"Mr. Simpkins is cool."

"Yeah, I guess. But kinda not really."

"Nah, maybe not. But, drones, right?"

Nodding. "It would be cool to get one."

"Yeah."

One of those very drones buzzed high overhead, beyond the reach of the towering trees. The dense canopy made it invisible, undetectable save for the thrum of its passing.

"Kinda like to get a cat." It was a simple statement, but Jeff confided it like a deep dark secret that had been eating away at him for years, robbing him of sleep, haunting his dreams.

"Maybe. Easier than a dog."

"Yeah."

They hustled through a swarm of gnats. Once through, Jeff asked, "You like Carla?"

"Nah, but you do," Owen said. Twiddling with a stick, he swung it like a fencing saber.

"I guess."

"Drinks a lot. So … you know." Owen shrugged.

"Yeah, she's like that blonde with the poofy hat that lived upstairs senior year."

"Heh, heh, just like that." Owen swung his stick through the air, humming lightsaber noises.

"No way these guys are meth guys," Jeff said.

"If you say so. I haven't seen the dark one, just the other one." Owen was the type to think he could adjudicate the nefarious intents and purposes of people with nothing but a single contemplative look.

"They're too clean and, like, spiffy. Not very meth-y."

"Yeah, but still, Ivy says they're shitty."

"But you know, Ivy can be sorta …" Jeff hesitated, shuffling through his mental thesaurus for the right term, but finding nothing that worked.

Owen relieved him of the burden of picking a word. "Yup," he said.

"Super-duper hot though."

"I guess so. What kinda cat?"

"I don't know."

Owen shrugged. "We could check the shelter this weekend."

Their half-formed conversation was interrupted by the cracking of branches and rustling of leaves.

A smell wafted over the trail, blowing in from the right, emanating from the heart of G12.

It was musty, like a reclusive curmudgeon's root cellar that had been sealed for months, packed to overflowing with jars of spoiled preserves, jams, and meats, their lids popping off from festering microbial growth. Jeff had smelled that particular funk before, in this very same place. That had been just before the tall dark stranger loomed from the leafy shadows. Yet the smell hadn't radiated from the stranger. It merely preceded him, as though he were towed in its foul wake.

Perhaps, Jeff thought, it was the smell of meth cooking. Could that be? One imagined such a process might be replete with smelly chemicals and vats of boiling gunk, each reeking more than the next.

There then came a robust stirring from deep in the foliage, originating from the same direction as the funk. It moved swiftly and violently, not cutting through its environment with nimbleness, but rather lumbering through it like a bone-crushing giant of yore.

"Mr. Simpkins is noisy," observed Jeff, although he knew deep down inside it wasn't the old surveyor. It was moving too fast. A possibility was that one of his drones had drifted below the canopy and was running rampant through branches, colliding and rebounding from limb to limb. But no, it lacked the distinctive humming whine of the drones.

"Nah," said Owen, "it's not him. He's over there somewhere." He gestured ahead of them, his tanned muscular arm flicking through the air.

"Oh yeah."

Jeff paused, as did Owen. Jeff was frozen like a rabbit trying to remain inconspicuous with a predator nearby. Owen, conversely, was a coiled spring, like the corresponding predator, waiting to see which way to dart after its prey. Both of them had their fight-or-flight response activated, just in opposite directions.

The crackling of branches moved rapidly, accelerating ahead of them, straight towards where Mr. Simpkins was, concealed amongst the far trees.

The trail darkened, the canopy overhead drawing together, as if concentrating on hiding Sector G12's activities from the outside world.

A grumbling roar, like a bear belching thunder, rippled through the still air, reverberating through the trees, the pine needles, their eardrums. It brought cold water into Jeff's intestines, sending emergency flares back and forth along his nervous system.

There was a yell, decidedly human, seeming feeble and sad in comparison to the booming howl preceding it, which still echoed in the liminal space between current reality and fresh memory. It was cut short almost immediately, falling away into silence.

Jeff took two shaky steps back, ready to bolt. His panicked gaze found Owen, who was also spooked. Seeing his gallant friend shaken was both reassuring and frightening. Owen hesitated for but a heartbeat before charging in the direction of the single human screech. Jeff hesitated considerably longer but his legs finally started moving, propelling him on a breakneck charge through wooden giants, each step bringing him closer to danger.

They were off the trail and Jeff was running blind, his arms up to guard against the stinging slaps of the beckoning limbs. Every scrap of good sense he possessed demanded retreat, but he plunged ahead, dragged along by the force of Owen's selfless will.

Owen was just ahead, pulling farther away with every step, yet the journey was short so he came to a jarring halt within fifty yards. Jeff arrived seconds later. Heart pumping and breath rasping, he nearly plowed into Owen, who was staring into the dense pool of shade before them. It was suspended between two burly tree trunks, a patch of midnight in the middle of the day.

It was murky within, but there appeared to be a beast, all gangly limbs, keen edges, and creeping movements. Only its pale face stood out in the ebony gloom, revealing shark's teeth below glossy eyes of flint.

Jeff froze, once again feeling like a prey animal, now captured within the spotlight of a predator's cold gaze. Whatever it was might decide to eat him, should he be so unwise as to stir.

But the monster was proven to be only a trick of the light, or rather the absence of light, when it transformed into the lighter-skinned stranger as he sidled from the shadows.

The area behind the stranger instantaneously brightened, revealing the previously hidden steep drop-off at his back.

"You should stay back, it's dangerous," the stranger remarked, winking at them. Hands in his pockets, long sandy-brown hair swaying in the light breeze, and an obscenely large smile on his beautiful face, he seemed entirely relaxed, impervious to any danger.

"You don't seem concerned," said Owen. He drew himself up to his full height, which was considerably taller than Jeff, but several inches less than the stranger.

The stranger's smile widened even further, revealing perfectly white teeth, the canines especially pronounced. His air was that of an adult humoring a child, too impatient to explain to them how the world worked or why they were completely mistaken about everything. Leaning forward, he confided, "Well, you see, it isn't dangerous to me." His eyebrows knit together, an iota of concern marring his face. "At least, not right this second."

Those words had barely escaped the stranger's lips when an uproar erupted behind him, just down the slope. They heard thumps, solid ones like something hard slamming into something soft, often ending with a snap or crunch. Also grunts, both low and high, as well as frantic cries and angry barks. Layered within that were wet tearing sounds, of the sort that lingered in the subconscious, emerging in nightmares when least expected.

As the horrid orchestra played, Jeff was immobilized by fear, inactivity proving to be his body's preferred reaction to emergencies. Mercifully, Owen was frozen as well, which was fortuitous, for to rush into whatever calamity was playing out down the hill felt like certain death.

The cacophony grew to a crescendo, ending with an awful reverberating howl lasting for seconds that felt like a lifetime. A sad, lonely lifetime that was cut short before nature intended.

The stranger giggled, as if thinking of some old joke that tickled his fancy every time he recalled it. Perhaps something with three men walking into a bar.

There was the briefest moment of silence, then the trees and branches shifted as something slowly moved below them, at the bottom of the steep decline. The forest regained its somber silence as the movement grew more distant.

As Jeff prayed he wouldn't pee his pants, Owen stepped forward and said, "Stand aside," in a commanding voice that wielded more innate authority than a computer scientist in his early twenties should possess.

The stranger's initial response was a smirk, followed by a lazy glance back over his shoulder as he said, "Relax, yellow-haired one."

Just then, the darker-hued stranger appeared, stepping over the rim of the steep decline as if gravity was not his concern.

A dark liquid glistened across his bare chest. The fluid was speckled with irregular chunks and might well have been red, but that was impossible to judge against his indigo skin. He was nibbling jerky, cut in the same wide strips as what Mr.

Simpkins had been carrying.

Sparing Owen and Jeff barely a glance, he nodded towards his lighter companion. The two of them shared a look that was unreadable to Jeff but seemed to convey great amounts of information, as if they'd spent enormous amounts of time together, making speech almost pointless, so accustomed were they to each other's looks and expressions. Despite that, an observer might think they had no great love for one another, beyond a begrudging companionable familiarity forged by time, or perhaps lack of alternatives.

"It happened as it happens. The passionate urges beckoned," the dark one said.

"Alas," replied the lighter one, "even the greatest among us falls from grace from time to time."

A flash of irritation played across the dark one's face, perhaps at an old indiscretion the other would not let go. "Mistakes get made. They're a part of life … and death."

"Indeed. Now, onward and upward. Is it safe for such as these?" The lighter one gestured towards Jeff and Owen.

"They don't interest me at the moment," the dark one said before turning and jogging off, almost immediately blending into the dense forest, but not before revealing a tableau of ragged scourge marks crisscrossing his back. The way he moved through the trees was oddly unsettling. There was a liquid grace to it, yet at the same time the branches, limbs, and roots almost appeared to move aside, parting for his convenience.

"Oh goody," remarked the light one, although his tone was dry as the desert, conveying no joy. Turning back to Jeff and Owen, he said, "I believe that Black man with the flying metal whatchamajiggers has taken a nasty fall." Maniacally leering, he paused, perhaps waiting for a response. An accusation, a query, anything.

Jeff was at a loss, but Owen demanded, "Where is he?" His hands balling into fists, Owen was the very picture of righteous indignation. On a lesser man it would have looked silly, but Owen wore it well.

"Let's take a look, shall we?" The towering stranger spun on his heel and jogged down the decline, light as a feather. Owen and Jeff followed more cautiously, picking their way over the thick roots and loose leaves.

By the time Jeff reached the bottom, the stranger had disappeared, fading into the forest like a firefly blinking its light out at midnight, there and then gone.

Mr. Simpkins looked as if he had taken more than a nasty fall. He appeared to have been dropped from a cliff, banging every rocky ledge on the way down. His remains were a misshapen pile of mortal litter, awash in blood, bones jabbing out of skin. The shapes were all wrong, bulges and flattened edges where they should not be, limbs twisted at right angles in the wrong direction.

A swarm of black pellets buzzed in the air and crawled across the ruptured skin, flies in a frenzy of avarice, desperate to sample the remains.

Jeff's stomach flopped, rumbled, and protested, gurgling in a mutinous fashion.

Stray tatters of bark were scattered near the corpse. They matched up to gashes in the trees, long horizontal grooves gouged inches deep into the wood, parallel groups of four or five linear marks running together.

Switching into detective mode, Owen squatted over the ghastly remains, studying every nuance of the broken man. Despite having never seen a crime scene, much less a dead body—except his grampa in an open casket—his confidence told him he would find something. If nothing else, he was committing the scene to memory, all the better to fuel his hunt for the killers, whether with the police or without them.

For his part, Jeff stood back, begging his stomach to hold its contents.

"Hmm." Owen reached down, prying something loose from Mr. Simpkins' hand. It took a moment, for it was held in a true death grip.

A queasy cold tremor shook Jeff as he watched Owen wrestle with the corpse's fingers. The idea of touching the dead body horrified him. Instead of disturbing the scene they should be running for help, but he knew Owen wouldn't leave until he'd had his look.

Standing, Owen held his prize inches from his eyes and nose, squeezing it between his fingers, subjecting it to a level of intense scrutiny usually reserved for master jewelers assessing the quality of a massive diamond, the likes of which they might never see again.

It was a greasy hunk of long, stringy hair. A gobbet of bloody flesh dangled from one end like a horrific pendulum. Sniffing it, Owen winced, wrinkling his nose in disgust.

"Well, the one that talked to us has long hair, sort of like this." Owen waved the grisly trophy in Jeff's direction. "Maybe Mr. Simpkins grabbed it during the scuffle?"

Jeff stared purposefully at the tuft of foul hair, anything to refocus his attention away from the fly-ridden corpse. "Yeah, but his hair is lighter and clean, not dark and oily and ... nasty."

"And smelly," added Owen, once again sniffing the grimy clump in his hand.

"Werewolf?" Jeff offered. He thought it would lighten the mood but it immediately felt disrespectful, standing as they were over a dead body. Plus, having said it aloud, it seemed possible.

"Maybe," agreed Owen, perfectly serious. His fingers continuously rubbed the hair like a good luck charm.

Having barely enough warning to turn his head away, Jeff threw up, spraying peanut butter, grape jelly, bread, beef jerky, and kettle chips across the forest floor.

Conversely, Owen retained his lunch. Heroes don't vomit.

10 CAN YOU KEEP A SECRET?

"Totally disappeared!" Jeff insisted.

"No, it didn't," Carla said. She was the skeptic amongst them, when sober, which she was right then. It was late afternoon and they were at Winterbottom's Coffee Shop, under the watchful eyes of her parents, who frowned on her drinking, even though they themselves started sipping brandy or wine well before dinnertime.

"It did so," Jeff said. He was getting flustered, since the most monumental, most scary, most story-worthy thing of his life had happened, and the girl he might sort-of, kinda like didn't believe it.

"Corpses don't get up and walk away. Maybe you were wrong and he was alive. In which case, you two waltzed off and left him alone and injured. He could be out there right now, lost, alone, and hurt," said Carla. She was accusatory, but also dismissive, not yet certain how much of the story she believed.

Disengaging from her straw for a second, Ivy sang, "Knock, knock, knocking on Heaven's door." She tittered and returned to her mocha. Sugary drinks made her giggly.

Shaking his head, Jeff said, "No, no, no, the cops scoured the area and didn't find anything, except his truck and drones and other equipment scattered around. He was definitely dead, and his body definitely disappeared."

"There were lots of serious men and women with guns and uniforms out there stomping through the woods, poking at bushes, making noise," Ivy added. Pulling one edge of the plastic cover from her drink, she poured in two more sugar packets and swirled. A pile of such packets sat before her, most of them already emptied, victims of her merciless sweet tooth.

Jeff sipped his coffee, his lifeline. He was tired. It had been another long night, chatting with the authorities about bodies and how they might disappear.

Carla shrugged. "Fine then, if he's dead and his body's gone, then something got him, like wolves or a bear. They would want the body but not the drones and gadgets. I'd imagine your meth-cooking male models would want the drones, not just the old man's dead body."

"That could be," Owen muttered. He'd been especially troubled since Mr. Simpkins' death, feeling solely responsible. Amongst Owen's few flaws was the propensity to bear burdens that weren't truly his.

"I completely believe you. Those meth dudes definitely stole the body," Ivy said around her straw, before adding with an evil grin, "Probably to eat it." She shivered, a full body one, everything from the tips of her toes to the highest curl of flaming red hair atop her head committing to it.

Looking at the people at his table, Jeff realized he was part of a Scooby gang. They had an attractive redhead in Ivy, a smart brunette with glasses in Carla, and an athletic blond guy in Owen. That must make him Shaggy. He didn't want to be Shaggy. Following that train of thought, he had to acknowledge the possibility that the mysterious men in the woods were actually crooked real estate developers or bankers perpetrating ill-conceived schemes in rubber masks.

His musings on how awesome it would be to have a talking Great Dane were interrupted when a woman entered the coffee shop.

Something about her immediately demanded his attention, since she entered like a gunslinger in a cheesy old western. A real shoot-first-and-ask-questions-later type, since her gun was already drawn. Except in this case, it wasn't a six-shooter but rather a y-shaped stick. She held the two shorter arms in one hand. The longer arm led her, bringing her straight to their table.

She was wearing an immense backpack of the sort made for a months-long expedition into the desolate wilds. It reached several inches over her head and was jampacked, with several cobbled-together doohickeys of unfathomable usage tied to the outside, as well as a bedroll strapped to the bottom. A pot and a pan dangled from one side, clanging into one another with her every step.

The overall effect was not so much that of a backpacker but more like someone panning for gold in a backwoods stream, far from civilization.

Her brown hair, tinged with gray at the temples, was pulled back in a ponytail. It wasn't to keep it from her face, but rather simply to hide the fact that it hadn't been washed recently.

The expression she wore was part wince and part smile. Her budding jowls and sagging face, when considered alongside her crow's feet, placed her at an indiscriminate age, certainly above forty but definitely short of sixty, although it was anyone's guess where in that range.

She was leaning forward several degrees, which Jeff took to be a consequence of the ponderous backpack, but would later learn was her continuous posture, as if she were resolutely striding into a strong wind.

After stopping at their table, the woman cradled the y-shaped stick, so like a divining rod, with great satisfaction. Smiling with delight, she slid it into a pocket along the side of her backpack and then set her hands on her hips and rocked back and forth, her brown eyes searching each of their faces in turn.

"Well, how's it going?" she asked, as if they'd been expecting her.

"Umm, fine," offered Carla. "You can order a drink over there." She pointed towards the counter, currently being manned by her mother, who was grinding beans. The satisfying smell of freshly ground coffee filled the room.

"Nah," the backpacker said, waving her hand enthusiastically. That was how she did most things, with abundant enthusiasm. "I'm here to help you. Just call me Coach." She spoke as if the words spilling from her mouth were a curiosity and she couldn't wait to hear what was next. Nearly everything Coach uttered, whether it was a question, comment, or statement of fact, emerged as an exclamation of dawning wonderment, as if she were experiencing an epiphany.

The blank faces worn by Jeff and his friends did nothing to hinder Coach's enthusiasm. Wrestling her way out of her backpack, she plunked it on the floor, then slid a chair between Jeff and Owen. Collapsing into it, she sighed a sigh of such contentment that it seemed she might not have sat in days. She set both elbows on the table and leaned forward, as if ready to plot a conspiracy.

"Ivy, Jeff, and Owen," Coach said excitedly, correctly pointing at each of them in turn. "I don't know you though," she added, pointing with both hands towards Carla.

"She's Carla," Ivy said. While the others were caught flatfooted by this new person's intrusion, Ivy was taking her presence in stride. Jeff assumed that was because she herself was a devotee of the unexpected.

"So, it sounds like you've got a bit of a fairy problem," Coach said, as if she were letting them in on some inside joke, one that only she could fully comprehend.

"Say what now?" Carla asked, even as Jeff muttered, "Huh?" The mention of fairies made him immediately nervous, recalling the night at the bar that ended with Murray swinging from a tree.

"You know, fairies? Mystical beings? Elves, from the sound of it." Coach peeked around to ensure no eavesdroppers lurked nearby, yet made no attempt to lower her voice, which was of the sort that carried well, finding its way into every nook and cranny of the cafe.

"Fairies or elves, which one is it?" asked Carla. "You've gotta get your bullshit straight."

"Oh, it's no bullshit," Coach crooned, brimming with exhilaration. "Ya see, the word fairies is a blanket term for magical folk, which includes elves as a subtype. So, all elves are fairies but not all fairies are elves, It's like how all robins are birds but not all birds are robins. Easy, right?"

"Either way, I don't think we have problems with fairies or elves," Jeff said.

"Not fairies, and definitely not elves," Carla agreed. She had no reservations against shooting down the impossible.

"Yes, probably elves," Ivy interjected, nodding stridently. Coach was absorbing her complete attention, with an absolute focus Jeff would not have thought Ivy capable of, like a child meeting Santa.

"They're definitely elves," Coach said, rolling her eyes, as if desperate to get this part of the conversation over with and move on to the good stuff. "Listen, you're having problems with two people, right?"

"Yes," said Owen, "but how do you know that?"

"It's my job to know stuff. Now, let me ask you, are they tall? Often in the woods? And are they handsome, but in a genderless sorta way? Are they somehow ..." She paused to scratch her chin, where a few wayward hairs lived. The leanest second later, her face lit up, as if the scratching had helped her conjure up the appropriate term. "Majestic?"

Jeff and Owen exchanged glances, trading silent moral support, acquiescing for the other to voice the truth howsoever they saw it. Finally, Owen said, "Well, yeah, all that stuff."

Coach was nodding before Owen finished, as if she'd

known the answer all along. "Do they have pointy ears?"

"I did sort of think that one time when I got a good look, yeah," Jeff admitted. A low-level blush snuck onto his cheeks and he looked away, towards the exit, as if he'd made a shameful admission of some secret he'd been withholding.

Wearing a look of complete disbelief, Coach managed to stifle her tone to one of polite, understated incredulity. "Uh huh, didn't you find that unusual? You're aware that people don't tend to have long pointy ears, right?"

Jeff squirmed, realizing he wouldn't stand up to cross-examination if he were ever on the stand. "Well, uh, yeah, but I wasn't too sure since their hair is usually in the way, so I could be wrong." Panic sweat charged down his forehead, seeping into his left eye.

"Sure, sure, I can see that," Coach said, letting him off the hook. "Anything else weird about them?" The question was merely a formality, for she obviously knew the answer was yes.

Owen offered no response. He was lost in the dense thickets of his own thoughts, his expression unreadable.

The folk-rock song in the background faded out, the resulting silence filled by the thumping of the espresso machine.

"Um," Jeff mumbled, swabbing the salty sting from his eye. "One has sort of bluish-purple skin."

Roused from his temporary reverie, Owen said, "Yup, it was, like, indigo."

Coach nodded, setting her puffy cheeks to jiggling. "Indigo, sure, of course. You sharp cookies are aware that humans don't often have blue skin, right? Although some elves do, just so you know." She seemed delighted by her own words, as well as enchanted by the opportunity to straighten out a table full of fools.

Jeff said, "Well that one could have a condition that affects his skin. And like, for the ears, they could both be wearing some prosthetics or something." That was grasping for straws, but the decidedly unlikely was still a better explanation than the completely impossible.

Coach sneered, although it was jovial, lacking any hints of maliciousness. "Wandering around the woods in Halloween costumes, huh? Well, you're not the brains of this operation, I can see that. But that's okay, you're a nice kid."

"Jeff really is very nice," Ivy confided in a breathy whisper, as she patted his nervously fidgeting hand. Her kind words and tender touch soothed him, making him wonder if perhaps it could be elves after all. Some people are resolute in their opinions, unlikely to be swayed without a convincing counterargument associated with persuasive evidence. Jeff was not such a person, mostly since he was too needy for approval. Blame it, perhaps, on his unwanted virginity, or possibly his overbearing father.

Coach looked overjoyed. "I'm sure he's just swell. Anyway, yup, those are elves you've got on your hands."

Ivy nodded. "That sounds right. And they're evil ones." Adventure sparkled in her eyes. She had the most sparkly eyes.

"Yeah, probably evil." Coach squinted at Ivy speculatively.

"And they've got a big weird black bunny," Jeff offered. That seemed like a silly thing to bring up, but Jellybiscuits had a lot of gravitas for a bunny. It deserved a mention.

Coach waved a hand dismissively. "I wouldn't worry too much over a bunny."

"Okay, so imaginary creatures are to blame," Carla said, her sarcasm just a step short of completely over the top. It rolled off her in waves.

Coach absorbed the sarcasm and reflected it in the form of utter sincerity. "Not imaginary at all. All magical folklore and fairy tales are based on reality, from Cinderella to seelies." She picked up one of the sugar packets from the table and began fiddling with it.

"That's totally not true," said Carla.

"Yeah, ya got me, they probably aren't all real." Coach spawned a sheepish grin. "But they're definitely parables carried down through the centuries, and there's a form of truth embedded within parables. No one can deny that."

After responding with a derisive snort, Carla sat back and sipped her coffee, rolling her eyes.

Oblivious to the implied derision, Coach ripped the sugar packet, spilling the contents across the table, a splash of ivory granules across stained wood.

The spilled sugar caught Jeff's attention for half a heartbeat, about as interesting as a stranger's sneeze.

Ivy, however, was transfixed, giving it a level of focused concentration commensurate with a unicorn walking in the door and ordering a latte. Leaning forward, green eyes gleaming as they raced over the pile, she twirled a finger through the granular heap.

As Ivy studied the sugar, Coach studied her, and Jeff studied Coach studying Ivy. Owen stared into space. Carla chewed her lip, staring at her drink.

Looking as if she'd come to a decision, Coach leaned down and rummaged through one of the side pockets in her backpack, extracting a sandwich baggie and placing it on the table. Within it were a pile of irregularly shaped brown clods, about the size of elongated dice. A transitory flight of fancy whispered in Jeff's ear that this crazy woman carried small animal poops.

"Chocolate-covered hazelnuts," she announced. "I made them myself. Anybody want some?"

That was an obvious no, in Jeff's mind. Any homemade candy extracted from a stranger's backpack was a hard pass.

He shook his head and mumbled, "No thanks," just as Ivy's hand shot out like a snake and grabbed a couple of the sloppy chocolate treats. She jammed them in her mouth, eyes not rising from the sugar, which she was studying like a puzzle she was on the verge of solving.

Owen took one as well, although less vigorously than Ivy had. Similar to Jeff, Carla stared at them as if suspecting their coating wasn't simply chocolate but might instead be augmented with poop.

Grabbing a few more candies, Ivy continued chewing voraciously. She had a ravenous sweet tooth, one that she never attempted to rein in.

Coach squinted at Ivy, inspecting her closely. When she spoke, she sounded distracted. "They're probably looking to save the forest from being wiped clean by your logging company. Fairies and elves do that sort of thing. Big nature fans, them."

"Well, it isn't really my company and we aren't chopping down the forest, just thinning it out," Jeff replied. That felt insufficient, so he added, "I work for them, but I also believe in environmental conservation." That sounded hypocritical, but the two were not mutually exclusive.

"Yeah, sure, right, me too. Anyway, elves. I can help, since I see this kind of thing all the time." Coach sat up straighter, sniffed, and straightened her khaki shirt, as if trying to look official.

Carla held up an index finger, signaling a point of order. "To clarify for the record, you see this sort of stuff all the time?"

"Well," Coach said, "I've suspected it more than seen it, if you really want to split hairs. Anyway, you're definitely going to need me. I'm here to help. This is what I do."

Concentrating squarely on the sugar pile, Ivy groped around

the table, her grasping fingers eventually finding the baggie of chocolates and claiming several more for her own.

"Would elves beat a guy to death and then hide the body?" Jeff asked. It felt weird playing along with Coach's nonsense, but something about her fostered a mild suspension of disbelief. Perhaps it was that she was so inordinately sincere in her belief in her nonsense. And she seemed harmless.

"They did that?" Coach's dull brown eyes grew wide with excitement. She looked impressed. The idea of fairy folk killing humans got her heart pounding. "Sure, they very well might do that, if they had a good reason. Of course, what they consider a good reason would be very different than what we consider to be one. Maybe the guy stomped through their favorite patch of bluebells."

"And two hikers disappeared a ways back," Carla said, having apparently decided to humor this unlikely interloper into their everyday lives.

"Probably got them too, I'd imagine," Coach replied, her voice an excited warble.

"And they've been messing with my company's stuff. I think they're trying to keep us away from a particular spot in the woods," Jeff said.

Meanwhile, Ivy remained distracted by the sugar, to the exclusion of all other things. Her fingertips traipsed through it, crafting distinct piles. She'd finished the bag of chocolates.

"A particular spot, huh? Interesting. They must be guarding something. That's the way they are. All their little fairy holes, hidden away from prying human eyes, each and every one chockful of wonders." Coach's tone implied that she had seen this a thousand times, like an exterminator discussing cockroaches, although cockroaches that they had a soft spot and admiration for.

Carla looked dubious. "You said you can help. How,

exactly, are you equipped to handle magical creatures?"

She was teasing. That was obvious. Yet, Coach accepted the question as being asked with complete sincerity, so she sought to answer it in good faith.

"Mostly rune magic, but also a few other alchemical tricks I picked up overseas." Coach enthusiastically leaned over the table, elbows in spilled coffee and a tremendous smile across her face, displaying teeth in desperate need of a deep cleaning.

"Where overseas?" demanded Carla.

"In the Middle East. I was in the military, doin' my time, stuck over there for a couple tours. In my spare time, I got the itch for runes. It's a long story if you want to hear it."

"No thanks," Carla replied. "But, rune magic, huh? That's perfect for this problem. Except, one question though, what does that mean exactly?"

"Thanks for asking! Ancient symbols that, when added to something in a certain way with certain materials under certain conditions, convey a type of magic. Powerful stuff." Coach produced a canteen that had been hanging from her backpack. Symbols were scrawled on it. Some were wavy like water, others were chaotic scribbles, another was a sun symbol with a line through it. "For instance, this canteen is always full and the water is always cool. Or at least, usually. I mean, you know, it's not infallible."

Inspired by her own ramblings, Coach continued jabbering. She did that a lot. It was mostly an in-depth dissertation on runology and magical symbolism, but alchemy also had its place.

Although Owen was mostly silent, Jeff could see him shifting. Charging. Activating. Every seemingly nonsensical word Coach said struck him hard, each syllable turning an internal crank deep within him, winding him up like a spring. If he was a spring-loaded automaton, he would be almost fully wound, ready for action. Coach's version of the world, ridiculous or not, suited Owen well. In her version, there was more to existence than the simply mundane. Danger called. Adventure beckoned.

Coach paused in the midst of a spirited babble on Nordic runes. Her smile was wide, but her face apologetic. "Maybe I'm telling you more than you need to hear. That's a thing I do. Ya know, this one time in Turkey …"

As if arousing from meditation, Owen interrupted Coach mid-sentence. "You said to call you Coach. Why's that? Are you a coach?" Owen had excelled at several sports and been offered a full scholarship for baseball. But a torn rotator cuff had ended those dreams. It was just as well, since he liked tennis more. But again, the rotator cuff ended those hopes. A single torn tendon had ruined many of his aspirations, yet he'd never uttered a single complaint, instead just stolidly soldiering on.

Coach was delighted by the query. "Great question! IDK. Is that what you cool kids say these days, IDK? Like, when chatting on your computer phones?" She brought her hands together over the table and flailed her thumbs in the barest approximation of texting, as if she'd seen it before but never tried it. She shrugged and said, "Coach is just what people call me," as if she'd never considered the question before but was fascinated by it.

A pause ensued, wherein everyone marinated in their own thoughts.

There are companionable pauses in the normal ebb and flow of conversations, wherein everyone is comfortable and contented, but just happen to all be silent at the same time. This was not such a pause. This one was awkward, as everyone except Coach reflected on the dialogue thus far, playing it back, assessing it for granules of sanity, but finding few.

79

Outside their paused microcosm, the workings of the coffee shop continued. An old man demanded a fifty-cent coffee. He rattled his cane threateningly as Mrs. Winterbottom tiredly explained it would be nearly four dollars. The codger's ire soared as his face turned deep red, stammering that a nickel would buy a bucket of joe back in his day. Sadly, it was a conversation they had most days. He had a touch of Alzheimer's.

Since no one else was inclined to fill the verbal void, Coach took it upon herself to do so. "Anyway, about those elves," she said, her words carrying all the wonder of a deeply meaningful eureka moment. "I'll need a day or two to get my ducks in a row. Then we'll meet in the woods, and I'll summon them to ask what they want. It's as easy as that, lemon squeezy."

Enough was enough. Listening to this loon in the coffee shop was one thing but meeting her in the woods was something else altogether. Jeff was preparing his polite refusal when Owen said, "Okay, I believe you. Let's do this thing."

Snorting incredulously, Carla shook her head in disbelief. For her part, Ivy continued twiddling with the sugar pile.

Owen's words surprised Jeff, but they also didn't.

"Fine," sighed Jeff. Being a sidekick was a full-time job, even when you couldn't muster up complete commitment to a course of action. Being honest, Owen tended to be right about most things, so his level of credibility was beyond dispute in Jeff's mind.

Besides, it couldn't hurt. Although she might be exceedingly eccentric, Coach didn't seem to mean any harm. But of course, that's what they say about most people that break down and crack open the rules of society. That serial killer next door? Seemed nice and quiet, perhaps he was a bit eccentric, but everyone thought he was harmless.

Finally tearing her attention from the scattered sugar, which she'd sorted into a single pile, Ivy's shining green eyes rose to stab at Coach's face. She said, "I won't be there when you talk with them. They're too scary." Her cheeks scrunched up, pulling her lips back to reveal her white teeth, forming a sort of nervous snarly grimace.

"Fair enough," Coach said, her voice an excited trill. She punched Owen's shoulder playfully, although awkwardly, as if it had started as a noogie but been redirected midstream. "Don't worry, we got this covered."

"This is awesome," Ivy said, hopping to her feet. "I've got things to do, but please do keep me updated." She ran out the door, her feet barely touching the floor, as if floating. Her exit was no surprise; Jeff had rarely seen her sit in one spot for so long.

After Ivy had floated out the door, Coach leaned forward and spoke with the air of someone planning a heist. "She's of the fair folk. You can see that, right?"

"Uh, yeah, she's very pretty," Jeff answered, thrown by the sudden conversational turn. Glancing at Carla, who looked annoyed by his agreement, he added, "I mean, you know, looks are subjective so not everyone would agree." Ivy was beyond his reach, but he sometimes thought Carla might like him, so he couldn't afford to alienate her.

Coach waved her hand. "No, no, not like that. She's a fairy, almost certainly a pixie, to be precise. Although not pure pixie. Nope, she's got some other lineage cooking in there as well. Sprite or nixie maybe. Gnome? Nah, no beard. Could be some nymph in there."

"She looks pretty nymph-y," Owen agreed.

"Sure does," said Jeff, while avoiding Carla's irritated gaze.

A few steps away, the old man stomped off with his four-dollar coffee, just as he did every day. He muttered of senior discounts, the price of coffee beans, and how fat cats were always trying to stick it to the little guy.

"Uh huh, yeah," Carla said. "To clarify, you are saying that not only are the guys in the woods elves, but also that Ivy is some kind of fairy."

Carla's sarcasm was so thickly slathered that even Coach detected it. On the defensive, she replied, "Yup, trust me, I can tell. For instance, the sugar counting. Pixies can't help themselves, they've just gotta count spilled sugar or salt or whatever. It's a compulsion."

"Really? They couldn't possibly not count it?" Carla asked. She remained a paragon of skepticism.

Coach's head rattled up and down in the most emphatic of nods. "Yeah, always count it, every single time." She planted her right elbow on the table, rested her chin in that palm, and gazed up speculatively, her eyes unfocused, as if she were staring into the depthless heavens. "Although, come to think of it, it probably depends on what they're doing. Like, if they were running from a blazing fireworks factory, the sugar might interest them less than if they were just sitting around a coffee shop, I imagine. There's not really a standardized handbook on this stuff, it's more just word of mouth. But, anyway, she's a fairy, that's for sure. She has an aura. Magic just drips off her. Oh, and my handy dandy divining rod found her." Coach patted the y-shaped stick in her backpack.

Meanwhile, the old man and his overly expensive coffee were prowling the coffee shop, looking for a discarded newspaper, of which there were none. It was another part of his daily routine.

"So, your stick points at her, she seems magic-y to you, and she looked at some spilled sugar. That's how you can tell she's a pixie," Carla said. As she spoke, Carla reached into the shopping bag at her feet and extracted a newspaper.

Grinning like someone who'd just had a surprise birthday

party sprung on them, Coach said, "And she'd be vulnerable to iron or silver. Like, if you jabbed her with an iron spike she'd be wounded."

"That would hurt anybody," Owen observed.

"True," Coach said, "but if you poked at her with most other materials, like plastic, she'd be unharmed. Well, mostly unharmed." She mimed poking a spear at an invisible foe. "Just try it," she urged.

"Okay, fine, if those guys are elves, then she can be a fairy," Carla said. She tossed the newspaper on the neighboring table.

"More specifically, a pixie. But maybe also something else." Coach looked troubled.

The sound of the newspaper hitting the tabletop drew the old man like a cat to a tuna can being pulled open at dinnertime. He snatched it up and retreated to a corner table. In the interest of keeping the peace, the Winterbottoms had started buying a paper just for him.

Ivy wasn't a magical pixie, obviously. Jeff refused to suspend his disbelief to that level until actual evidence presented itself. Some evidence beyond a magical pointy stick and spilled sugar.

Although, Coach's story did allow a few observations and events to align, clicking into place in a reasonable order. Odd things happened around Ivy. For instance, Snakebite wouldn't usually spin himself to the point of injury on the dance floor. And, when she was leaving someplace but still at the corner of his eye, Ivy did appear to float. Or just outright disappear.

His thoughts were interrupted when Coach leaned forward, signaling them all to lean in as well. Her eyes became shifty as she inspected the other customers. She was the very picture of someone ready to mount a secret rebellion.

"Can you keep a secret?" she whispered, once they'd all tipped their heads forward attentively.

"Sure," said Owen, which was true. He was a lockbox, holding all Jeff's secrets.

"Well, I can't," murmured Coach. She peeked suspiciously at the old man at the corner table, who was now rifling through the paper, grumbling that he couldn't find the funnies. "The truth is that the pixie invited me, although I didn't know she was a pixie at the time."

"Ivy did?" asked Owen, just above a whisper. In the last few minutes, he'd seemed to grow, expanding in some ill-defined way. His inherent valorous spirit of adventure was stirring, activated by having a path forward, however indistinct and unlikely it might seem. It made him loom large, inflated by burgeoning valor awaiting an outlet.

"Yup."

"So, your stick thing didn't actually lead you here?" Owen asked.

"Divining rod," offered Carla.

"Correct!" Coach said, beaming at Carla. "And no, it did not," she continued, talking towards Owen. "Although it works up close, it wouldn't lead me all the way here from another state. Its mojo isn't that powerful."

"And that's rune magic?" asked Owen, pointing towards the fancy stick in question.

Excited, Coach snatched the stick from the backpack. She traced her finger along the small symbols carved into its side. "Also correct! I scribed these symbols of seeking into this ash stick with a bent iron knife under a full moon on an unmoored vessel adrift in a lake." The way she said it, the procedure seemed like a completely normal hobby for a person to have.

Carla rolled her eyes and huffed. Neither Owen nor Coach noticed, excited as they were by the quest at hand, which was to track down two apparently murderous elves in the forest and demand to know what they were up to. And then, presumably, to demand they cease and desist all evil activities.

Tracing his index finger along the stick, Owen was enraptured. "Does that other stuff aside from the runes matter? For instance, the knife being bent."

"Yup," Coach barked enthusiastically, excited to have at least one member of her audience enthralled. "Or, I think so anyway. It's hard to tell." It seemed she would continue along that train of thought, but changed her mind, and gave her head a shake. "Back to the point, Ivy's the one that contacted me."

"So, she's paying you?" Owen asked, reluctantly disengaging his finger from the seemingly magical stick.

"Nope, it isn't like that. I go where I'm needed," Coach said. She grunted as she leaned down to jam the magical divining rod back into its backpack pocket home.

"Then this is a goodness of your heart thing," said Carla, ever skeptical. "Straight-up good Samaritan?"

"Honestly, no. It's curiosity and adventure and the experience. Plus, to be frank, where there are fairies of any kind there's often treasure." Coach's face became deadly serious. "And let me tell you, if that pixie was scared enough to call me, there's definitely something dangerous in these woods. Those two elf lads are trouble, and we're gonna figure out just how much trouble in a few days."

11 AN INFESTATION OF FAIRIES

Those few days passed. It was now a warm and windy Saturday. A good day to sleep in, eat fast-food burgers, play video games, and relax. But instead, Jeff and Owen met Coach at the logging site.

No trees were being felled that day. They only worked weekends when there was some monumental rush, and even then Uncle Chet tried to avoid it. Overtime costs cut into his margins, which were already dangerously thin. Or so he said, although Chet had a lot of expensive toys and gadgets for someone whose business was barely scraping by.

Ivy and Carla weren't there. Carla's patience for silliness did not extend to tromping through the forest on a Saturday. Ivy stayed away since she insisted the guys in the woods—the presumptive elves—were entirely dangerous and meant her harm. Her sincere pronouncements of their evil natures did nothing to settle Jeff's frayed nerves.

Also fraying his nerves was the hefty object in his pullover hoodie's front pocket.

It wasn't actually that heavy, but then again it was, containing the weight of destiny within it.

The bulk was a Glock 43, which Uncle Chet had described as a single-stack, double-action polymer 9mm semiautomatic pistol. Jeff wasn't sure what single-stack meant, or how many stacks someone might need. The same for the double-action part. How many actions did someone require? Two seemed ample. All he knew was that the pistol made him feel safer, but also horrified. The black polymer gadget of death felt like evil deeds waiting to unfold.

Declaring the Glock's operation to be foolproof, while providing no other instruction, Chet had pressed it into Jeff's hands a few nights ago, insisting he needed the protection in the unlikely event he ran across whatever had gotten Mr. Simpkins. Chet was a big believer in guns, and thought everyone should have one, which wasn't a notion Jeff agreed with. The weapon came with an innocuous nylon bag, big enough for a bowling ball, meant to contain the pistol, boxes of bullets, and magazines. Also, a holster whose function Jeff couldn't fathom. It was meant to be worn such that the pistol was inside his belt. That sounded like an efficient method for accidentally shooting himself in the ass, so Jeff instead reluctantly tucked the pistol into his hoodie pocket.

He'd instantly told Owen about the Glock. Owen didn't approve, mostly on the grounds that neither of them had ever used a firearm before.

Jeff told Coach as well. Having been in the military, the presence of the pistol didn't upset her. She simply shrugged and said, "Couldn't hurt, I suppose."

They drove one of the company Jeeps bumping across the backroads, stopping just at the border of Sector G12.

Climbing out of the passenger seat, Coach hitched up her britches and sniffed, her eyes overflowing with excitement at the adventure to come.

Jeff, conversely, was immediately jumpy, spooked by the pervasive shadows within the denser confines of G12. The invasive hum of what must be cicadas was everywhere, calling out from several spots, sometimes in disjointed harmony, other times separately.

Coach's attention was immediately drawn to G12, even before they pointed her in the proper direction. She marched off, directly into the denser forest, coming to a stop several paces in, at a meager widening of the trail, just broad enough to feel like a clearing.

With little recourse, Owen and Jeff followed. The fragmented cries of the cicadas died away, as if a veil had dropped.

Scratching her chin, disturbing the few stray hairs decorating its bumpy surface, Coach said, "Good gravy, this place has an infestation of fairies. Reeks of it." She waved her hand before her scrunched nose. "And not just elves and pixies, but other sorts. There might actually be things besides your standard-issue fairies." She was marveling at the dark woods surrounding them.

Coach wafted the air towards her nose and delicately sniffed like a crazed wine connoisseur. "And it's not just smell. You can feel the magic pulsing like a giant heart," she insisted, sounding as if she were sharing an inside joke, although one that she herself didn't understand.

Both Jeff and Owen remained silent. How did one answer such statements? Did magic have a scent? A feel? The area smelled like pine trees, mud, and wet leaves. As for the feel, it was definitely creepy.

With a flourish normally reserved for stage magicians and street-corner card sharps, Coach produced an object from one of the thousand pockets she possessed, even in the absence of her backpack. Raising her arm and opening her hand, she revealed a silver bell resting on her palm.

It was modestly sized, with a dark wooden handle barely thicker than a pencil. Along its humble metal cup were a multitude of symbols carved into the silver. The small clapper was wrapped in tissue paper to prevent premature clanging.

With great care, as if handling a bomb, Coach pulled away the tissue paper, wiped her nose with it, and shoved it up her sleeve.

"A ring from this bell will summon them," she announced with great glee. The pride she seemingly took in the bell surpassed what Jeff had felt for any of his major life accomplishments, few as they were.

Far away, deeper into Sector G12, turkey vultures wheeled, circling above the treetops, just visible through a gap in the trees. Squinting into the sun, Jeff couldn't make out their number. Whether it was two or twenty, they were a bad omen.

"How does it work?" asked Owen. While Jeff retained a healthy dubiousness of Coach's various fantastic claims, Owen was invested in her abilities. His skepticism had been banished when they'd sipped from her 'magic' canteen yesterday, finding the water far cooler than they expected. Whereas Owen experienced magic in the canteen, Jeff suspected advanced materials and a vacuum lining. However, as a proper sidekick, he followed Owen's lead.

"Rune magic," answered Coach, as though it were obvious. Presumably, they were to assume anything in her possession with cryptic symbols slashed into the surface contained magic of the highest order.

"Neat," said Owen.

"Uh, okay," said Jeff.

"Fascinating," said the lighter-skinned stranger. Without warning, he was amongst them, leaning in to inspect the bell.

Jeff was equally dumbfounded, startled, and confused by the stranger's sudden appearance, but Owen reacted quickly, as if he'd been expecting it. He stepped back and raised his hands in some semblance of a ready position, in case this should come to fisticuffs. At the same time, Coach jumped back, accidentally ringing the bell, which released a light tinkle, muffled by the wind shuffling the leafy branches like playing cards.

The darker one then materialized, emerging between Jeff's panicked blinks like a subliminal message that, once visible, refused to fade. Although, when Jeff later reviewed this moment in hindsight, he would picture the second stranger walking out of the woods in what could only be described as a casual, yet resolute, meander.

The hypothetical elves were both wearing faded jeans and brightly colored polo shirts. The lighter-skinned one wore loafers while the other's feet were bare. Like the rest of him, his bare feet were indigo, with scars traced into the skin, either as purposeful markings or evidence of old wounds. His body was a canvas of pain and sacrifice, the evidence in elaborate patterns etched into the surface.

Stepping back to a respectful distance, the two newcomers looked entirely placid and harmless, just a couple of guys out for a regal walk in the woods. Even several steps away, they smelled splendidly, of wildflowers and sandalwood.

Their wretched rabbit Jellybiscuits was nowhere to be found, which was a kindness to Jeff's eyes.

Embarrassed, Owen dropped his dukes. His tanned hands, hanging by his sides, looked lost, the fingers incessantly flexing and releasing, unsure what to do with themselves. The adrenaline surging through his system was urging him to action.

Those flexing fingers were a concern, since Jeff was seized by the sudden unassailable certainty that these guys were not to be trifled with. They were serious men, possibly even evil, just as Ivy had insisted. Any clenched fist thrown at them in anger would be returned with grievous damage. Possibly a finger bitten off.

The compact pistol in his pocket now felt like a necessity, even if he wished that Owen held it instead. He was better suited to cope with the responsibility.

Jeff jumped like a startled cat when Coach bellowed, "I have beckoned and you've arrived, powerless to resist my summoning magic." She was so intensely pleased with herself that it seemed she might explode. She clutched the bell as if it were the only lit candle in a pitch-dark cave.

The darker stranger scrunched up his face in confusion. "You didn't really beckon us. Did she?"

"Nope, I was already here," said the lighter one. His hands were tucked in his pockets. He looked like a model at a photo shoot who'd been told to act casual, yet with some smolder.

"I haven't been properly beckoned in some time," said the darker one, followed by a weary sigh.

"You're elves," Coach announced. She said it accusingly, although lightheartedly, as if pronouncing someone was 'It' in a game of tag.

Bemused, the lighter-skinned one said, "That should be obvious." Shifting his flowing brown mane, he revealed his ears. They were long and pointy, poking up like little flags. "The ears give it away," he added.

"Many of the fairy folk besides elves have big pointy ears," replied Coach.

"Yes," said the light-skinned elf, "but unlike some silly pixie or ugly hobgoblin, elves have a certain, well, let's just say we inspire …" He paused before poking a finger into the air triumphantly, signifying a lightbulb moment. "A stately sense of wonder."

True, thought Jeff, they were indeed stately. Regal, even. Beings of true purpose. Their close presence fostered a sense of unreality, like standing near a zoo's lion enclosure when the mighty cats strutted by. It simply felt primordially wrong to be so close to them.

"Reveal your names, foul creatures," roared Coach. She gave the bell a tiny ring-a-ding. "The power of my summoning compels you."

The indigo elf sneered. "Foul? She's rather rude, isn't she?"

"Yes she is," agreed his comrade. "Vulgar woman, you're off to a bad start." His eyes varied in color depending on the viewing angle, but right then flashed a furious gold.

"What are your true names? I demand you reveal them as required in the ancient agreement between our peoples," yelled Coach. Her face was a cherry red. She was not a yeller by nature.

"Whatever agreement do you mean?" asked the indigo one. After the question he smiled, displaying a set of teeth that looked suitable for a toothpaste commercial. Until he shifted slightly, at which point they looked like interlocking arrowheads, well-honed for tearing flesh. Jeff would see those teeth in nightmares.

Looking sheepish, Coach shrugged. "I thought there might be something like that ..." She trailed off to inaudibility, scuffing her feet and kicking an acorn into the trees.

The elves exchanged glances, exhibiting a heady mixture of annoyance and humor. The lighter one said, "It is about time we did introductions, I suppose. Tell us your names first." It was a command more than a request.

Owen stepped to the fore, planted his hands on his hips, and tried to match the authority emanating from the elvish pair. He failed, but it was a valiant effort. Pointing at the members of their party in turn, he said, "This is Jeff, and Coach, and I'm Owen."

Waving limply, Jeff smiled halfheartedly.

Inclining her chin towards the imposing pair, Coach said, "Howdy." She held the bell in a white-knuckled grip as if it were a winning lottery ticket.

The lighter-skinned elf bowed, sweeping his hand out to the side. "I am Yoric, who contested the goblin king for Matilde's heart, now stored in a vault of ice. Wounded at the aerie of Grimton. Swain of Gorrhyl and bane of the Infernal Baron's High Guard. He who challenged the pillaging of Atlantis. Born in sleet. Seeker of the southern winds. Who bears the shame of having lost the fair Belltruckle to the Sulfur Riptide."

The darker one dropped to one knee, bowing his head. "And I am Ackley, whose heart was shorn in the Elder Trenches and built anew. He who strode the Slate Wall and helped turn the tide of the western hobgoblin hordes. The twice impaled. Scourged by the dragon of Madagascar. Past sentinel of Dunwich. Once and future general of the wyvern cavaliers and slayer of the wendigo of Verglas. Thane of the Cinnamon City for a scant decade. Bearer of the cursed blade Banderhaunt, whose thirst will never be quenched."

Jeff's mouth hung open. He shut it quickly, with a louder slap than he would have liked. His hand cradled the ugly black plastic Glock, praying he wouldn't need it.

Uncoiling himself, Ackley arose and crossed his scarred arms. He was defiant, scornful of the overwhelmed looks on the faces of the humans before him. The lighter-skinned Yoric, meanwhile, appeared amused.

The wind silently howled as it poured over the elves, whipping at their clothes and hair, painting a majestic portrait. Their ruse of humanity having diminished, their appearances subtly changed. No less beautiful, but now faintly alien. Their ears aggressively poking through their hair, their eyes overlarge, their chins and faces too long and sharp and perfect to be those of humans.

The elves waited patiently, as only the ageless can. The humans were locked in place by incredulity, uncertain how to proceed.

The idea that Yoric and Ackley were fabricating their outlandish credentials never crossed Jeff's mind. He could feel them for what they were. Magical beings, ferocious warriors, slayers of all manner of beast. Life swung on a precarious balance in their presence.

At the edge of the clearing was a brown and white bunny, its head cocked to one side, ears flopped over, watching the impromptu meeting. It was chewing clover and had gotten several bites along before anyone spoke again.

"Huh," Coach peeped, finding her voice. There was no denying she was impressed, nor did she try to hide it. "So, you're both really fancy. Got it. Super-duper."

"She says we're fancy, Yoric," said Ackley.

Yoric nodded. "I suppose we are, Mr. Ackley. These things are subjective, but I tend to agree. Our histories are rather storied."

Ackley nodded, scratching at the scars running along his muscular indigo arm. "Indeed."

After adorably scratching an ear, the bunny resumed chewing clover.

Coach abruptly jabbed a finger at the pair. It set her shiny silver bell to tinkling. She bellowed, "Do you mean to harm these humans? You can't lie to me while I hold this." She brandished the bell as though it were a crowbar. It was very melodramatic, but the ringing was so weak as to be lost to the breeze.

The elves shared a look of purest wonderment. "Whyever do you think that?" asked Yoric.

"That you might want to hurt us?" asked Coach. She poked the bell at them as though it were a torch and they were made of straw.

"No, that we can't lie," said Ackley.

"Oh, uh." Coach traced a finger along the runes inscribed into her bell. "Just a thing I'm trying. These runes are of my own design. They're supposed to summon you and make you unable to lie or hurt us." She shrugged. "Some work better than others. I thought I'd give it a shot."

Ackley sighed. Yoric giggled, a madman's giggle. No, a mad elf's giggle, which was probably immeasurably worse. He flexed his hands. They were larger than they had been, out of proportion to his height.

"Those runes don't work," said Ackley.

Jeff wondered if he meant all runes or just the set Coach was referring to. Was Coach delusional? Were they delusional for believing her?

Coach looked disappointed for a moment, then shook her head and continued as if nothing had happened. She rang the bell. Ding ding. "Yield to my rune, elf, and answer my questions truthfully. Are you intending to hurt these people?" She yelled it in such a way that she sounded like a maniac, especially when considered in contrast to the elves' calm demeanors.

After careful consideration, Ackley replied, "Not without good cause."

"The term 'good cause' covers a lot of territory," remarked Yoric. "It could mean almost anything."

"True," said Ackley.

Coach poked a threatening thumb at Yoric. "And what about you?"

"I can't read what the future holds," he replied, "but perhaps. I make no promises."

"And what do you mean exactly by hurt?" asked Ackley. "Just curious, would a swift painless death count as hurting?"

Yoric nodded. "Excellent question."

Scowling in deep thought, Coach had no answer. She squinted at them, looking suspicious.

Ackley's indigo face split into a wolfish grin that unnerved Jeff, sending him an unconscious step back. The increased distance actually helped settle him. Being in the elves' close proximity was odd, unnatural. If the world were a clockwork mechanism, then people would be cogs within it. Yet, the elves were cogs of a different size or shape, their very presence subtly upsetting the workings of reality. Nothing felt quite right, even if the changes were invisible to the five senses but instead simply stirrings of the soul.

Meanwhile, the bunny continued watching them, perfectly content in its bunny world. Nibbling clover. Sitting in the grass. Feeling the breeze.

Coach maintained her scowl. It was perhaps meant to be intimidating but came across as more of a lopsided frown of angry confusion. "Moving on, what is your purpose in these woods?"

"It's a sacred duty," whispered Yoric. The words sent a chill down Jeff's spine.

Ackley sneered. It was a common expression for him. One that fit his face well, as if his lips and cheeks were made for that exact purpose. "Well, not really sacred, is it?"

Yoric flailed his hands in annoyance. "Sort of sacred. Regardless, it is our duty."

"Does it involve killing people?" asked Owen.

"Killing is often associated with sacred duties, even if not the direct purpose," said Ackley. He seemed confused as to why a petty issue like death was such a concern.

"Is it your mission to guard this forest?" asked Coach. Ring-a-ding-ding went her bell.

"We are guardians of a sort," Yoric said begrudgingly.

"You seem like kinda heavy hitters to be doing a simple job like guarding some trees," observed Owen.

The elves shared a meaningful look. "We are not simply guarding some trees," growled Ackley, clearly offended.

"Our mission is an important one," said Yoric. "Many of us take turns, traveling here to serve when our time comes. It happens that right now is a rather energetic time for this task."

"Uh huh," Coach said. "I get it. There's a hoard here, isn't there? A cash stash?" She turned to Owen and Jeff. "They're guarding their fancy fairy treasure in their snuggly fairy holes.

Or possibly in a tree." Taking a step to the side, she knocked on a tree trunk, as if expecting a hollow thunk indicating a treasure trove. The brown and white bunny inquisitively watched her.

"Any particulars of our business aren't your business," Yoric said, folding his arms across his chest.

"Fine. Besides, it doesn't really matter what your mission is. Whether it's to protect treasure or pick strawberries, it has to stop. At least one person's been killed and you're standing in the way of industry. Your activities here must come to an end," said Coach, folding her own arms, which shook loose a tinkle from her supposedly magic bell.

"No," the elves declared in unison, with a resolute solidarity that made it clear they'd given the final word on the matter.

As if resigned to the inevitable, Coach spoke in a tired voice that lacked her usual gusto. "Alrighty, then, if that's the way it's gonna be." She'd expected that answer, which landed them at a stalemate. But even though she'd expected a stalemate, she lacked a plan for how to break it.

Examining a low-hanging pine bough as though it held answers, she made little popping noises with her lips as she pondered what to do. They were distracting, each tiny pop its own individual hurdle to everyone's train of thought.

Throughout the discussion, whenever he wasn't speaking, Owen had been regarding the elves intently, inspecting their every move, sizing them up. There was a challenge in his stance and in his gaze, a challenge the elves seemed unimpressed by. For his part, Jeff had fidgeted and sweated, growing increasingly alarmed.

Seconds passed, Coach's popping noises rapidly expanding from merely distracting up to entirely irritating.

"I have a question of my own," declared Ackley.

"Okay," said Coach, excited at a possible break in their

impasse. Regardless of the burgeoning tension, she was simply thrilled to interact with the elves. It made Jeff wonder how often she truly met such beings. It had to be less than she had implied.

"Do you even know how this works?" asked the indigo elf, offering up his hand. The compact Glock rested on his palm. His attention was fixated on Jeff, his ancient regard as unwavering as a mountain.

A fresh squirt of panicked adrenaline coursed through Jeff's arteries. He patted his pocket, finding the weapon was indeed gone. It was impossible that it was gone, yet it was. Either fairy magic was in play or he was losing his mind. "Yes," he gasped defensively.

"Do you really?" asked Ackley, lifting the pistol to point it at him. The action wasn't particularly menacing and had no additional implied threat beyond what was inherently involved in directing a deadly weapon at someone's chest.

Panic invaded Jeff's mind, quiet but pervasive. The world became lopsided, the trees spinning, as he felt everything fade around him. Sounds were muffled. Light became muted as his vision dimmed. Everything narrowed to the bleak dark hole at the end of the pistol. The lub-dubbing of his heart boomed.

With a hiss, Owen leapt forward, sweeping Jeff behind him, blocking his view of his impending death. But that wouldn't save him, there were enough bullets in the pistol for everyone.

"Hey!" yelled Coach. She threw her hands up placatingly, but it was too late. Ackley pulled the trigger, a satisfied smile on his face.

There was a tiny hollow click, but no furious boom.

Owen jerked, looking down in expectation of seeing a tunnel blown through his abdomen. Mercifully, there was no tunnel.

Jeff patted himself, feeling for gaping bloody holes, but

finding none. He was certain he'd been deafened by the blast, and that was why he hadn't heard it. The shortcomings of that logic failed to take root in his panicked mind.

"I think you don't know how to use it," said Ackley. Yoric giggled.

"The safety was on, I guess," mumbled Jeff. His heart raced, the words tumbling unconsciously from his mouth, even if he couldn't immediately imagine their meaning.

"There is no safety switch on this weapon," said Ackley. He was almost unbearably smug. "You simply failed to load it. You should do so in case you need it. Shall I show you how?" He handed the Glock to Jeff, grip first.

Holding the weapon again, with the immediate threat passed, Jeff's mind recommenced functioning, the gears beginning to turn, the nerves to fire. Barely audible, he whispered, "Thanks." It didn't seem that elves would use firearms. Yet, Ackley's knowledge and handling of the pistol spoke of intimate knowledge. This was a creature possessing an inborn familiarity with all instruments of death.

"Enough," roared Coach, stepping forward and brandishing the bell as if it were a cross and the elves were vampires.

Ackley feigned a look of utmost innocence as he backed away, his hands held at shoulder height.

"Well done, Mr. Ackley. An unloaded firearm never saved anyone. Except, I suppose, the villain being shot at," Yoric said. Stretching luxuriously, his hands high in the air, he snickered. His polo shirt rose up to reveal his flat stomach. There was no belly button. No innie, no outie, nothing.

The air hissed as Ackley abruptly slid to his right, striking towards the edge of the clearing. For the scantest of seconds, a black blur extended from his hand, appearing at the seam of the unseen and the seen, the real and the unreal. Assuming it wasn't imagination, it was a long blade, incredibly broad, blacker than the bleakest starless midnight. It was perhaps some sort of polished obsidian, but it wasn't shiny, it didn't shimmer. Rather, it swallowed the light, like a rip in reality.

The bunny's head tumbled to the ground, released from the confines of its cuddly body. A second later, the torso followed, slumping into the delicious clover.

"A sad usage for a grand weapon," said Yoric, shaking his head with extreme gravitas.

"Indeed," replied Ackley. He toed the bunny's corpse, so as to ascertain the factuality of its death. Considering its headless state, the conclusion seemed inevitable.

Just then, Jellybiscuits coolly ambled from the bushes with a crooked swagger. Hunkering down next to its decapitated cousin, it didn't spare the furry corpse a shred of concern.

Silent and unmoving, Jellybiscuits commenced staring at the humans. Its lime-green eyes followed them, tracking their every move. Yet, they would later disagree on who it was watching, since all three of them were convinced it was focusing on them, with no mind for the others. Ultimately, they would agree that the bunny's gaze was like one of those paintings in a murder mystery movie, always watching everyone everywhere.

"Why did you do that?" asked Owen. No matter what the elves might say, it was certainly a demonstration, a millisecond drama displaying their power to rapidly lay claim to a life.

"We intend to eat it," said Yoric, stating the obvious to a dullard.

"It is the closest fresh meat to hand," added Ackley. His hand now held a knife. It wasn't a majestic blade, as the sword had been. This was a simple pocketknife, with a slight curve, tipped with a gut hook, as could be found in a standard sporting goods store. Wherever the elf had summoned the massive ebony blade from, it had returned to once again.

"Well, not really," said Yoric, his voice like an uptight professor correcting a thoughtless student. "There is other, more bountiful meat nearby." He flashed those shark teeth, like gleaming ivory razors. His inhuman gaze roved Jeff's body in an unsettling way.

"Not to my taste," said Ackley. He'd collected the headless bunny. It hung at his side, blood draining from its stump of a neck.

Coach's voice was shaking, her attention fixed to the dead rabbit. "You are dismissed," she announced. "I'll let you know if and when we need to talk to you again."

The elves didn't move. Time stretched, possibly minutes and possibly hours, but most likely just a few awkward seconds.

Unwavering, Jellybiscuits stared, its green focus unsettling Coach and Jeff. Owen was unperturbed.

In an attempted alpha move, Coach flicked the back of her hands at the regal duo, attempting to shoo them away as if they were a pair of troublesome puppies trying to chew her slippers.

They didn't move, just stared at her. Not hostile, just indifferent.

"Go on, get," she yelled.

Nothing. Ackley shook the dead bunny a bit, jarring loose a few crimson drops.

"Shoo!" Coach thundered.

No movement. Uninterested in commands from a human, they obstinately stood their ground.

In this miniature battle of wills, Coach blinked first. "Okay, well, we're leaving anyway." She spun and walked away, Jeff and Owen at her heels like obedient beagles, haughty elf stares gouging their backs.

Once in the Jeep and a safe distance away, Jeff asked, "Was Yoric implying he would eat us, or was that just me?" He was driving entirely too fast, every bump in the trail roughly jostling them.

"I believe he was." Owen's tone said he found the insinuation amusing. Jeff didn't agree.

Coach sighed. "Those boys are nasty. I'll have to get my togethers together, and then we'll deal with them."

"Can we deal with them?" asked Owen, sounding uncharacteristically doubtful.

Coach grinned, awash in glee. "Sure, I just need some prep time. I've got a plan. Well, I'll have a plan soon. I need to do some thinking, but then we'll gather reagents and do some questing."

"A quest?" Owen asked, his eyes glowing with excitement.

Coach waggled her thick eyebrows. "Sure, there's always a quest when it comes to fairies."

12 SUNDAY MORNING

A hand-painted sign proclaiming 'Gertie's Gifts and Delights' hung outside a standalone store in Cayuga's meager business district.

Inside, the mildewy stench of desperation hung heavy, feebly stirred by the slight breeze through the open door. Motes of dust mottled the air, eager to drape themselves across whatever they could.

The largest overhead light buzzed loudly as it considered dying. After a moment's hesitation, it elected to cling to life, at least for a few moments more. Yet the buzzing continued, receiving accompaniment in the form of blinking, as the light tended more towards off than on.

There were two other lights, in the form of bare bulbs hanging from the ceiling, but they provided few lumens.

Coach picked up a lawn gnome and rotated it around in her hands, studying it as though it were the Rosetta Stone. Its nose was chipped and the paint around its mouth had faded, making it appear shocked at how its life had turned out. Setting it down, she moved on.

The shop was a tangle of folding tables packed tightly together. They were stacked with old jeans, foldaway baby strollers, oil paintings, and all manner of nearly useless knickknacks and gewgaws. A rack of used power tools stood alongside a wheelbarrow of battered laptops and tablets.

Despite the signage, this felt like more of a pawn shop than a gift store. Perhaps even a secondhand store, or consignment shop, since it seemed unlikely anyone could pawn stained jeans.

Sidestepping a cardboard box full of heavily used rollerblades mixed with stringless rackets, Coach continued picking through the offerings, hoping for treasures.

Behind the counter, an old woman, presumably Gertie, watched Coach's every move like a wrinkly hawk. She looked to be pushing ninety, much like the loaded double barrel shotgun she kept close to hand. She'd blow someone's guts out before she'd let them steal so much as a plug nickel from her shop. Her lips, topped with dark bristly hairs, pulled back into an evil grin at the thought, revealing a set of bent, yellowed dentures.

Feeling the malevolent gaze of the ancient shopkeeper, Coach paused to inspect a pair of iron candlesticks. Scratching at their surfaces with a fingernail, she nodded and carried them to the counter. They were a no-brainer. She returned to shopping.

Sorting through a box of jewelry that was kept locked away when not in Gertie's direct view, Coach found a pair of silver earrings. Holding them up to her ears, she appraised herself in the dusty mirror. They were low-grade and ugly, but silver, nonetheless. She kept them, eventually adding a silver pendant, silver pinkie ring fit for a mobster, and another two sets of silver earrings. It was all the silver Gertie had.

Never pass up silver. Keep your iron supplies stocked up as well. Both substances were kryptonite to most types of fairies. That's what the folklore said anyway, even if Coach had received few chances to put it to the test.

After completing her purchases at Gertie's, Coach stopped at the grocery store. She grabbed bologna, mayo, white bread, and a six pack of a nice IPA. And also a few baking supplies. Chocolate, sugar, butter. They constituted an important failsafe for her plan.

Grocery shopping took longer than she'd intended, since her cart had a bum wheel. It wobbled and turned sideways but refused to spin in any way that promoted forward motion. That hurdle proved to be fortuitous since it extended her trip, giving her a chance to pick up on the gossip, which started as a background murmur but grew to a roar as word spread.

There'd been a fire last night, and the town was abuzz. Well, mostly just the old and the bored were abuzz, but that included most of the workers and shoppers at the grocery store.

Coach barely stifled her smirk as she listened to various recountings of the events. It was the same in every small town. What they lacked in action, they made up for by blowing everything out of proportion. Usually, but that wasn't the case here. No, Cayuga had real problems, and she suspected the fire was a part of them.

The flaming events occurred at a goat farm on the far outskirts of Cayuga. A goat farm that Coach couldn't help but notice was situated on the forest side of town, in the general direction of Sector G12.

It was a hobby farm, someone's passion project, started later in life after quitting the rat race. Coach didn't care so much about the backstory. The farm had no more than ten or twelve goats, not for meat but to make soap and cheese from the milk.

There'd been a fire in the barn early that morning, before the sun rose. It had raged through the modest structure, sending screaming goats fleeing as everything collapsed under the weight of the inferno.

Amidst the charred remains, firefighters found puddles of wax, appearing to be the sad remains of melted candles. Also, an empty wine bottle. And a pair of burnt goat carcasses that had been chewed at by large predators.

Not one to let an opportunity to jump to a conclusion slip away, Coach was immediately convinced the elves were involved. This was the sort of wanton destruction evil creatures thrived upon.

She wasn't yet sure what their game was, but her working theory was that they were guarding fairy treasure tucked away in the forest. That was her preferred theory, mostly since it involved gold. They could just as easily be magical psychopaths who enjoyed lurking in the trees, but that was far less appealing, mostly because of the lack of gold.

In the first version of the fire story that Coach heard, it was a devil summoning gone awry. She found that unlikely, since summoners wouldn't consume large portions of the goats during a sacrifice. And it didn't jibe with her elf angle. Elves weren't big on goat sacrifices, so far as she knew.

In the second version, it was a monstrous romantic dinner gone haywire. That didn't ring true either. Neither of the elves seemed the romantic type.

The third rendition, which included an arsonist escaped from a mental asylum, added the breaking news that there was a firefighter missing. She'd been tromping the field near the trees, hosing down the underbrush to ensure no smolders remained, when she'd vanished. The storyteller, a teenage bag boy with a face full of aggressive acne, admitted that the firefighter news was fresh, and perhaps was a mistake. Coach didn't think it was a mistake, though. The firefighter was probably a victim of opportunity, snatched away by elves. She did, however, doubt the human arsonist part.

Whatever deviltry the elves had underway, their dark hijinks were escalating.

The story of the crisped goats occupying her thoughts, Coach next visited Winterbottom's Coffee Shop. She found her partners wasting the day, as kids tend to do, in her considered opinion. They preferred to treat life like a sitcom, lounging about while complaining about how they couldn't get ahead. Coach knew better. Life wasn't a sitcom. It was a tragedy waiting to unfold. Despite her sunny disposition, she knew that to be true.

They were gathered around a table in the back corner,

slurping eight-dollar drinks, most of which Carla got for free from her dad, who was working the counter. Must be nice. All Coach ever got from her dad were bruises, the knowledge that you should always keep your door locked, and the need to leave home as soon as possible. That bastard was dead now, but strangely she mourned him still.

Anyway, the others were listening to Jeff complain about his job. He was supposed to be leading his work crews into Sector G12, but he was failing. And failing in such a way that the boss couldn't understand. "The elves don't want us there" was an excuse that probably wouldn't fly with the boss, even if Jeff had the gumption to use it. Just the other night he'd received a tongue lashing from his Uncle Chet on the matter. It had been delivered over burnt fish sticks while Jeff's pinched-faced aunt squinted at him in disappointment.

Only nepotism was ensuring Jeff's continued employment. Little did Uncle Chet know that their failure to forge ahead into G12 was probably saving workers' lives.

Jeff wasn't Coach's favorite member of their little team. He meant well, but he was a spectator in his own life. A watcher, not a doer.

Carla was drooping, like a flower lacking sun and water. Her unwashed black hair was knotted atop her head, and she wore sunglasses in place of her usual eyeglasses. She was hungover, a state Coach could easily recognize, often winding up there herself. Forehead down on the table, she reeked of gin and regret. She wasn't good for much either.

Owen, though, was the real deal. If Coach had ten Owens, she could rule the world. Or at least start a few fairy-hunting franchises. He glowed, a sheen of dried sweat coating his brow, the result of a pair of CrossFit sessions.

Folded back into the corner was Ivy, who appeared drained, as if she'd been partying all night, which rumor said was not unusual for her. Wearing a sparkling sundress and a hat fit for the Kentucky Derby, she sagged listlessly. Yet her bright eyes roamed her companions, taking everything in.

Coach leaned into their caffeine-infused orbit, interrupting their pointless chatter. This was a good time to put everyone's cards on the table. If they were going on a quest, and then confronting murderous elves, it was best to have everyone on the same page.

"Let's get one thing straight," Coach said, before pausing for dramatic effect.

Ivy took advantage of the pause. "Good morning," she chirped, her voice like a bell.

Waving the greeting off, Coach jabbed a finger at Ivy. "You're a pixie." She was expecting denial, mostly in the form of hurt feelings and tears, both of which would bring the boys to Ivy's side instantly. Most young men were simple, predictable creatures, with obvious strings to pull to manipulate them. A pretty young woman's tears were string number one, containing power beyond measure.

Carla's eyes rolled, while the boys both looked startled, their attentions suddenly riveted to Ivy.

Emotions rippled across Ivy's lovely face, although the exact constituents were unclear. Perhaps embarrassment, perhaps relief, perhaps anger. Whichever they were, they were quickly covered by a wide smile. She studied the room before quietly responding. "That's true. Thanks for clearing the air. I wanted to tell you all but didn't think you'd believe me." Her green eyes widened and sparkled, basking Jeff and Owen in their majesty.

"Huh," said Jeff.

Owen nodded knowingly.

"Do you believe me? Truly?" The pixie leaned back, hugging herself tightly, looking lost.

"Of course," said Coach. She'd known it all along.

"Oh, thank you," Ivy said, tears descending slowly down her cheeks, leaving sparkling lavender trails in their wakes. "Since we're being so honest with each other, I can tell you a little bit more, but not much, since it's fairy business and you wouldn't truly understand." Her breath hitched, barely containing a sob. She visibly gathered herself before continuing.

Her body quivering, Ivy whispered, "You're my only hope. I need you to save me from those elves. They want to kidnap me and chain me away in their lair, a pit dug deep into the cold hard earth somewhere in their domain, the area you call G12. They'll make me their slave and they'll do things to me. Awful things." Ivy's lips trembled and she stared down at the table, as if shamed by what she was revealing. "Those evil elves mean to molest me and make me bear their foul offspring deep underground where I'll never see the sky again. You won't let that happen will you?" Tentatively, she reached out, laying a small, fragile hand in the crook of Jeff's arm.

Jeff looked lost and scared. Staring incredulously at Ivy's hand where it rested on his arm, he asked, "Can't you just run away?"

Shaking her head, scarlet curls whipping back and forth, the pixie said, "I can't leave this place."

Setting both hands flat on the table, Owen looked furious. He said, "We'll save you. None of that will happen. Not on my watch." Much like a German shepherd, Owen was certain that all the watches were his watch.

Jeff nodded, swept up in Ivy's tale and Owen's enthusiasm. Carla appeared dubious of the whole thing, but that was her constant inclination, particularly when hungover.

Coach's heart went out to the pixie. Originally, she'd been in this for the adventure. And the treasure. Mostly the treasure.

But now, there was a heroic purpose driving them.

Moments later, Coach took her coffee to go and hopped into her Subaru. She had iron to grind, bologna to eat, and a seashell to scribe runes into.

13 FIEND MANAGEMENT SYSTEM

The wind was gusting and the sky exuberantly weeping cold tears, working together to create an inauspicious beginning for a major undertaking. Thus far, the midmorning sun had yet to peek through the charcoal clouds blanketing the sky. Yet Owen, Jeff, and Coach were gathered in the forest by G12, preparing to embark on Coach's quest.

Coach was facing into G12, an intense expression on her face. She'd looked nowhere else since exiting the Jeep. It seemed she was concentrating, but she might simply have been listening to the whispers of her own internal muses. Or perhaps to mental carnival music as she watched clowns caper around imaginary carousels while they made balloon animals.

Lacking a better idea, Jeff stared into the trees as well. Without a doubt they stared back. Not at him, but rather into him, their wooden gazes examining his soul, critiquing his shortcomings and contemplating his innermost fears. They had a deep dark consciousness, these woods, and he was squarely in their sights.

This venture into the trees was a bad idea. Perhaps it wasn't too late to turn back. Nothing good lurked within these arboreal borders, just elven killers with dreams of kidnapping and molesting pixies, possibly while cooking meth. Jeff's only potential saving grace was that he was probably beneath their notice.

His gaze slid to Owen, hoping to see a bit of doubt, a foothold for uncertainty, any crack in the facade of his confidence that could be pried open and turned into a reappraisal of this course of action. Then perhaps, leveraged into a sudden full retreat.

There was a solid set to Owen's jaw that Jeff could read like a book. There would be no retreat. This was a windmill Owen would tilt at.

Owen was determined, and Jeff would be swept along by the power of his friend's convictions, just like always. As his dad often said, Jeff was a follower. But that was okay, since the world needed followers, second bananas, lackeys, and nameless rabble. In fact, there was a nobility in fighting the good fight with anonymity, even if he'd never actually, really, truly fought in his life. In the eternal struggle of fight versus flight, he often chose the third option, to freeze.

"Let me tell you what you really need," Coach yelled, struggling to be heard over the pounding rain. She paused to cinch up her rain jacket's hood, tightening the opening such that her face could hardly be seen. It barely helped, for the rain found its way in regardless. It always did. Sputtering through the deluge, she continued, "You need a proper fiend management system specifically directed towards magical fairy folk. Luckily, I've got some ideas." Her delivery sounded like nothing so much as a car salesman offering a deal on undercoating.

"That sounds expensive," Jeff said.

Patting his pockets, he confirmed he had food bars, phone, bottled water, and the Glock, which was loaded this time. The bullets made the pistol heavy, imposing, and disconcerting to carry. They also seemed to make the weapon cold, for it sent a chill into his ribs where it touched him.

"Won't cost you a dime," Coach answered, her thumbs hooked around her backpack straps. She continued staring blissfully into G12.

"Cool," said Jeff, gazing between tree trunks, certain he saw movement in the branch-shrouded distance. The shadows moved and shifted, possibly like tree limbs, but also possibly like evil sentient observers. However, even if the confines of G12 felt evil, at least the trees were densely packed, so they would provide some refuge from the downpour.

"The first step," said Coach, "which is why we're gathered here today, is the quest. We need to pick up a few things. Won't be much, since I've already got some of the stuff."

"What stuff, exactly?" asked Jeff. That earned a scowl from Owen, as if questioning Coach's fanciful planning was bad form.

"You'll find out," Coach replied. She slapped Jeff on the back, making the few words sound merry, when he actually found them completely ominous.

The rain intensified and the gusts strengthened, as if redoubling their efforts to waylay their quest via a solid sideways soaking. As far as Jeff was concerned, it was working. His feet were soaked, and he hated that, which was why he'd worn high-end waterproof hiking boots. But sadly, they were no match for the internal wave of water his drenched socks were wicking all the way down to his toes.

"Stuff like moss from the north side of a dying willow, or something like that?" Owen asked. He was already at G12's border, which was a very apparent boundary, seeing as how the trees quickly became close packed and more gnarled. As his friend and de facto sidekick, Jeff knew Owen was itching to start this adventure, a feeling he wished he shared. Much like when they visited amusement parks, Owen made straight for the roller coasters, while Jeff was content with the ring toss or, at most, bumper cars.

Coach beamed like a starving, saturated rat that had stumbled upon a bag of potato chips. "Good guess, but no. We need some standard magical reagents only available from vendors found in the wilds."

"Vendors out here?" Jeff asked. "Can't you get good magical reagents online these days?" If one accepted that magic existed in some form, one could also anticipate vendors popping up to sell their wares over the internet.

As if in answer, the wind howled, ferociously shaking the trees at their back. Jeff was just beginning to notice that the trees before them, in G12, were barely swaying.

"Proper reagents are only obtained through questing." Coach snuffled, then held a finger to one nostril so she could blow forcefully out the other. A gush of snot shot forth. "We could get some reagents online, but they're more effective if obtained through questing. Plus, you can verify authenticity this way."

Best to let that go, since arguing nonsensical absurdities was a game for fools. "Those elves are in there somewhere." Jeff gestured vaguely ahead of them, indicating all that they surveyed. "Aren't they gonna, umm, get us or something?"

Coach waved dismissively. "Probably not. I assume they respect a good quest. They're like bees probably, if we don't bother them, they won't bother us." The deluge nearly drowned out her words, millions of incessant, strident wet plinks working to muffle her.

"No time like the present," Owen said. Pulling a size-twelve boot from the mud with a splucking noise, he plopped it onto the path leading into the dim leafy confines of G12.

Within seconds, he'd disappeared, with Coach right behind him.

Suddenly alone, Jeff hesitated, terrified at the prospect of entering the elves' territory. Frozen yet again.

In seconds that stretched to eternities, his fear of being alone gradually overcame his anxious dormancy, forcing him to put aside his visions of impending doom. Like a marionette unable to control its movements, he was dragged into G12, his strings pulled by the twin hands of fear and the need to not be alone.

The quest had begun.

14 BUSHY-TAILED EXECUTIVES

There was a certain indefinable sense of unreality associated with being on a quest. It felt weird. That included the internal bit, where you were forced to accept the unlikely hard turn your life had taken wherein you're suddenly on a magical quest, whereas normally you'd be at work or napping or watching Netflix. But there was more to the weird feeling than that. The very world around them had changed.

Once within G12, the rain ended immediately. At first, that seemed to be a consequence of the thick forest canopy acting as an umbrella of sorts, as the background murmur of raindrops slapping leaves and needles instantly faded. However, breaks in the trees revealed blue skies, with hints of sun peeking through, although those stray rays seemed to come at random angles, as though the sun were erratically hopping about.

And the winds blew differently, first from one direction then another. They carried strong scents, intensifying and waning seemingly randomly. Flowers from one direction, then pine from the other. The smells of large animals came from everywhere, drifting in and out as if large herds of something grazed nearby.

The forest was alive with wildlife. The scurrying of unseen animals thrashed the limbs above them, while furtive movements stirred the leaf litter just off the path. Other times it was dead silent, as active as a landscape of seared skeletal trees after a forest fire.

They walked in silence, an almost funereal hush upon them, part awe and part disorientation. At the first clearing, Coach called a halt to get her bearings.

Jeff checked his phone. There was no reception, which was perhaps not terribly surprising. The sun was straight ahead of him, just visible through some pines. But then it shifted to his left, then back again. For an instant, he thought there were two.

The inconsistencies he was experiencing were subtle, and transitory. It was easy to explain them away as the mistaken workings of his overstressed mind. None rose to a level of certainty where he was compelled to say anything. He lacked the confidence to make the bold proclamation that the world around them had changed.

Owen, however, did not lack the confidence to call it as he saw it. "It's like we're in some other world. Everything smells different, looks different … feels different, just slightly off-kilter." He plucked a needle-covered twig from the ground, sniffing it and rubbing it between his palms, before dropping it with a shrug.

"We're in quest mode," said Coach, with a level of barely restrained excitement that might be associated with unveiling the revelation of the century, as if she'd unearthed an ancient alien spacecraft in the desert. Giddiness oozed from her pores. One hand was planted on her hip, while the other sat atop the satchel she wore slung across her body. It was weathered and well worn, much like Coach herself. Unlike her, it had symbols scrawled along the side, presumably sigils of power. "Quests angle the world to the side, revectoring how we move through it."

That statement impressed Owen, who looked about in renewed wonder. Jeff, who was less prone to suspension of disbelief, remained confused. And still a bit dubious.

"How'd you make that happen?" asked Owen. "Putting us in quest mode, that is."

Coach beamed with a level of unbridled enthusiasm that normal people rarely displayed, yet she wore like a favorite baseball cap. Again, Jeff questioned her mental stability. She said, "This section of the forest is magic. It knows questers when they enter it."

"Are you saying it has a consciousness?" asked Jeff. He doffed his rain jacket, shook it out and tied it around his waist. Owen did the same. On Jeff it looked like a cocktail dress while Owen's looked like a cool old-timey Scottish battle kilt.

An uncharacteristic frown prowled onto Coach's face, hunkering there for a second before moving on. "Not as such. But it's best not to dwell on such matters. The knowledge could break your mind. It's one of those don't-stare-into-the-abyss-since-it-might-stare-back-at-you type of deals." The way she said that made it seem like she had no idea of the actual answer.

Without another word, she turned thrice counterclockwise, once back the other way, and strode purposefully onto a needle strewn trail that Jeff hadn't noticed before. They followed. What else could they do?

Hours passed, or possibly minutes. Whichever it was, it allowed Jeff's feet to dry out. And get sore. Coach led the way, turning at odd spots, searching for split trunk trees for guideposts. They walked trails that probably didn't truly exist, finding occasional impossibilities in their path.

At one point, a thousand-foot drop-off loomed at the side of the trail, yawning into oblivion, both its bottom and far side lost in grayish-red mists. It was there one moment and gone the next. Jeff knew the regional relief maps, and such a canyon didn't exist.

In one particularly dark stretch, a lime-green glow shone from beneath a bush full of brown and purple berries. Its eyes fluorescing in the gloom, Jellybiscuits was watching them tromp by.

The bunny's mouth was probably hanging open, but it was hard to say, since its teeth, tongue, and gums were black, blurring into the spiky fur of its face.

"Hey there, Jellybiscuits," said Coach, as if greeting an old friend.

It didn't respond. Being a rabbit, they shouldn't have imagined it would.

They kept going. It didn't follow.

A moment's walking later, Jeff said, "That's a nasty bunny rabbit."

"That's no ordinary rabbit," said Coach.

Intrigued, Owen asked, "What is it then?"

"I'd guess it's some poor animal entranced to do their bidding. Like a fuzzy little scout, or a witch's familiar," said Coach.

They dropped the subject and continued on.

They passed four squirrels sitting at a tree stump. The squirrels had been chattering to one another but paused to watch the trio pass. It felt as if they were interrupting a business meeting, as bushy-tailed executives of the forest discussed whatever corporate affairs interested squirrels. Perhaps nut futures.

"Always turn widdershins when you can," Coach mumbled occasionally, just loud enough for them to hear. Whether she was advising them or herself was unclear. Hopefully herself, for neither Owen nor Jeff knew what she meant.

It was primarily just the three of them on their trek through the forest, but the elves made appearances as well.

Yoric walked with them for a bit, alarmingly close, nearly shoulder to shoulder with Jeff. The elf refused to speak with them, instead choosing to murmur to himself. Indeed, he generally ignored them, as if their paths just happened to coincide.

Coach urged the elf to scat but he disregarded her, eventually peeling off at a split in the trail, electing to go the other way.

Ackley made an appearance as well, although it was shorter than his partner's had been.

He was sitting atop a tree stump fashioned to look like a throne.

As they passed, he watched with cold charcoal eyes. They swallowed the light, refusing to gleam as Yoric's did.

"We're on a quest," Coach announced. She said it with great pride, like a kindergartener who had tied their own shoes.

The dark elf said nothing, grimacing with the clear intent to display his razor teeth. Ackley appeared decidedly inhuman now. He was very tall with enormous hands like grappling hooks. His facial features were long and sharp, his face thin. Although different than humans, he was still entirely beautiful, in the way a tiger is, an exquisite and ferocious being that could, and might, tear your arm off.

They continued on, chasing the trail to its end, relieved when the dark elf faded from sight.

Following the trail as it ascended a steep incline, they arrived at a clearing. Unlike the other clearings they had passed, this one felt purposeful, as if intelligent beings had fashioned it for some purpose all their own, as opposed to it having been haphazardly trampled flat by deer, foxes, and beavers over the years.

Emptied of grass and most vegetation, what remained was a bare patch of flattened earth. The dirt was rich in clay, and decidedly red.

On the far side was a massive owl, big as a Saint Bernard. It was a great horned owl, although an unnaturally large one, stretched beyond the boundaries of what nature allowed. Jeff knew what type of owl it was from a documentary. He'd always been better with animals than with plants, as evidenced by the fact that the trees around them carried acorns, but that didn't tell him what kind they were. Acorn trees?

Despite its impossible size, the owl's plumage was unremarkable, with a motley assortment of brown, gray, and white feathers ranging its wide body. Yet, it wasn't just the owl's immensity that was unusual. Its eyes shone red like a forest fire, blazing brighter than the meager rays of sun filtering through the leafy canopy. Also, unlike a true horned owl, this one had actual horns curling up from over its eyes, devil style.

The owl also kept unlikely company, in that next to it was a hedgehog. The hedgehog was completely standard. Small and adorable, although with a roguish glint in his eye. Such an animal would probably be a meal for a normal owl, but that wouldn't be the case here. They looked to be companions.

The owl spread its wings wide, fluttered them about, and took a few mincing steps back and forth. Owen immediately stepped to the fore, ready to face down the huge predatory bird. It regarded him warily as it resettled itself next to the hedgehog.

Dropping to one knee, Coach bowed her head. "We are on a quest," she said in reverent tones.

The owl and hedgehog exchanged a fleeting look, then turned their attention back to Coach. Neither the two animals nor the woman stirred. Nor did Owen. Jeff stirred enough for everyone, nervously shifting about, hoping the owl didn't decide they were lunch.

Somewhere far off, a creature bellowed. If forced to guess, Jeff would have gone with it being a moose.

Setting her palms in the reddish-brown dirt, Coach sunk lower. Her head mere inches from the ground, she was almost groveling. "It's very important."

The owl huffed. It was a humanlike sound. Very much like a sigh.

The hedgehog scratched at its chin, staring at the nearly prostrate woman.

A moment passed, during which Jeff realized they were truly being steered by a madwoman.

"I come in search of stygian dyes," said Coach, nearly inaudible from the clay she spoke into.

"What sort?" asked the owl. It had a deep rich voice, one that you would want to narrate audio books or nature documentaries. Not what you would imagine from an owl, if you ever imagined such a thing. When it spoke, their surroundings hushed, as if time had been drawn to a lull and nothing moved outside the borders of the clearing.

Coach leapt to her feet, clearly shocked, although she sought to recover her composure quickly. Her stunned look told Jeff she actually was sane, since she was as amazed by the owl's speaking as he was. And yet, he was less surprised than he would have thought. Within the context of recent events, a talking owl wasn't entirely unreasonable.

When Coach didn't immediately respond, the owl exhaled sharply. It acted terribly inconvenienced by the delay. "What sort of stygian dye?" it said slowly and precisely, as if speaking to someone without a firm grasp on the language.

"The blackish-red kind derived from the blood and humors of a chenoo," Coach said. She thrust her hands in her pockets and winced, looking uncertain, like someone making an elaborate specialty order at a fast-food burger place.

"Chenoo?" the owl asked. It snorted, then raised its eyes to the sky, perhaps seeking patience. "Whatever for?"

"Like, to add power when crafting a rune," she said, although timidly. It sounded a bit more like a question than a statement.

"What's a chenoo?" asked Owen. He'd taken the talking owl completely in stride.

Although she remained facing the owl, Coach tilted her head and lobbed her response back towards Jeff and Owen. She flapped her hands nervously as she spoke. "Kind of a North American giant ice-monster predator maneater sort of a creature."

The owl's head bobbed up and down, then twisted to the back, as if searching for witnesses. Whiplashing its predatory face back towards Coach, it said, "I'll need something in return. A trade."

"There is always a price," Coach said gravely, far more serious than they'd ever heard her speak before. "And it must be paid by whomever requires the quest." She stood aside, her eyes down, offering nothing further.

The owl's horned head swiveled to Jeff, fixing him in an unwavering gaze. The massive bird was a somber being, not inclined to waste time with fools. By its side, the hedgehog scratched at its nether regions.

The owl's stare probed Jeff. It spoke with the deep gravitas only a talking owl can muster. "I'll require your firstborn son, hale and hearty, delivered to me on a full moon, his lips still wet with mother's milk."

The silence was deafening, broken only by a tiny gasp from the hedgehog. Frozen by a sense of unreality, Jeff didn't immediately respond.

Owen thrust himself to the fore, sweeping Jeff behind him. If there was a sacrifice to be made, he would prefer it to be his to make. "What if I never have a son?"

"Sadly, you won't. Not ever. But I wasn't speaking to you," replied the owl, dipping its great head. It raised a wing to point at Jeff. "I meant the other one. The scared one with trembling knees."

Some notions are too ludicrous to be taken seriously, with proposed magical transactions wherein you barter away your firstborn son being one of those. The prospect was so farcical as to be beyond comprehension. Yet, the presence of a talking owl negated the impossibility of the proposition, making it feel all too real, forcing Jeff to take the question seriously, even though he had a fleeting thought that agreeing really couldn't hurt anything. After all, the logistics of enforcing such a deal were bafflingly inconceivable. He wasn't even dating anyone, so any kids he might eventually father were certain to be many years and miles away. How would an owl even discover the existence of a son? And how long did owls live anyway? In many ways, it felt like a deal easily made and broken. And yet, there was magic involved, so who knew what was truly at stake.

The risk felt minimal, but the stakes were too large. "That seems awfully steep to me. No deal," he said.

Relief washed over Coach's face, scouring away the blank countenance she'd been wearing. She nodded approvingly, confirming Jeff's logic.

An owl's face is not crafted for optimally displaying human emotions, but the owl made a valiant effort to appear irritated. "Very well then. The price shall be your secondborn daughter, apple of her mother's eye, such a beauty, presented to me on the summer solstice."

"Nope."

This time, disappointment played across the owl's beak and eyes. "You sure? You'll lose little in that deal. It saves you having to pay her dowry one day. Think on it again." There was a hint of wheedling in the owl's rich baritone.

"Nope, sorry."

"No?" the owl asked, as if incredulous that Jeff was such a fool as to pass up that bargain. The feathers over its left eye rose quizzically, simulating the eyebrows it did not have. "Very well, then. I'll take five years of your life."

"Do you mean, like, in servitude?" asked Coach.

"No, no, taken all at once. Wicked away from you and stored in a vessel that I'll keep in reserve and use whensoever I want." The owl drew itself up, giving its wings a vast melodramatic flap, stirring the crumpled, dried brown leaves in the clearing.

"Done," declared Owen in a throaty whisper. The opportunity to sacrifice for the greater good thrilled him.

The owl shook its head, doing nearly full rotations each time. "Still not you, hopeful hero."

Again, Coach looked uncharacteristically solemn. She directed a finger at Jeff. "This is your quest. It's your call, your price to pay."

A crossroads had been reached. The required response had to be from Jeff, and Jeff alone. For once in his life, he could be the one that stood up and played the hero. Truthfully, he couldn't imagine why he wouldn't agree. He could accept talking animals, which was probably a group hallucination anyway, best blamed on too many cartoons. But he couldn't accept magic that stole years from people's lives. Utterly impossible. That was where he suspended his belief. His line in the sand of gullibility.

In hindsight, the deals for his future kids were probably fine as well, but that ship had sailed. Anyway, to be safe, it was just as well he'd passed on that one, since, in the astronomical chance that this owl wasn't full of crap and would actually show up to claim his kids someday, he couldn't imagine explaining that away to his future wife. Although she was imaginary in this scenario, Jeff feared her wrath.

"Yeah, sure, why not?" he answered. Besides, he could be hit by a bus tomorrow, so what would it matter?

"Wonderful," said the owl, looking as pleased as an owl could. The hedgehog clapped his tiny paws together.

The owl gestured vaguely at the hedgehog, who charged into the bushes, returning seconds later with a wee little bellows, like one would fan a flame with. Although a very small flame, no larger than a match, for the bellows was tiny, undersized even for the hedgehog that held it.

With no pomp or ceremony, the hedgehog scrabbled up Jeff's body and sat upon his shoulder, perched like a quill-y, furry parrot. It jabbed the business end of the bellows into Jeff's neck. The tip penetrated a millimeter or two at most, but depth didn't matter. The simple act of penetration did.

It was barely a pinprick, yet Jeff instinctively said, "Ow."

The hedgehog slowly pulled the handles of the bellows apart, drawing away something that had been within Jeff. Cold spread from the wee puncture. Not a cold of temperature, but rather one of hollowness.

As the hedgehog hopped off, Jeff sagged to the ground, the world fading at the edges of his vision. Emptiness closed in, whistling like a tornado. He slumped forward to meet the ground, out like the proverbial light.

It was a dreamless unconsciousness, brimming with fathomless adjustments as Jeff's body acclimated to its lost lifespan. Yet he remembered none of it.

Branches swam back into view. A mossy scent filled his nose. Hardpacked dirt dug into his back, a rock projecting into the base of his spine. He sat up like a bolt, grunting at the effort. A sour taste sat in his mouth and a ringing filled his ears.

As a reward for the herculean effort of sitting up, Jeff received concerned looks from Coach and Owen. Off to the side, the owl and hedgehog looked far from concerned. In fact, they appeared entirely pleased by the bargain.

"Are you okay?" asked Owen, who was almost, but not quite, distraught. "You were out for several minutes there."

Rising to his feet, Jeff received a hearty slap on the back that nearly sent him sprawling, although whether it was from Coach or Owen he couldn't tell.

"Sure, I'm fine," he said at last, placing his hands into the small of his back and stretching. His bones were stiff, and he was exhausted. Every movement shook loose a skeletal creak or an audible groan, like he was an out-of-shape nonagenarian trying to do calisthenics.

Coach cast an accusatory look towards the pair of animals. "You sure you didn't take too much? His whiskers are all gray."

Jeff felt his chin, which was rougher than it had been moments ago, several days growth having sprouted while he was unconscious. It wasn't long enough for him to see, so he'd have to take Coach's word on the color.

"It evens out over time," the owl said, flapping a wing dismissively. "He'll feel ragged for a bit but should be fine. Well, except the lost years, but that's water under the bridge."

The hedgehog chittered in excitement, sniffing the tip of the bellows like a wine cork. The adorable little beast held the bellows out to the owl, who took a huge sniff of its own. Beaks don't smile, but this one did its best. "Simply succulent," crowed the owl. "Five years from a virgin! How lovely for me that you haven't yet felt the touch of a woman, or man, or whatever suits your fancy."

The hedgehog pointed at Jeff and giggled, or so one might describe the noise. Certainly, it looked overjoyed.

"What? A virgin?" snorted Coach. She grinned and laughed, her eyes goggling wide as she searched the clearing for someone to celebrate this discovery with. In the absence of drunken frat guys or teenage boys, there was no one, so she stifled herself, keeping her guffaws marginally contained.

Jeff's face was aflame. Being a virgin was nothing to be ashamed of. He knew that. And yet … still, it bothered him.

Owen said, "Let's move on." It was a command, not a request. He took his best friend and wingman duties seriously, and having a runecasting lunatic and two forest animals giggling at Jeff's lack of luck in love was more than he could stomach.

The hedgehog continued giggling as the owl gathered itself, returning to business.

"One other thing," said the owl. "Give me your cell phone for a second." It extended a wing towards Owen and flicked its feathers, the equivalent of a human's gimme gesture.

Shrugging, Owen handed it over.

"Passcode?" the owl asked.

Owen told the owl his code. After, his square jaw hung open in wonderment.

The owl input the code, adroitly manipulating the phone despite having no fingers. Somehow it just worked.

It began flicking through his apps. Obnoxiously, the signal was strong and the reception fine for the owl, despite having been nonexistent for the humans. More magic at play, Jeff supposed.

"And I'll require this cell phone as part of the deal. With the bill paid for an entire year." The owl's full attention was glued to the screen, a movie trailer reflecting from its large eyes.

"Really?" asked Jeff. Of all the paraphernalia a magical talking bird might require, he wouldn't have guessed a smartphone to be on that list. Did it need the phone for calls or for games or to find movie times or what?

"You gotta be kidding," exclaimed Coach, as if she'd just heard the punchline to the world's funniest joke, the one that made her whole life make sense. She was overjoyed, effusively thrilled, as if having the time of her life. She slapped her knee in glee and sipped from her supposedly rune-blessed canteen.

"You can't fool the telephone companies," the owl said sagely. The hedgehog chattered, disturbing its companion with a lengthy string of squeaky jabber. The owl waved the hedgehog to silence and continued, "Magic doesn't help, such arcane trickery struggles to bypass online billing and passwords and carrier services."

"Fine," said Owen, enthusiastic to make a sacrifice for the cause. The loss wasn't a great one. It was a two-year-old iPhone with a crack in the corner of the screen. He'd been considering getting a new one for months but hadn't yet pulled the trigger. In fact, he and Jeff had been at the mall a few weekends ago playing with the newest models. They'd also gone clothes shopping, to the movies, and out to dinner, spending the day like an old married couple.

"We have an accord," the owl slurred, generating a fair impression of Jack Sparrow, a character it was hard to imagine how it knew of.

"Yup," said Jeff and Owen in unison, as Coach nodded vigorously.

The owl signaled to the hedgehog, who scuttled into a nearby stand of berry bushes. It returned within seconds clutching a stoppered vial of dusky glass wrapped in a mesh framework of thin copper wire. There was a murky liquid within, like beet juice mixed with squid's ink, thick and chunky.

With great reverence, the hedgehog handed the vial up to Coach, who accepted it greedily, immediately gazing into its swirling depths.

The scant sunrays that penetrated into the clearing were clean and bright when they entered the vial. Once filtered through the glass they exited profoundly diminished and with a crimson tinge.

"Stygian dye," Coach muttered reverently, staring intensely into the depths of the vial and tipping it about for different views. She gripped the vial tightly, as though it contained the antidote to a poison she'd just ingested.

With a herculean effort, she tore her attention from the concoction in her hand and looked at Jeff and Owen.

"Perfect for scribing powerful runes," she said, eyes agleam. "I'll carve the appropriate runes into the metal with a diamond knife, then color this brew into the grooves."

Jeff wondered what metal she was referring to but chose to save that for later. He asked, "So, we're good here?"

She nodded. "Perfect."

In the barest split instance where the humans' attentions were focused on one another, the owl and the hedgehog disappeared without so much as a rustled leaf or flapped feather.

The sounds of the woods resumed. Chipmunks wandered. Leaves fluttered in the breeze. Crickets chirped. A pinecone plummeted to the ground.

Coach pocketed the elixir, circled twice to her left, and ambled confidently off, resuming their quest with a magnificent treasure in her possession.

"That wasn't too bad," Owen remarked, setting off after her. In the next ten minutes, he would pat his pockets twenty times, his mind refusing to believe that his phone wasn't there.

Jeff dragged himself along, back aching, knees creaking, feeling the accelerated loss of every one of those five years. He wanted to believe the throbs and twinges were probably psychosomatic. And yet he knew they weren't. They were entirely real.

15 AN UNCOMFORTABLE NIGHT

They continued their trekking quest over virtually nonexistent trails, turning at whatever questionable landmarks Coach perceived. Whether they were truly real or figments of her overactive imagination was unclear. Sometimes it felt she was making it up as she went along.

Jeff trudged along, running on fumes. Each step was a journey; every tree passed a milestone. His legs were dead, his feet sore, and his back stiff.

Was the loss of five years of his life real? He talked himself into believing it and then disbelieving it, back and forth ten times a minute. Who knew what to trust in this weird alternate world they were journeying through.

Eventually, he walked off the discomfort of his bargained-away years, returning to semi-normal, if incredibly drained. It would have made his dad proud that Jeff had walked it off. Walking it off was the old man's answer to everything, from a skinned knee to a broken arm. One of Jeff's clearest childhood memories was of his dad insisting he walk off what turned out to be a broken ulna. Dad had dropped into a fit of passive-aggressive shame when Jeff's mom took him to the hospital for x-rays and a cast. At least passive-aggressive shame was better than explosive rage and strident belittling, so that was something.

It was starting to get dark, the blue of the sky giving way to gray as the sun slipped away, losing its ability to penetrate the dense canopy above them.

The trio were walking in silence, each of them lost in their own thoughts. It was that silence that allowed Jeff to hear the furtive noises that were growing louder, approaching them from behind.

"What's that?" he whispered. It was as though his words

invigorated whatever was out there, for it immediately became louder and charged towards them.

The intensifying crunching shook the woods, the terrible cacophony interrupted only by a tremendous snap, followed by a symphony of fluttering crunches that could only be a tree tumbling over. The mind's eye envisioned the tree pushed over or brushed aside by something of immense power.

After a frightening moment of staring at each other in wonder, they ran. It followed, stomping the earth in its fury. A bellow tore loose from its throat, sending ice into their veins.

Pee soaking through his underwear, Jeff fled as fast as the trees allowed. Faster than he would have dreamed possible, yet the thundering presence narrowed the gap, inching closer and closer to them.

They fled along what was not a trail by conventional standards, but rather a slim corridor mildly bereft of vegetation as if a lazy woodsman had stumbled along it decades ago and begun to clear a way but stopped for a nap and never resumed.

The crashing clamor pursued, shuddering the surroundings, as if a giant were on their heels. Yet, in the few panicked peeks Jeff stole behind them, he could see nothing. Nothing he was certain of anyway. Many shadows shifted and branches were purposefully flung aside, but the creature doing it never came into view.

Hundreds of yards into their breakneck dash, Jeff's lungs were burning from a combination of fear and lack of regular exercise. Coach was laboring as well, but Owen was moving at what seemed a casual, if concerned, trot, lagging so as to stay with them.

Just ahead, an exceedingly large tree loomed in their ill-defined path, dwarfing its neighbors. A titan of the forest, its leaves were shaped like a frog's feet, but with claws. The bark ran like dried rivers of molten chocolate, chips dropping away at the edges. Its branches spread their leafy embrace wide along twisted routes conjoining it with the nearby pines. The base was wide as an SUV, marking its age as hundreds of years older than its neighbors, by Jeff's inexact guessing standards.

Carved into the thick trunk was a slit of purest black, reaching from soil to shoulder-height, like a window into perpetual midnight. Coach dove in and they followed.

The rough bark gouged Jeff, scraping skin from the back of his neck, as he thrust himself into the hasty refuge.

The cleft within the tree was large, stretching the boundaries of likelihood, such that it felt as if they'd slipped into yet another world, journeying through sideways realities as if they were floors in a skyscraper. Although hale and hearty on the outside, the titanic tree's innards were dried and rotting, forming a roughcut floor of sorts.

Jagged branches sprouted from the inner walls. Lacking bark, they pulsed and oozed, dripping an ichor that had to be sap. Cold dribbles persistently fell from the yawning darkness overhead, generating regular plops that acted as acoustic counterpoints to a scuttling sound far above them.

Even knowing as little as he did about the arboreal sciences, Jeff knew such a hollow should not exist within a living tree. Nor should the poking branches reside on the interior. Yet they did. This was a tree that should not be.

The lumbering presence passed by outside, scraping against the outside of their sanctuary as it went, releasing a cascade of insects, spiders, and wooden clods to rain down upon them. The sounds of snapping limbs receded, moving away in the falling night.

Not knowing what else to do, they stayed inside, hoping the creature wouldn't return. Above them was a porcupine's bristling hide of poking branches, so Jeff squatted, finally sitting once the burning in his thighs got to be too much. Sitting wasn't comfortable either, as the uneven rotting wood, shot through with roots, knobs, and branches, poked incessantly at him.

Above them, something slithered. Slowly, luxuriously, it dragged itself along the wood, creating a rasping wheeze of sorts.

The interior was darker than it possibly could be, particularly above them. The darkness resisted Coach's flashlight's weak attempts at illumination, refusing to let the beam penetrate its gloom, instead swallowing the luminance like a black hole. Indeed, the flashlight barely illuminated the three of them, and they were mere feet apart.

The darkness made noises, forming words that dropped down onto them like shovelfuls of dirt onto a fresh grave. "You hide from that which stalks the woods."

His body bypassing fight and jumping immediately to flight, Jeff scrabbled for the opening, but Owen blocked the way. When they discussed this later, Owen would say that his instinct told him that the lumbering giant outside was the greater threat.

"What's the thing stalking the woods?" Coach asked. She held the flashlight under her chin, pointed up, as a child does on Halloween when trying to look creepy.

"It is gone, is what it is," the voice replied in a dry hiss. "Gone for now, anyway." The voice was cold unwelcome fingers along the spine.

Pausing to consider that, Coach moved her flashlight from her chin and itched at her left nostril. Through the impossibly deep gloom, it appeared her fingertip lingered inside, searching for something to clear out. Finally, she asked, "Can we stay here for a bit?"

Its voice a tumble of flailing cockroaches erupting from an attic door, the thing above them said, "Night is upon us. You should not go outside. Tasty ones such as yourselves are at risk. Greedy hungry beasts walk the woods after twilight."

There was then more slithering and scuttling, closer than it had been. It felt as if one could reach up and brush their fingers against whatever the being was.

"Are we safe here?" asked Coach, flicking a finger into the gloom.

"The beast cannot enter this place," it replied, its voice the crunch of walking on dead cicadas.

"No, I mean are we safe from you?" Coach asked conversationally, as if inquiring about the creature's health after a bout of hay fever.

A dry clicking fell from above, in what might be a monster's chuckle, but there was no other response.

The creature's failure to confirm that it wasn't murderous hung heavy on Jeff but seemed to satisfy Coach.

"I'm Jeff. What's your name?" Introductions would make him feel better. If the thing knew his name, it would be less likely to murder him. That was only logical.

It didn't reply, beyond a bit more skittering, perhaps indicating that it was getting cozy, or perhaps that it was coiling to strike.

Giving Jeff the evil eye, Coach muttered, "It doesn't care about our names." She sounded embarrassed, as if he'd made a monster greeting faux pas by even suggesting such a thing.

Deflated, Jeff shrugged, looking helpless, which was apt, because he felt helpless.

Jeff looked to Owen for support, but he was busy wedging himself just inside the entrance of their temporary sanctuary. The opening wasn't very wide and hid him well from whatever might pass outside. Regardless, anything that wanted to enter would have to go through him.

"Should I hold the pistol?" Owen asked, putting his hand

out.

It was a reasonable request and made sense no matter how Jeff looked at it. Owen was the coolest under pressure, and he was guarding the door. And yet, Jeff didn't care for the idea.

"I'll keep it for now," Jeff replied. It was hard to say no, but it felt safer that way. Not that he wanted the responsibility of holding the awful thing, which he didn't. Jeff just didn't want Owen charging out after whatever was out there, which seemed like something he was simply dying to do.

If anything, Coach should carry the weapon, since she'd served in the military and had actual training in firearms. Yet she'd shown no interest in the pistol, as if she saw it as an incidental tool with no purpose or utility in their mission. Perhaps she was correct.

Squeezing himself into a ragged hollow as far from the entrance as possible, Jeff perused the tree's innards. Of the creature above, he could see nothing, but he imagined this to be its home. Although, there was nothing homelike to be found. No bed, no books, no furniture, nothing of the sort. Just a hollowed-out space, fit for nothing except gobbling up trespassers and unwanted guests. Perhaps, he pondered, when not fretting over being eaten by the thing above, there were all the amenities of home upstairs where it was roosting. It could be listening to music on headphones for all he knew.

He was almost, just barely, on his way to getting comfortable, except for a root poking into his left buttock, when the lumbering heavy tread passed again, just outside the tree. It made noises like a lovesick humpback whale as it trampled along, shaking the earth.

They all froze, hearts pumping, hoping it would pass them by.

It did, although it was in no hurry to do so.

After it was gone and silence had cloaked them for a

reasonable amount of time, Coach whispered to Owen, "What was it? Could you see it?"

He shook his head. "Must have gone by the other side."

Again, the dry clicking from above, which Jeff suspected was laughter. The creature was enjoying the terror of its houseguests.

Moments later, as Jeff was rearranging himself to set the offending root into the cleft between his buttocks, which was a little better than jabbing into his left one, there was a stirring outside.

It was a soft thump, as quiet as a badger lying down for a nap on a bed of grass. It happened again, as if the badger were turning in the bed and resettling itself.

Owen turned his head such that he could peek outside but they could see his face. He mouthed a single word. "Ackley."

Owen's left index finger was up, requesting silence. Neither Coach nor Jeff stirred, while the creature above chose that moment for some inopportune slithering.

Seconds ticked by as Jeff pretended to be a statue, cradling the Glock like a lifebuoy. His eyes were still adjusting to the unnatural gloom. He saw a pile of bones close to hand, the remains of past meals. Small bones and skulls, perhaps robins and chipmunks. The finding was oddly reassuring, since no human remains inhabited the pile.

Silence held sway over the hollow for minutes, until Owen eventually dropped his finger and nodded, as if signaling the start to a race. "Gone," he whispered.

"So that's who's out there," Jeff hissed, quietly as he could. Any sound, no matter how insignificant, felt as if it could call the dark elf down upon them.

"Whatever was behind us was no elf," Coach countered. She said it as if unveiling an epiphany. It seemed the flight through the woods had both terrified and delighted her, like a ride on a roller coaster.

"Maybe he's a were-elephant or something," said Owen. The phrase was ridiculous, the conclusion inconceivable, yet when Owen said it, Jeff could believe it.

"That's silly, right?" asked Coach, directing her question up to the darkness. But there was no answer from the clicking, slithering inhabitant of the tree.

"He didn't see you?" Jeff asked.

The grimace that came across Owen's face was an unusual one, a look of uncertainty and trepidation. "I kind of thought that he did, but those black eyes just kept on going, sliding over me, like he didn't care."

"He's just trying to freak us out before coming back to murder us." Jeff squeezed the compact Glock. Despite his shaking hands and complete inexperience, he was fairly confident he could hit whatever he was aiming at. Especially if it stood within four feet of him and didn't move. Realistically, even closer than that would be better. It would be most ideal if he could reach out and touch the target with the tip of the barrel. Then, and only then, he was sure he could hit it. Probably.

They waited, hunkered in the gloom, uninvited visitors in a monster's home.

"Want to tell ghost stories?" asked Coach, as chipper as a troop leader at a boy scout jamboree.

"No!" Jeff and Owen hissed in unison.

"Fine, be that way," she replied. "If nothing else, I guess I can gather some tree sap. It'll have extra oomph since we got it on our quest. That'll help hold the seashell together."

That made no sense. Jeff asked, "Seashell?"

"You'll see," she said. Selecting a desiccated bone from the heap, she used it to scrape up a trickle of brown goo from a jagged stick angling down from the darkness. Slowly and carefully, she maneuvered the bone, perhaps a rodent's thigh bone, to wipe the sticky goo into a sandwich baggie. Over the course of several minutes, she managed to transfer a decent amount from branch to bag.

Beaming widely, Coach tucked the sap-laden baggie into a pocket and patted it proudly. She then leaned her head back against the deadwood and settled in. Almost immediately, she was fully asleep, a feat that neither Owen nor Jeff were able to properly accomplish.

And so, they spent the night in a hollowed-out tree that served as a creature's home. A home they were possibly guests in, or perhaps future breakfast.

It wasn't a great night. Insects and spiders crawled over them like visitors to an amusement park on Fourth of July weekend. Slithers and skitters scraped by overhead, portending horrors that would fuel nightmares for weeks to come. Any lingering hopes for legitimate sleep were expunged when a wet probing brushed gently against Jeff's forehead. It made for an uncomfortable night, containing all the luxuries of an evening spent in an iron maiden.

At one point, it seemed like a lime-green glow flashed at the entrance. But it was gone before it fully registered in Jeff's mind. Perhaps he imagined it, or perhaps Jellybiscuits was checking in on them, its lantern eyes falling on them for a millisecond.

As he shivered in the dark, hugging himself, Jeff took the opportunity to consider his life, the decisions that had gotten him where he was, and what he should do next.

Was his employer's right to cut down a few trees worth facing a giant monster in the woods? That one was easy. Nope.

Yet, it wasn't about logging, was it? Not really. It was actually about Ivy, the beautiful damsel in distress. Admittedly, discovering she had a boyfriend put a minor crimp in that motivation. But still, they had to help her or what kind of people would they be? The answer was bad people.

So, the elves were harassing Ivy, but wasn't that a matter for the police? Probably yes.

Was all this worth losing five years of his life in the blink of an eye? Definitely not, but did that even happen in the first place? Unknown.

Was he delusional? Maybe. But if he wasn't, and the world actually did hold fairy tale creatures, then what business did he have meddling in the affairs of sexy pixies and meth-cooking elves? None.

Should he go back to school? Probably.

If so, should it be medical school? Probably not, since his smarts and drive were average, at the very best. Perhaps below average, if he was being honest.

Maybe law school? No, that sounded just as hard. And boring. What made some juries so grand, anyway? And torts sounded like something sticky and sweet you should eat, not a legal something or other.

Exhaustion finally took its toll, forcing him into a light fitful doze, even as he pondered whether being a veterinarian, or more likely a veterinary technician, might be the best course of action, while dreamily acknowledging that he was intimidated by large dogs. And ornery cats.

16 OGRE DUST

When dawn came, the trio crawled out of their arboreal sanctuary. They were greeted by a light drizzle tickling the leaves. The patches of sky they could see were grayish-white, with streaks of black and glimpses of blue.

There'd been no other words from the slithery inhabitant residing in the dim recesses of the tree's innards. They mentioned it no further, as if not discussing it would make it have never happened. With luck, one day the experience would be expunged from their memories. As a beginning to that untrustworthy process, Jeff packed his memories of the night into a corner of his mind and labeled them figments of his imagination. That was a good start on the road to forgetting.

Brushing soil and cobwebs from her pants, Coach chirped, "Just one more thing, and we'll be all set. Then we can start crafting our victory." She was particularly bubbly, considering they'd just passed the night wedged into a tree trunk.

Scowling at his perky companion, Jeff dreamed of coffee. He would kill for a cup, especially with a shot of espresso and some hazelnut creamer. Speaking of killing, he pawed at the pistol in his sweatshirt. Still there, although touching its hard polymer surface reminded him that killing was nothing to joke about.

"Do you have a specific shopping list, or are you winging it?" Jeff asked. The question sounded snippy, even to his own ears.

Coach's face became thoughtful, her lower lip pushed out to wrap around the upper. After a moment of bobbling her head left and right, she said, "There are some must-haves and some nice-to-haves, as long as they're attained through a quest." Her dull brown eyes twinkling merrily, she thrust a eureka finger into the air. "The quest is the key!"

"Yeah, yeah, you've said that," Jeff said as he stretched out his lower back. It was tighter than he would have expected, even considering where they'd spent the night. Perhaps it was those five years he'd lost. And the rain didn't help. He was tired of this quest.

Emerging from peeing behind some bushes, Owen looked uncharacteristically glum. "I miss my phone." He doubtless did, but not for reasons of text messages, calls, or emails. Owen's waking up routine centered around game apps. They were his replacement for that first cup of coffee that got Jeff going in the morning.

Misreading the proverbial room and all its prevalent grumpiness, Coach grinned and clapped. "The phone is a small loss. Let's get it together team, we still have quite a ways to go. The next thing we need is an exotic reagent. It could take us days to find it."

She backed away, beckoning them to follow, which they reluctantly did.

Less than three minutes later, they entered a larger clearing, several steps across, yet still covered by the prevailing canopy.

The ground was a tumble of rotting brown and orange leaves. It smelled of late autumn, which it wasn't. An especially wet late autumn for that matter, where all the dropped leaves and dying plants were soaking in a continuous puddle of murky water, well on their way to moldering. The twin scents of rot and ruin dueled for supremacy.

"Well, this is great," howled Coach, her gold medal in enthusiasm remaining untarnished. "Can you believe our luck?"

Her excitement was generated by a bedraggled pushcart. It had four wheels, two worn wooden handles for pushing, four tiers of shelving, and was laden with unlabeled jars, vials, and pots containing powders, liquids, crystals, and granular substances. Around the top ran a frilly maroon curtain, drawn up and held in place with fraying twine.

At the cart's side, swaying unsteadily with one hand braced on a push handle, was a person of some sort. If not a human, it was at least humanoid, having the rough shape of a man with thin arms and an immense belly. The stench of rotting meat rolled off him.

His greenish flesh was mottled with patches of gray. And it was aggressively flaking, with deep furrows and cracks crisscrossing its surface. Chapstick was an obvious stranger to him, for his lips were two continuous sleeves of dead dried skin, barely housing a lopsided pair of what were nearly tusks jutting up from his prodigious underbite.

A comb-over started amongst the hair protruding like a thistle bush from his left ear and boldly swept across the top of his otherwise bald pointy head, covering a sea of protrusive lumps. A cobweb strung between his left ear and shoulder was gathering dust and flakes of dead skin. A fat red spider nestled within.

His eyes slowly focused on Coach. He paused and looked lost before speaking. "What do ya need?" he asked, with a wooden accent lacking intonation, as if English were an unknown language and he was merely reading the phonetics, sounds, and acoustics from a cheat sheet. Whenever not speaking, his face either hung slack or looked quizzical, as if receiving orders from a commander who was difficult to hear.

He stood up a little straighter, although he moved awkwardly, stringy muscles rippling under his skin, not aligning well to where the joints or skeleton were. Between his disjointed movements and lackluster intonations, he seemed nothing but a hideous marionette unaware of his own movements and motivations, as if an alien creature had crawled inside an ugly humanoid husk and taken up residence but hadn't quite gotten the hang of how to work it just yet.

"What do I need? What do I need?" Coach said, slapping a merry tune on her thighs as she stepped up and perused the wares on the cart.

"I don't know," the awkward peddler said.

"First things first, I'd like to know who I'm doing business with. Hi, I'm Coach." Coach was in the initial stages of thrusting her hand out to shake when she quite obviously, and visibly, thought better of it. Instead, she waved, rapidly back and forth, as an exuberant child might. "Nice to meet you. And you are?"

"Uhh," the peddler murmured, as if unprepared for such an exotic and confusing question. His eyes rolled back, revealing yellowish whites.

During the ensuing awkward pause, Jeff wondered why Coach hadn't felt the need to do an exchange of names with the owl. Perhaps names weren't an owl thing.

The drizzle continued pattering the foliage. The peddler mumbled a horrid string of consonants under his breath for a few seconds, then went quiet.

They waited for him to come up with an answer, although it stretched into unbearably long seconds. Jeff watched the spider on the peddler's shoulder going about its business as it hungrily lurched about the web, shoring up weak points, testing tension, and whatever else spiders do.

Eventually, Coach decided to move the conversation along as graciously as she could. "How rude of me. I forgot to mention these two." She gestured at Owen and then Jeff. "This guy is Owen and this one here is Jeff."

The peddler nodded, then cocked his head as if listening to an inner muse. Finally, he said, "Umm, Owenjeff is my name." The words tumbled from his mouth as if in a language he didn't understand.

Coach's mouth hung open, catching raindrops in her incredulity. She raised her eyebrows and stared at the peddler. "Your name is Owenjeff?" she asked, unable to hide her skepticism.

"Yessss," Owenjeff confirmed in a hissing whisper.

"That's quite a coincidence," said Owen.

"It is a family name," Owenjeff replied, completely deadpan. "But, more important than ... appellations," he stumbled tremendously over that word, "you are seeking magical artifacts. Or unguents perhaps. Or a nice mystical amulet. Some wolfsbane, maybe?"

"Ogre dust," declared Coach. She crossed her arms resolutely, entering into bargaining mode.

"Ogre dust, that is most wise," Owenjeff rasped, his voice the harsh rattle of polar wind through a sewer tunnel. He snatched a jar from the cart. It looked like a repurposed jelly jar. The contents were a gray powder. Jeff imagined the powder to look like charcoal briquettes that had burned down to gray ash and then been ground into powder with a mortar and pestle.

Coach excitedly reached for the jar but Owenjeff snatched it away, holding it close to his chest.

Owen leaned in for a closer look. "What's it made of?"

Confused, Owenjeff rocked back on his heels to think. Or to listen to that magical inner muse he seemed to follow. That subtle shift brought him under the flow of channeled raindrops funneling off a wide leaf overhead. The resulting drizzle soaked his shoulder, sending the spider scurrying into a hole in his sleeve. Eventually, the blank look on his horrid face realigned itself into one that mixed disdain and insult. "It's made of dried ogre, painstakingly ground into a fine powder, ya dumb bastard. Nothing but the finest."

"Excuse him, he doesn't get out much," insisted Coach.

Although she wore a huge smile, as always, Jeff could see she was mortified by Owen's lack of magical bargaining etiquette.

"But nothing's free," added Owenjeff. He'd shifted so that the spider's web was clear of the funneled drizzle. Instead, the rivulet flowed over his face, running into his left eye, which didn't blink.

Staring at that unwavering eye made Jeff feel increasingly uneasy. The lack of so much as a flinch convinced him that Owenjeff was nothing but an ugly simulacrum of life, moving that bold assertion from vague notion into absolute certainty.

"Well, of course nothing's free. We wouldn't expect it to be. How much?" Coach groped her pockets, as if searching for her wallet so she could whip out some cash. Owenjeff seemed unlikely to take credit cards or online payments, though.

The weather chose that moment to swell, expanding from background nuisance to attention-grabbing discomfort. The drizzle switched to a downpour, pelting the leaf-strewn clearing. The breeze amplified to a gale, sending dead leaves skittering along the undergrowth.

"Answer my riddle and we'll be square," Owenjeff said. He paused, mouth hanging open, then said, "My puzzle."

"Just answer a riddle, or puzzle, or whatever?" Owen asked, squinting suspiciously at the listless being before them. "That's it?"

Whereas Jeff was squirming under the increasingly heavy rain, Owen was undisturbed by the dowsing. He was not someone overly concerned with his own comfort, which was one of many reasons that Jeff's dad liked Owen more than him.

"A riddle puzzle," Owenjeff clarified, although he looked confused, as if interpreting the word from another language. He made a vague, expansive gesture. "Puzzle master," he mumbled, although the second word was easily heard as monster instead of master.

Coach gulped from her canteen, which seemed an odd thing to do with the rain pouring onto her upturned face. When done, she wiped her mouth, which was already soaked from the rain anyway, and asked, "So, we just solve a puzzle? That's it?"

Lightning lit the snug clearing, two quick flickers as bright as amplified flashbulbs. Seconds later, thunder rumbled, far off and ominous. The cloud-choked sky swirled evilly.

"Answer a puzzle and you get your ogre dust. Otherwise, if you get it wrong, I win, and I get my thing," Owenjeff said. His mouth hung open as if there were more. But there wasn't.

"What's your thing?" asked Coach. Again, lightning flickered, bathing them in white light.

Owenjeff's eyes rolled back into his skull. When they returned seconds later, a queasy grin came along with them. The rare facial expression approximated delight, although a twisted version of that happy emotion. "Just don't get it wrong," he whispered, the words nearly lost to rumbling thunder.

"What does that mean?" asked Jeff. He found his hand was on the Glock, clutching it like an emergency eject lever.

A fleshy ripple crossed Owenjeff's forehead. "If you get it wrong, there are consequences." He chose not to elaborate.

"What consequences?" asked Coach. Her eyes were glued to the jar of ogre dust. Whatever its purpose, she clearly coveted it.

Owenjeff had not yet assembled a response when Owen said, "We accept. Give us the puzzle." He was rubbing his hands together. Such was Owen's unbounded confidence that there was no need to hear anything more. He'd always considered himself a master puzzler, so the consequences of failure didn't bear consideration.

The puzzle contest had been accepted, even if the conditions were unknown. Coach cringed. Yet, she didn't complain. Jeff fretted, but he'd been doing that regardless.

As if a switch had been flipped, the weather eased, returning to a steady drizzle with the mildest of breezes.

There was a pause as Owenjeff hummed tunelessly with his eyes once again rolled back in his head. His white-knuckled grip on the jar of ogre dust remained firm. Jeff pictured him downloading data.

When Owenjeff spoke at last, it was in a lurching monotone, containing regular pauses, as if someone were whispering the puzzle in his ear as he recited it aloud.

"I am an item. I contain a tale yet to unfold. Inklings of epics, wrapped in stiffer stuff, currently engraved in old repetitions. I sit upon a throne of boards, waiting to be inscribed, situated in a home amongst the pines in a gully, within a river station. One of three, I am, each bedecked in beige, black, and red. Garbed in the axe man's words, never having shone and never shall. What am I?" Once finished speaking, Owenjeff's expression approximated a sneer. It was the most authentic expression they'd seen on his ghastly face.

Coach and Jeff exchanged confused looks. The puzzle was far too open-ended and vague to be answerable. Suddenly, the consequences of failing to answer the puzzle loomed large, whatsoever they might be. In a perfect world, it would be something replaceable, like a smartphone, as had delighted the owl earlier in this venture. Owenjeff, however, wasn't an inhabitant of a perfect world. His price was likely to be more drastic, assuming they were forced to pay it.

"Totally unfair," Coach barked.

Enraged, Owen said, "That puzzle's impossible."

"Impossible," Jeff repeated. He'd echoed Owen since he was too confused and panicked to generate a fresh synonym for the same concept.

His sneer had faded and once again Owenjeff was slack-jawed, his face devoid of expression. "Seemingly impossible," he conceded.

"You didn't give us enough information," Owen growled, his handsome face coloring itself red. Few things upset him as much as an uneven playing field, especially when he'd been confident in his own success, which was pretty much always.

A poor replica of a shrug flowed along Owenjeff's body, his shoulders moving back and then hunching forward. "You didn't ask for an easy one."

"Can we switch riddles?" Jeff asked. Coach nodded briskly.

"Too late," mumbled Owenjeff. "What is your answer?"

There was a knife on the cart. It was not a magnificent magical one, but rather a hefty butcher's blade that had doubtless hewn many a carcass, worn down from decades of sharpening. Owenjeff fingered it distractedly, his hand skittering across the well-worn handle as though it possessed a mind of its own. A mind with a craving for cutting.

"What if we choose not to answer?" Owen asked. He was already calming himself. Heroes such as him took hurdles in stride, never being swayed from their mission. For him, pressure formed diamonds.

"Yeah, what about that?" asked Jeff. He was becoming more upset, picturing the gory repercussions of a wrong answer. Born sidekicks such as him tended to be worriers. For him, pressure made small cracks that turned into larger fissures that turned into catastrophic ruptures.

"Failure to answer is even worse than a wrong answer," said Owenjeff. His wayward hand continued its blind perusal of the knife.

"We're gonna need a minute on this one, so we'll just step aside to discuss," said Coach, herding Owen and Jeff back out of the clearing.

"Don't come back until you have an answer. But don't make

me wait too long," called Owenjeff. As an afterthought, he added, "Don't go too far."

"Don't worry," Coach called back to the grisly peddler. "I'm pretty sure I have the answer. Just wanna confer with my associates."

They moved down the trail, out of Owenjeff's likely earshot.

"You know the answer to that mess?" Owen whispered, clearly impressed. Relief flooded Jeff's mind, pushing away the panic that had been building.

"Nah," answered Coach. She snorted.

The panic came thundering back, claiming Jeff's full attention.

The prospect of running felt like the best option so far as Jeff could imagine. Avoiding problems wasn't generally the best course of action, but right then it felt like the wisest, considering the situation. He was planning how to best frame his running-away proposal for sharing with the group, when some branches to their left stirred.

The tree limbs and bushes parted, and out stepped Ivy. Her eyes were alert, scouring the trail, the trees, the sky, the undergrowth, and everything else in their surroundings, as if a meth-cooking elf could spring from anywhere.

It was still lightly raining, but she was bundled up against it. Her cherry locks were safely contained within the hood of an oversized raincoat. She was like a cat, in that she detested being wet.

"What was the puzzle?" she asked. "I couldn't quite hear."

17 SPLATTERED WITH CRIMSON

Initially, Ivy was a sight for sore eyes, and not just because of her nearly cartoonish attractiveness, like an anime brought to life. No, Jeff was excited to see her since she was a pixie. One of the fairy folk. As such, it seemed reasonable to think she might know the riddle's answer, or at least have an inkling of where to start.

But his relief didn't last, for they were unable to relay the riddle to her in its entirety, try as they might.

First, Coach tried and failed. Owen failed as well. Then Jeff gave it a shot. He failed most miserably of all, his mind seizing the opportunity to fold under pressure, as it often did. Sadly, even when putting their heads together, they were unable to exactly recreate Owenjeff's riddle. In fact, the more they talked about it, recounting their individual versions, the more confused they became.

That was making Jeff increasingly nervous. If they couldn't remember the riddle, they couldn't answer it. And what then? Not only would they not get the ogre dust, which Coach said they needed, but they would also face the consequences of failure. The specifics of those consequences were unknown but certainly constituted a box that he didn't want opened.

His thoughts turned to the butcher's blade, which was quickly becoming the lodestone of his attention.

Owenjeff had been stroking the knife's handle luxuriously when they'd left. He seemed eager to snatch it up and go to work. The ill-formed peddler might even now be whetting the blade, scraping his thumb along the edge to test its sharpness. From several steps away, it had appeared razor sharp, although not surgical. It was far too filthy for that. Any slicing done by that squalid blade would leave festering sores in its wake.

"It was an impossible puzzle," said Coach.

"Just gibberish, with no rhyme or reason to it," confirmed Owen.

"Plus, I think he was just making it up as he went along," added Jeff.

Nearby, some leaves rustled, just beyond one of the larger trees, a wide monster of an oak with sweeping, low-slung branches. Rustling was a thing leaves did in the rain, especially when the wind was blowing. Yet, this particular rustle felt nefarious. Ominous, even. Jeff could feel eyes upon them. The only thing that allowed him to tamp down his fear was that he'd already been certain they were being watched on and off since this questing caper had started and it hadn't amounted to anything thus far. He had a history of being the boy that cried wolf and was gun-shy to raise the alarm until he was certain.

"Forget it," Ivy huffed. She snugged her hood down as a stray drop dared to wet the tip of her nose. "I'll go ask for myself and get it straight from the horse's mouth. Which way is it, exactly?"

"I'll go with you, for protection," Owen said, stepping forward resolutely. The only thing lacking was a cape regally flapping in the breeze.

Ivy rolled her eyes. "Ugh, I made it this far dodging those horrid, pervert, numbnut elves without you, so I think I can manage twenty more steps."

Chuckling, Coach pointed towards Owenjeff's leaf-strewn clearing. "Thataways, you can't miss him. Go get 'em tiger." Energized by Ivy's confidence, Coach clapped twice and whooped loudly. Again, Jeff questioned her sanity.

Snorting in derision, Ivy stamped along the trail in search of Owenjeff. Although her boots slammed the soil, very little sound came from them. "I have to do everything myself," she grumbled.

Once she was gone, Owen asked, "So, what was that thing,

exactly?"

"Yeah, what the heck?" Jeff echoed. If only he knew what Owenjeff was, perhaps it would be easier to keep it from his nightmares. We fear the unknown, shivering in terror during the night at that which we don't understand. But if he could label Owenjeff and fit the creature into some logical framework, perhaps it would slip more easily into the land of the forgotten.

"What thing?" Coach asked. She craned her neck and scanned the area. The sheer earnest sincerity upon her face during the scan almost tore a nervous giggle from Jeff's throat. It was as if she'd accepted Owenjeff's existence without question, and the thought of pondering his origins hadn't crossed her mind.

Caught flatfooted by her uncertainty, Owen clarified, "Owenjeff. What is he, or it?"

"Ohhh," she said, in dawning realization, drawing the syllable out across several seconds. Perhaps to give herself time to think. She shrugged, beaming wildly. "Who knows? Maybe a flock of industrious boggarts or deranged fairies dressed up in a goblin suit. Beats me. Pretty stinky though. Whatever he is, he has what we need."

"Do we actually need the ogre dust, though?" Owen asked.

"Oh yeah, totally," Coach said. Her tone was pure reassurance. The few words were delivered with a you-gotta-be-kidding-me look.

Jeff said, "Do we really, really though? I mean really?" He was not an eloquent arguer. His presence would have made any debate team a certain loser. Words failed him during any situation that involved a dispute or even meager amounts of tension.

"Yeah," Coach replied incredulously. This time she included a have-you-lost-your-mind look. Her eyes bugged, as if amazed they would ever question the utility of powdered ogre.

It was obvious that the running-away proposal Jeff was preparing wouldn't fly, so he changed tactics. "Maybe we can just make up an answer. I mean, the puzzle riddle is so vague that we could just tell him our answer works. If he's vague and sketchy, we can be too."

"I suppose we could," Coach replied. She crossed her arms and cradled her chin in her left hand, settling down into deep thought. Like a shroud, pensiveness fell across her face, replacing the jaunty enthusiasm otherwise always found there.

Within seconds, they were each engrossed in contemplation, grappling with the impossible riddle. The downpour had increased, the fat drops partitioning the trio from one another, giving them each solitude in which to think.

Jeff was ruminating on the ominous "axe man" portion of the riddle when a high-pitched shriek ripped through the forest. It was pure terror, rising in fractions of a second that felt like forever, before abruptly halting as the voice cracked.

Jeff leaned away, his subconscious mind instinctively selecting flight, even as it also registered the voice to be Ivy's. Rejecting the possibility of fleeing, Jeff's legs took it upon themselves to race towards the clearing where Ivy should be. The split second he paused was enough to let Owen and Coach get a head start, so they were several steps ahead.

Bursting into the clearing, Jeff witnessed a gory tableau that would haunt him.

Ivy knelt over Owenjeff. She was screaming incoherently, her mind cracking, grinning like a lunatic. Her hands were raised before her face, clutching frantically at air. They were splattered with crimson, as were the upended cart and surrounding fallen leaves.

The blood was from Owenjeff. A generous scoop had been

torn from his torso, running from breastbone to belly.

Ivy, the cart, and the ground were painted in a denser coat of blood than seemed possible, considering Owenjeff's body was largely intact, beyond the yawning gap crossing his chest and belly. Yet, that corporeal chasm was empty, scraped clean, his innards having been scooped up and flung across the clearing, where they decorated the tree limbs with festoons of gore. Unlike the bright red blood, the organs littering the clearing were black and dry, almost withered.

Ivy tore her attention from Owenjeff's remains and looked up at them. Behind the bloody mask, her eyes shimmered a pastel palette. She raised a shaky, blood-soaked hand to point vaguely out of the clearing, towards where the trees were mostly pines. "Yoric," she gasped, her voice breaking from terror.

Like a one-man posse, Owen was three steps into a charge after the villainous elf before Jeff finished processing that single word—Yoric. Yet, before Owen reached full speed, Coach flung herself at him. Her tackle was clumsy but effective, almost bringing them both to the ground.

Owen staggered to a halt, Coach hanging from his waist. Her arms encircled him, hands clasped tight, her face pressed into his lower back.

"Nope, no time for that," she said. "We've gotta go."

"Fine," Owen said, giving up uncharacteristically easily, as he realized that Owenjeff's murder wasn't his responsibility to avenge. He stared into the pines, seeking any hint of the elf.

Extricating herself from Owen, Coach snatched up the jar of ogre dust from where it sat by the cart. Unlike most of the cart's contents, the ogre dust was sitting neatly upright, completely intact.

Nearly all the other jars, vials, flasks, and vessels of fabled, esoteric materials lay amongst the leaves. Many were broken, spilling substances that steamed where the meager sun kissed them, hissed when they contacted water, smelled of corruption, issued cloudy miasmas that seemed unwise to breathe, or formed wispy tornadoes.

Ivy slowly shook her head, as if trying to clear the shock from her system. She stared with disgust and horror at the blood on her hands, transfixed by it as if it were acid eating away the outer layers of her skin. The rain was already sluicing Owenjeff's blood from her jacket. Trembling, she staggered away from the stinking corpse.

Jeff scrubbed her face clean with his shirt. Ivy offered no help or resistance but instead remained thunderstruck.

"We have to get out of the woods," she whispered. "It's not safe here. There are monsters lurking everywhere."

Ivy smiled, a grin so wide it threatened to split her face. Her sparkling round eyes expanded to comical proportions. There was a manic quality to the expression. Hers was not the face of a stable mind. She was in danger of cracking, mentally if not physically.

"Roger that," said Coach. "Let's beat feet."

Owen and Jeff, each of them over two decades younger than Coach, regarded her blankly. Ivy, who was far, far older than the others, was equally confused. "What are we beating?" Owen asked.

"Beat feet. It means to run. Get those legs pumping." Coach jogged in place, her boots mashing the magical reagents scattered across the dead leaves. "We need to get out of here. We have the ogre dust, so let's skedaddle before we end up like him." She inclined her chin at Owenjeff. Her hands jealously clutched the ogre dust like it was the crown jewels.

"Yeah, but what about him?" Owen asked. He stood over Owenjeff, studying the ragged remains. Jeff was on the other end of the clearing, squatting over the dead leaves and sticks, trying to calm his nerves. The sooner he could get away from the dead body, the better.

Coach stared at Owenjeff for a few seconds, considering him carefully. Her brown eyes roamed the clearing, inspecting his organs and bloody spray. She shrugged. "The world's probably better off without that thing in it," she said. "And, we don't have to answer the riddle anymore."

After that, Coach grew thoughtful, as if she'd stirred up a line of reasoning she couldn't yet see the shape of.

"Just leave him like this?" Owen asked.

Coach shook her head violently, not as if disagreeing, but rather as if clearing it. She snorted. "Yes, we leave him to rot. You got a better idea? Would it make you feel better to report his death to the cops?" She snatched up an imaginary phone and held it to her ear. "Hi, 911? Yeah, I'd like to report the murder of a magical scoundrel. It happened in the mystical woods. We were in the middle of a puzzle bargain where I was hoping to obtain some ogre dust. Yup, that's right. Anyway, I think he was some sort of miniature troll. But good news! I know who killed him. It was an elf named Yoric who lurks deep in the woods, hopping barefoot from tree to tree."

Jeff looked at Owen. Owen looked back. Unspoken communications flew. Simultaneously, they shrugged.

Yoric murdering Owenjeff was, frankly, convenient, if terrifying. But it didn't feel like a real murder, since Owenjeff hadn't seemed truly alive. This was more like Yoric had slashed up a puppet of meat and bone, although one that contained a surprising amount of blood.

"Should we take other stuff?" Jeff asked. The clearing was full of magical substances in various stages of spillage, wreckage, and splatter. But some of the containers were unbroken, leaving quite a treasure trove of unknown mystical materials. The value must be phenomenal, assuming any of it had the value that Coach insisted it did.

Coach shuddered. "No, no, no, that's tempting the fates. There could be curses for stealing. Can't risk it."

"What about the ogre dust?" asked Owen. "Wouldn't that be cursed?"

"Nah, we earned it," Coach said, waving her hand. Yet, she looked uncertain.

"But we didn't know the answer to the puzzle," said Jeff, who very much did not want to be cursed.

"We would have figured it out sooner or later," Owen said, sidestepping a steaming pile of green powder.

"No need to fret," Ivy whispered. She was markedly calmer than she had been, preoccupied by the bloody portrait they stood within. Solemnly, she continued, "You entered the bargain in good faith. It isn't your fault you couldn't finish it. Anyway, I didn't hear the exact words, but it sounds as if he didn't offer a square deal, since the puzzle was nonsense, its answer unknowable." She kicked at the butcher's blade, sitting amongst the dregs of Owenjeff and his spilled wares. "He just wanted some easy meat."

And then, just like that, they gathered their belongings and retreated, keeping a careful eye out for elves.

Jeff draped an arm around Ivy, helping steady her thin, shaky frame. She smelled of wildflowers and sunshine, with undertones of bloody murder. As she walked, she absentmindedly dug bits of flesh from under her nails, occasionally spitting on her palms to wipe away the crimson stains.

Within an hour they were back at the Jeep. Their exit from Sector G12 was obvious, as the normal world resumed. Birds chirped. Insects buzzed. The sun was in a single, dependable location, no longer swiveling about the sky on a whim. Never had Jeff felt so relieved by the mundane.

18 A SEASHELL AND A BEAR TRAP

The entire crew, as Jeff thought of them, were in Jeff and Owen's apartment. Besides he and Owen, the crew included Coach, Ivy, and Carla.

Normally the presence of women would have driven them towards a vain last-ditch effort at cleaning. Mainly for Ivy and Carla, but not so much for Coach. But sadly, there'd been no time. As a better-than-nothing measure, Owen had raced ahead and doused the place in fresh linen air spray, emptying the can just seconds before the others walked in the door.

The apartment was pretty typical for two young men to inhabit.

There were two bedrooms, nearly identical. Each had a mattress with no box spring or frame. Overflowing wicker laundry hampers. No proper dressers, just an array of plastic storage drawers and plastic tubs, much like huge Tupperware containers for clothes. Identical small desks to hold their laptops. A desk chair in each room.

Amongst the few differences were that Owen had a lamp in his room. Jeff did not. Also, Owen had an exercise tower for pullups, ab exercises, and dips. Having discovered one drunken night that he couldn't do so much as a single pullup, Jeff had never again touched that tower, generally ignoring its very existence.

There was a single bathroom. In the way of young men everywhere, it didn't get as much cleaning as it should. The toilet, in particular, had a nasty ring around the water line that refused their infrequent attempts to scrub it away, always clinging to existence and regaining its habitual girth days after scouring. There was no standalone shower. Instead, there was a shower set up in the bathtub, complete with a dingy shower curtain that had been left by the previous tenants. A mildewy smell tickled the nostrils.

The kitchenette was barely dirty, since it received more cleaning than the bathroom. Owen was in charge of kitchen cleaning, while Jeff handled bathroom cleaning. True to their individual natures, Owen did a more fastidious job than Jeff. Regardless, cleaning the kitchen was the easier job, since they cooked very little, beyond what went into the microwave. In fact, Jeff had never tried the oven or stove and just took it as a given that they worked.

The little kitchen opened into the living room. There was no rhyme or reason to the living room furniture. Instead, it was a mishmash of what they'd had forever, gotten cheap, or found for free. It held two wooden end tables, a battered coffee table, two loveseats, and a recliner, none of which matched. One loveseat aggressively mismatched everything they'd ever put alongside it, its stiff plaid exterior studiously denying aesthetic congruence with any neighbor.

The only aspects of the room receiving any planning or care were the video game systems, the television stand, and the 75-inch television that swallowed one side of the room, nearly blocking the sliding door to the small balcony that looked down on the parking lot two levels below.

Coach was working at a little butcher block table at the interface between the kitchenette and living room, seated atop a wobbly chair salvaged from Owen's grandma's basement.

She was wearing half-glasses, occasionally leaning her head backwards for the added clarity of the lenses. Other times, she swapped them out for glasses with surgical loupes, the ultra-magnifiers surgeons use for precision work.

Atop the butcher block table were a few old books, each page laden with runes. One book was written in Latin and the other in something that Jeff took to be Nordic in origin.

There were also paintbrushes of all sizes and some fine tip

Sharpies. Off to the side were the spoils of their quest, including the stygian dye, tree sap, and jar of ogre dust. They were set to the side primarily since there was precious little room in the center of the table. That was taken up by a seashell and a bear trap.

The seashell was a rusty reddish pink, long, with a spiraling pointy end across from a broader smoother end. Very standard, although in nicer shape than most.

The bear trap might have been standard as well, but Jeff couldn't tell, having never seen one before in real life.

It was brand new and black, made of thick steel. The trap was more compact than those he'd seen on television, without the big arms sweeping out to the side. It was mostly jaws to clamp shut and a plate underneath. Also, there were no teeth. Mercifully, the jaws were closed.

"Don't they usually have teeth?" asked Ivy. She'd quickly recovered from the horror of the butchered peddler in the woods and was back to her usual bubbly self, wearing clothes that looked more appropriate for a garden party than for preparing to battle evil elves. Her floral sundress was light blue and low cut. Crimson strands of hair exploded from her straw sun hat. In truth, she looked ready to model for a women's spring clothing catalog. More exactly, a catalog put together in such a way that teenage boys would wish to tuck it away beneath their mattresses for personal investigative purposes.

Coach winked mischievously. "Usually they have teeth, yes. But there are questions of legality there. This particular model is technically functional, but built for collectors, so there are no teeth. Doesn't matter, since the teeth aren't important for our purposes, anyway. It's about the intent of the device. This was crafted as a trap, even if made and sold for display purposes, so it'll work for us. And it's a good size, if a bit heavy."

"How heavy?" asked Carla from the loveseat, where she sat shoulder to shoulder with Owen.

"Thirty pounds," answered Coach. "Which is a lot to have to haul through the woods."

"Lucky we've got Owen. He can do it," said Carla, patting Owen's wide shoulder, giving it an exploratory squeeze. Jeff's ego deflated, dried up, and fell into bits.

"Yup," Owen agreed. His attention was affixed to his laptop. He was a human being of great focus, and being squeezed, fondled, or poked at by attractive women did not distract him.

"Yeah, I figured Owen would have to carry it," said Coach, stomping Jeff's ego into tinier bits. She returned to her art project, supervised closely by Ivy.

Throughout the course of the day, Coach decorated the bear trap with a series of runes. First, she would consult the rune books, then practice by drawing each symbol on a piece of paper. When satisfied with her drawing, she'd sketch the rune on the bear trap with a Sharpie and then score it with a diamond knife. Finally, she'd paint the slashed Sharpie doodle with the stygian dye, applying it with a tiny brush whose soft hairs were from a marten.

As Coach diligently worked, Ivy studiously oversaw every step, while saying very little. Ivy knew a bit about runes, perhaps as part of her education in pixie middle school. Sometimes they discussed the symbols Coach was considering using, ruminating on their power, their meaning, and what import they had in the current project, which was meant to be an elf trap, so far as Jeff could tell.

Meanwhile, Owen and Jeff researched local legends and any unfortunate events or other bad happenings in the nearby woods, looking back as many years as the internet would allow. They were trying to get an idea of whether the area had a storied history of danger, since that would provide hints as to how long these elves had been at work and how malevolent they truly were. There were occasional short video game breaks. Jeff enjoyed those tremendously, for they were the one arena he could often best Owen.

Carla was alternating watching Coach's handiwork, looking over Owen's shoulder, refilling her drink, and staring at the television while tirelessly flipping channels.

With the exception of Coach, who needed to concentrate, everyone was drinking. Carla was outpacing everyone in that regard, getting a little slurry as the session stretched out. Nevertheless, she didn't get sloppy. She rarely did. She could handle her liquor.

Coach mumbled from time to time, her inner thoughts spilling into the light. Often, Ivy would respond.

"Runes drawn in stygian dyes are hugely powerful. They direct the whole deal. Amp it up to a higher level," mumbled Coach, staring resolutely at a symbol she'd drawn that looked like a duck in the wind.

"Was the dye being from a chenoo important?" asked Ivy.

"Maybe yes and maybe no. But either way, it brings power to the table," said Coach. She crumpled up the windy duck and began again.

It took hours, but Coach finally got the bear trap decorated with enough runes to make her happy. Then she started on the seashell.

"What magical quest is that seashell from?" asked Carla from across the kitchenette, where she was pouring a vodka and root beer. She hadn't wanted beer, so she was working her way through combinations of the available mixers and liquors. The grape juice and bourbon she'd just finished had been, according to her, a delight.

"It's from the Outer Banks," replied Coach, holding the

seashell up proudly. The way she gazed lovingly at it, the seashell might have been the finest one ever pulled from the Atlantic. "I was there a few years ago."

"On a magic beach?" asked Carla, over the fizz of freshly poured root beer.

"I wish," Coach enthused, charging the words with animated wonderment. "I got it from a gift shop. You can't find shells this nice very easily." She returned to her work, oblivious to follow-up questions on the non-magical nature of the seashell.

"What have you two found?" asked Carla, returning to the living room and snatching up the remote. She slid into the loveseat next to Owen, scooching up close to him. Her increasingly blatant fawning over him went unnoticed by Owen, but Jeff found it irritating. Jealousy was stoking that particular fire.

Owen consulted his notepad. He'd been taking studious, well-structured notes, as if preparing for a test. Jeff's piece of scrap paper had some useful jotted information but was mostly full of illegible scribbles.

Brows knit in concentration, Owen studied his notes and said, "There's quite a local history of mayhem. Most of it seems pretty standard, but there was some notable well-documented trouble over the span of a few seasons, way back hundreds of years ago. Lots of farmers and villagers were murdered. Others disappeared and were never seen again. There was plenty of finger-pointing, mostly at Native Americans and the French. Let's see, besides the murders, there were lots of shadowy assaults, both sexual and physical. Livestock were killed. Human bodies were found that were partially consumed, with theories including cannibalism or attacks by large forest monsters. Umm ... creatures wearing people's skin. Things like that."

"You know not everything on the internet is true, right?" Carla asked.

Owen flashed a megawatt smile and nodded. "Yeah, yeah."

Jeff had the distinct feeling Owen wanted there to be monsters, even beyond the elves. Heroes need monsters to battle. It was a wonder he hadn't gone into law enforcement. Instead, Owen studied computer science, with a focus on cybersecurity. In many ways, that was the battlefield of the future. Internet viruses and computer worms were modern-day dragons.

Jeff said, "They suspected lots of possible creepy things. Witches were big for a few years. A wendigo, devil monkeys, lizard men, giant weasel monsters, you name it. Lots of skookum legends as well." It all sounded ridiculous, but since he'd accepted Ivy was a pixie, it seemed anything was possible.

"What's a skookum?" asked Carla. She sipped the vodka and root beer, smiling contentedly.

"Like a big forest monster thingy," said Jeff. "Anyways, legends of monsters have persisted since then, along with what seems to be a more than average rate of violence in these woods, although I'm not a historical forest criminologist so it's hard to say."

Owen glowered resolutely at the notebook before him, trying to conjure facts from scribbled conjecture. He said, "So maybe it's always been the elves causing trouble, down through the centuries, but people just guessed that the trouble was caused by whatever monsters struck their fancy that season."

"Probably just always these same elves, then? Over hundreds of years?" Carla asked, while returning her attention to the television. Her patience for the topic was slim. She wasn't yet a true believer.

"No, the elves told us they rotate in and out on this mission of theirs," said Owen. "Whatever that mission is."

"Protecting the piles of gold squirreled away in their fairy house, that's their mission," mumbled Coach. Right then, she was staring through the surgical loupes at a symbol she'd practiced that looked like jagged concentric circles.

Ivy said, "Whether it's those elves or other ones, it doesn't matter. Other elves are just like them. Each and every one is an evil bastard." Her tone was angry, guttural, not what one would believe would come from a charming pixie. Beneath the sun hat, her face formed a vicious snarl.

Conversation died back down, everyone returning to their tasks, whether it be drawing runes, researching on the internet, or swigging vodka.

Hours later, Coach finished the seashell. Once it was appropriately rune-laden, she poured a generous dollop of ogre dust into the aperture, then closed it up with duct tape, sealing the nasty powder within. As the final step, she used the tree sap from the quest to seal the edges of the duct tape. She leaned back from the table, stretched, and loudly sighed.

As Coach proudly showed off her crowning seashell achievement, Owen asked, "Why a seashell?"

"To hold the ogre dust," said Coach matter-of-factly.

"Yeah, but why?" asked Carla.

Pointing at her books of runes, Coach shrugged. "Says to do it. One thing is, instead of tree sap, I could have used the wax from a fisherman's ear. Unfortunately, I'm fresh out."

That might have been true or a joke, Jeff had lost his hold on the reality of their situation.

Coach unrolled a sleeping bag and crawled inside. "Okay, tomorrow we do this thing," she announced. Snores followed shortly after, rising from the sleeping bag like muffled thunder.

The party broke up, rather anticlimactically. Ivy left almost immediately, stepping out onto the balcony and disappearing.

Owen retired to his bedroom. Once Owen had gone to bed, Carla left for her own place, but not before staring forlornly at his bedroom door, which was yet another blow to Jeff's vanishing ego.

Left alone in the living room, which was silent except for Coach's snoring, Jeff fretted. Coach had spent a tremendous amount of time getting the seashell and bear trap exactly as she wanted them, but that didn't mean they would do anything. Although she insisted she was a practitioner of rune magic, they'd yet to see actual undeniable proof of it. The questing trip in the woods had been magical and weird and unexplainable. That was true. But sometimes, he wondered if Coach had somehow dosed them with a psychedelic and led them through a shared group hallucination. All he knew was that Ivy was being threatened by two weirdos in the woods, who might be meth cookers, or might be elves, or might be flaky nature lovers. And that those same weirdos, or possibly the worst run of bad luck ever, were keeping his company from moving into Sector G12. The lack of progress was making management nervous and irritated, imperiling Jeff's job. Uncle Chet was a great guy, but nepotism only went so far. Something had to give, and soon.

19 OBTUSE ELDRITCH LOGIC

Without so much as a word, or a note, or a text, Ivy did not appear on the morning of the monumental bear trap experiment.

Nor, for that matter, did Carla. Unlike Ivy, Carla sent her regrets, saying she had to work at her parents' coffee shop. The implied sentiment was that field trips to trap imaginary elves weren't worth burning a precious day off over. Also, being honest, she was not the biggest fan of bug bites, wild animals, or long hikes in possibly haunted forests.

It was a nice day for rune magic. Not too hot and not too cold. Neither overly sunny nor overcast. A gentle breeze carried the smell of pine from the woods.

Jeff's plan had been to use a company Jeep to get out to Sector G12. It was better suited to the terrain than Coach's Subaru. The Subaru was a capable enough vehicle, but the tires were balding and slid on any stretch of road that didn't provide perfect traction. Plus, it was packed floor to roof with Coach's life, bag after bag, most of them garbage bags but a select few actually designed to be luggage.

However, when Jeff arrived at the worksite to pick up the company vehicle, all was chaos. The logging company had once again set its sights on G12, since the area had black cherry trees that Chet had a need for.

Yet, as always happened, the reorientation towards G12 had stirred up trouble. A vast expanse of pricker bushes had sprouted overnight, multiplying with a speed that defied logic. The thorny shrubs had grown to ridiculous size at an impossible pace, as if mutated by radiation. They reached up into the various vehicles, intertwining their prickers into wheels, treads, and engines. The prickly branches and vines had thickened, squirming themselves into every apparatus they had access to, putting a temporary halt to progress until they could be cleared out.

In a gloriously frothy rage, Pinkie was stomping about, swearing at the top of his lungs and yelling at everyone unfortunate enough to cross his path.

Still on the boundaries of the worksite, Jeff cautiously slunk away before Pinkie saw him. Trouble like that, he did not need.

Creeping back to meet Owen and Coach at the Subaru, he texted Chet that he would be scouting for the black cherry trees in G12. There were several texts from Pinkie and Chet, none of which did he read, although he did do a quick internet search to familiarize himself with what a black cherry tree looked like, in case it should come up. The bark of a black cherry was described as resembling burnt potato chips, so Jeff was relieved to finally see an identification scheme that made sense to him.

As he retreated from Pinkie's roving enraged notice, Jeff saw Ackley.

The elf, if elf he truly was, lingered at the edge of the worksite, floating like a soap bubble, sliding between the porta-potty, deadfalls of shorn branches, and piles of delimbed trunks.

From straight on, the dark elf appeared as an old Black man with white hair, a hard hat, and what looked like a minor league baseball jersey colored brown with yellow sleeves. The lettering on the jersey was nonsensical, like the writing in a dream, where you think it makes sense until you really focus and find it to be gibberish.

Yet when Jeff shifted his gaze away and allowed Ackley to sit at the corner of his eye, he could see the elf for what he was. Tall, menacing, and inhuman. The elf watched Pinkie's tirade, seeming moderately amused by the chaotic scene. He wore a smug look of self-satisfaction, although in a majestic fashion.

Jeff quickened his pace, hoping to escape Ackley's notice. He didn't consider himself to be fleeing. No, he was wisely avoiding an adversary, although with fear in his heart.

Thankfully, Coach's Subaru got the job done, precariously bumping them along the trail to just outside Sector G12, where they parked and unloaded the bear trap.

Venturing into the darkened confines of G12, the temperature dropped and sounds fell away, a hush settling over the trees. It was like walking into a parallel reality, similar to our own, but distinctly different in some intangible way.

The trio trooped through the woods with varying degrees of excitement. Coach and Owen were floating sky high, buoyed by enthusiasm, yet counterbalanced by the lead weight of Jeff's trepidations.

Owen lugged the heavy bear trap. It was nestled in a greasy pizza box, which had been the best option at hand to hide it from prying eyes. Coach carefully held the seashell in her cupped hands. Jeff held nothing but misgivings.

As was his habit whenever venturing into G12, Jeff had the Glock in his pocket, where it fit surprisingly well. Something so deadly should not fit casually into a pants pocket, but it did. This particular model was referred to as a pocket Glock, after all. Despite its modest size, its very presence was upsetting. He wasn't becoming accustomed to carrying it, nor would he ever. The faster he could give it back to Uncle Chet, the better.

They thrashed through the trees and bushes of G12 until they found a small clearing that Coach found suitable. Trees leaned in from all sides, stretching their roots. Some grasped with their pine needle-covered arms, others groped with their leafy talons.

The area held sufficient space to take several steps. It was perhaps fifteen feet wide at its fattest point.

Owen set the bear trap down in the middle of the clearing.

After inspecting the contraption's positioning, Coach gave a thumbs-up.

"Let's try this puppy out," she said, squatting and gently setting the seashell atop the bear trap. She nudged the shell this way, and then that, and then back again, fine-tuning its placement. As she pushed and prodded, Jeff couldn't shake the feeling they had aligned themselves with someone who should perhaps be in an institution whose rooms had rubber walls.

Coach's grand scheme for trapping the elves consisted of a bear trap covered in scribbles. Atop that, she was carefully situating a doodled seashell filled with grayish powder of dubious origin. The powder, by the way, had an underlying reek. Jeff couldn't describe it, but it was bad. Rotten. Spoiled. Holding the dust within the seashell was duct tape, sealed with tree sap. Not to mention, the various scribbles were written with a dye that was apparently the blood of a type of ice giant called a chenoo. And those scribbles were where the magic originated from, since they were ancient runes of power.

So, Coach was either crazy, in which case magic didn't exist, or she was sane, and magic was real. But if magic was real, it felt like nonsense, as in, making no sense. Or, if it did make sense, it was a very separate kind of sense than the regular world abided by, with rules all its own, outside of known science and aligned to an obtuse eldritch logic.

When Coach had the shell exactly where she wanted it, she pulled her hands back like she'd just finished assembling the top of a triple-decker house of cards. Pressing her hands onto the top of her thighs, she arose, grunting loudly at the effort.

"Here we go." With a thumb, Coach rubbed away one of the symbols from the bear trap. It looked like a squiggly emulation of a cat on a ledge. She quickly stepped back, joining Owen and Jeff in the trees. "That was a dampener, sort of like a brake."

Seconds ticked by. Nothing happened. The leaves sang their song, rubbing elbows and brushing against one another in the gentlest of breezes.

Beyond the susurration of the leaves, the forest was still.

Owen fidgeted, shuffling his feet in excitement.

Coach stared confidently at her rune-coated creations.

Jeff felt foolish.

No animals crawled, dug, or climbed, either boldly or furtively. That was the way Sector G12 often was, devoid of apparent life. If there were critters about, they were hiding, struggling to avoid whatever larger predators stalked the trails.

The ticking seconds, stacking one atop the previous, threatened to become a minute. But that never happened. Abruptly, the trap hummed. Or rather, the clearing did. Then the world seemed to tip, and there was a muffled thump. Perhaps more of a whump. It was felt in the inner ears more than heard, reminiscent of an underground explosion.

20 ADD-ONS

The elves weren't there, and then they were, appearing in a fraction of a blink of an eye.

All pretenses of feigned humanity were gone, discarded like cheap Halloween costumes. Both elves were taller than they had been, towering at seven feet. And unnaturally lean, with bodies like harsh anatomical displays of corded muscle, pulsing veins, and steely sinews. Strikingly, their hands were overly large, with powerful fingers custom-made for grasping and tearing. Their ears were pointed, framing faces that remained disconcertingly attractive, despite the obvious inhumanity of their sharp elongated features. And despite their teeth, which were pointed, jagged, and sharp, yet pearly white.

Yoric held a bone in his hand. It was long, with a rounded knob jutting out crookedly from one end, much like the femur of a large mammal. Lightly roasted pinkish-red meat with scant tatters of fire-crisped skin coated the top, while the bottom was already chewed clear down to the bone itself. It smelled of pig, or something much like it. He was wearing nothing but frayed gray sweatpants, with crimson stains dried around the waistband and smearing down towards the thighs. He looked like nothing so much as a slovenly bachelor interrupted during a barbecue. Outright hostility flickered across his surprised countenance but was almost immediately hidden by a veil of studied indifference.

Ackley had shed his disguise from the logging worksite. Instead of a baseball jersey, he was clad in a faded black leather jerkin and pants. His indigo flesh was decorated with a sea of scars, many of which were purposefully applied in intricate patterns that vaguely resembled Coach's runes. Others were earned in ferocious combat, occasionally gouged deep into the underlying meat, running close to the bone. He looked puzzled, certainly. Yet, he did not seem overly concerned. Rather, he appeared mildly irritated at an inconvenience, like a person who has just missed their bus.

Surrounding the elves, encasing them within its confines, was a hazy orb, centered around the rune-marked seashell and bear trap contraption.

The surface of the orb glistened dully, although that wasn't exactly right. Perhaps a better means to describe it would be heat waves shimmering above a blacktop road baking in the sun. But not quite that either. Regardless, it was a sheath of distorted air, cordoning the elves away from the world.

The orb pulsed with a lazily throbbing energy. The power emanated from within, but also seemed to wick into the orb from the surrounding atmosphere. It oozed, popped, wriggled, and fizzed, although not in a way completely discernible using the five human senses.

Abruptly, everything clicked into place, the pieces locking together in Jeff's mind like a solved puzzle box. Things made an unlikely sort of sense. Everything was exactly as Coach had said. She had actual, legitimate magic at her command. The runes were real, and they had power. Elves and pixies were not a figment of his imagination. The seashell and bear trap formed a conduit to eldritch power, a pinprick in the fabric of reality, perhaps reaching back to centuries ago, when magic ran rampant. The runes provided guidance, a set of instructions delivered to vast entities, asking for power shaped towards a particular purpose. Suddenly anything seemed possible.

In a fleeting second where he tore his attention from the elves, Jeff glanced at Coach. She looked as shocked as he felt. Her mouth hung open, her eyes wide and dilated.

Similar to the elves, Ackley's broad obsidian sword wasn't there, and then it was. With a cold look of malicious intent, he swung it casually, the lazy slicing motion tearing through the air, producing a cry, and a whimper. The cry was from the air itself, torn by the wicked blade's passage. The whimper was from Jeff, who'd just viewed his own death.

Heart pounding, Jeff stumbled back, meeting a wall of needle-covered branches, his entire focus glued to the blade, convinced it would be his last sight before death.

"Ah, don't worry," said Coach. "They can't get out of there." She hiked up her pants and grinned, supremely satisfied.

"Well done," said Owen, as if he'd seen many magical traps in his day, but this one took the cake. He punched Coach's shoulder appreciatively.

The obsidian broadsword dissolved, leaving Ackley's hand empty. He filled that emptiness by stroking his chin thoughtfully, treading closer to the edge of their shimmering magical cage.

Realizing his bloody, hacked-apart death wasn't imminent, Jeff stepped forward again, his speeding heart slowing to the point where panic-induced cardiac arrest didn't seem as strong a possibility.

"This is an inconvenience, isn't it?" remarked Ackley, through gritted teeth. Very sharp, very pointy, gritted teeth. His expression, normally one of grim purpose, or mildly malevolent humor, was agitated. Yet he had regained his calm in spite of the threat, as only a creature who has watched the millennia march by can do.

"It is," replied Yoric, merry insanity flickering across his pointy visage.

"And yet, this does not trouble me greatly," said Ackley, stepping nearer to the limits of the haze and studying it closely. His charcoal eyes remained bound to the blur as he turned his head towards Yoric and asked, "Does it trouble you?"

"It does not. I've been in worse spots," said Yoric. He set

the meaty bone down on the grass near the bear trap, as if saving it for later, unsure how long this incarceration might last.

"Yes, such as when you tracked that unhinged Wampus Cat down into the coal mine." Ackley reached a long-fingered indigo hand towards the haze, pushing at it experimentally. The haze resisted the gentle shoves, not pushing back, but not giving so much as a hair's breadth.

"I was in those dust-choked diabolical tunnels for days," said Yoric. He chuckled, although with no humor. A swarm of fat mosquitoes encircled his face, yet he didn't wave them away. Unlike the elves, the insects freely flitted in and out of the orb.

"But still, this is insolent," said Ackley. He took his hand from the haze and stabbed it towards Coach, thrusting his index finger at her as if it were a dagger. It was easy to imagine that bold digit poking through human skin, hooking around innards, and pulling them out into the light of day. "Mark my words, blood will be spilled."

"Oh, yes, it will be. And after it is spilled, it will be slurped." Yoric's lips drew back in a sneer. His attention scoured the three humans, eventually settling on Jeff. The elf's expression was ominous, and his face an evil scowl. It was the darkest, most malevolent, look that Jeff had ever received. You have not received a truly wicked scowl until you've received one from a regal, ageless, inhuman murderer. It sent chills along his spine.

"No blood will be spilled, not with you in there," said Owen. He'd already circled the hazy orb holding the elves, inspecting it from all angles.

"It will happen, especially with us in here," countered Ackley. It was unclear what that meant, but Jeff didn't much care. Ominous threatening lies were still just lies, despite their menace.

The initial squirt of adrenaline that had kept her aloft expended itself, and Coach slumped down, hands on her knees like she'd just finished a race. "Channeling the sorts of forces needed to trigger that trap really takes it out of you."

Owen nodded. "Great job though. Problem solved now, right? The good guys win. They're stuck in there?" The disappointment coursing through his veins spilled out into his words, expression, and tone. He had wanted a confrontation, a chance to make these elves pay for their transgressions. Despite his attractive blond athletic exterior and generous, friendly demeanor, something lurked within Owen. Something that sought to lash out, funneling his carefully cultivated secret aggressions towards those he considered wrongdoers. Those aggressions sought release. His large hands flexed, fingers curling, in and out.

"They're stuck for now," Coach said, confirming their victory. "Of course, the trap will wither away over the next several days, and they'll escape."

"Wither?" asked Jeff. His hopes, which had started to rise, came crashing down. This victory might be short lived.

With a melodramatic grunt, Coach sat, propping her elbows onto her bent knees and leaning back against a tree trunk. Jeff thought it might be a maple. Or maybe a sycamore. Or something else. In its crooked branches, several black birds sat in silence, warily watching the humans.

Taking a sip from her canteen, Coach looked pensive. Finally, she said, "Wither, crumble, break apart, just generally fall to bits, starting soon and continuing for several days, until it fails. And then, no more trap." She fluttered her fingers like an escaping butterfly.

Jeff felt resurgent panic nibbling at his stomach lining. He was spending entirely too much time panicking these days.

"What then?" he asked, applying every scrap of serenity at his disposal to make those two words not sound whiny.

He pictured the trap falling to pieces over the course of days, during which time the elves would be pacing and becoming gradually more infuriated, like a savage pair of wolverines slowly working themselves into a frenzy. Eventually it would fail and they would escape, taking out their frustrations on some helpless prey animal. And he might just be that prey animal.

"Of course, I can keep the trap going, but I'll have to renew the mojo regularly. That won't come cheap," Coach said. Her eyes twinkled with delight, although whether at her success in trapping the elves or in consideration of future wages, who could say. She'd fully shifted into business mode, catching her companions by surprise.

"Won't come cheap? You gotta be kidding me," said Owen. He cracked his knuckles, infuriated that someone would charge money for doing the right thing. Heroic deeds were for the public good and therefore should be performed free of charge. That was his worldview.

"Here we go with the damn add-ons," grumbled Jeff. Classic bait-and-switch, provide something they need and then jack up the price. She had them over a barrel, as his dad would say. It wasn't exactly blackmail, since she was providing an agreed-upon service as per her deal with Ivy. However, they had little choice but to pay her what she wanted, if they could.

Shock and surprise washed across Coach's visage. "No, no, no, not like that. No payment required, not from any of you. My pay will come from their fairy hidey-hole. It'll have oodles of treasure. We'll collect some gold and jewels and whatnot, easy enough. Should be plenty there for all of us to retire, I'd imagine."

Treasure sounded good, but robbing from evil fairies

sounded ill-fated. And stupid. And like begging for trouble. Jeff was just beginning to protest when Yoric did it for him.

The brunette elf said, "You will, I suspect, be sorry if you try that." His pale skin stood in stark contrast to the curtain of pines on the far side of the hazy orb.

"I know what to do to safely enter a fairy house. I've read about this kinda stuff," Coach said, as if chiding a nephew over a rules infraction while playing Chutes and Ladders. Her drooping, tired eyes remained fixed to the elves while she held a straightened hand to the side of her mouth and spoke to Jeff and Owen as if in an aside, although a very loud one. "The main trick is to leave the door open. It's like a little pocket universe inside, and if you close the door anything could happen." She held her other hand away from her body and opened it theatrically, leaving her palm facing down, performing a mic drop. "Door stays open," she reiterated victoriously.

"Like what sorts of stuff could happen if the door closes with us inside?" asked Jeff. His emotional roller coaster continued, from the dizzying high of ensnaring the elves to the baffling lows of needing to poke around in their magical pocket-universe home. Perhaps Coach was wrong and it was just a happy little hobbit hole full of comfy cushions and copious snacks. But if there was some treasure, that would be nice too.

"What could happen?" Coach asked incredulously. She threw her hands up helplessly. Coach talked with her hands a lot. "Trapped forever, maybe. Or our skin turns inside out, or a sea of infernal cockroaches carries us away. If we're lucky, it'll be a flock of sexy sprites to play checkers with. Beats me."

Owen nodded. "Leave door open. Got it."

"The door is one consideration, it's true. But there are others," said Ackley in a voice that practically begged for questions.

"Yes, other concerns," said Yoric. He was glumly examining the haze orb they were trapped in.

"Yeah, yeah, lots of problems, sure. That's enough out of you two," Coach said. She gestured lazily towards the pair of ancient killers, waving their warnings away. "Traps and stuff, got it. Don't eat the food, I know. Not too worried about it, I've got rune magic ready to go that should keep us safe. I've been waiting quite a while for a sweet payoff like this." She hesitated, a guilty look inhabiting her face as she ran a hand through her sweaty lank hair. "By which I mean waiting for a heroic opportunity such as this."

Coach slowly sat forward from the tree trunk. Setting her hands on her knees, she planted her feet and levered herself up. A grunt of maximum effort sprang from her chapped lips.

"But no fairy tree houses right now," she said. "We'll have to find it first, and that'll require some magic. I'm a bit tapped out for the day, so tomorrow is soon enough."

"So, we're just going to leave them here, like this?" asked Owen.

"Yup, just right here," she replied exuberantly and with great gusto, as if she were revealing the existence and location of Atlantis.

Owen regarded the elves skeptically. "Two guys sitting around a bear trap like it's a campfire. Someone will see them."

Coach did another of her patented waves, dispersing perceived problems like smoke from a barbecue. "They'll hide themselves. It's their nature."

"So, to recap, your plan is to keep them trapped here forever?" Owen asked. Second thoughts had taken up obvious residence on his handsome face. He was enthusiastic to best the elves in some gentlemanly fashion, but eternal imprisonment was not a punishment he was willing to be a part of.

Coach frowned, as though the question had never occurred to her. "Well, not forever. A few weeks maybe? Or until Jeff's company moves on to fresh territory? We'll have to consult Ivy on that. She's the boss."

Ackley perked up, transitioning from grim, yet bemused, agitation to focused interest. "Ivy, you say? The pixie?"

"I work for her," Coach said, grinning triumphantly, as if she'd just scratched a winning lottery ticket.

"Aha," mused Ackley. He and Yoric exchanged meaningful looks, with rage, curiosity, and resentment fighting for supremacy.

"They shouldn't heed her words, should they, Ackley?" Yoric said through a smile that displayed his pointy, razor-sharp teeth, like ivory arrowheads.

"She is … not to be trusted," Ackley agreed. It seemed he would say more, but he did not. The dark elf looked vexed.

Owen huffed a huff of deepest indignation. His mild countenance dropped away, replaced by red-faced fury. "Of course, you'd say that. Trying to cover your asses. She told us all about the meth cooking and how you two were stalking her and trying to kidnap her for whatever perverted sex games you want to play." He shook his fist. It didn't impress the elves.

The mention of meth cooking visibly confused Ackley but he quickly recovered, dismissing it from consideration. "That is not why we want her," he said in a clipped tone.

"Well," Yoric said with a casual shrug. "Perhaps the perverted sex games part. We all have needs, some more … dramatic than others." He grinned lasciviously, running his tongue along his upper lip as he swiped a long tumble of deep brown hair out of his face and hooked it behind a pointed ear.

With a soft rustle of pine needles, Jellybiscuits slouched into the clearing. Its presence immediately stifled any conversation.

It awkwardly meandered past Jeff, who cringed at its passage, shrinking away from the stench of death that clung to the rabbit's matted spiky fur.

The bunny stepped into the hazy orb. Whatever magic the seashell and bear trap evoked, the macabre animal was immune to it.

Ackley spoke to the rabbit, unleashing a string of chattering grunts and grumbling snarls. It was an ugly dialect, making Jeff's ears sore just to hear it. Whatever it was, he knew it couldn't be the elves' native language. Elven, presumably, was mellifluous, regal, and lovely.

Yet, whatever Ackley was saying, Jellybiscuits listened intently. When the dark elf finished, the horrid rabbit turned and crept away.

Looking up from the departing black bunny, Ackley spoke with urgency. "Whatever you do, don't lead her to our home. It would be …"

He was cut off by Coach blowing a thunderous raspberry, launching the rude noise out into the world like a rocket.

She drew in a deep breath, then repeated the noise, a long and hard wet blatting sound, accompanied by a spray of spit. Afterwards, she said, "She could be there right now for all I know, so give it a rest." Coach's excitement at her unexpected victory was making her cocky. Jeff wasn't a fan of cocky. It never ended well.

Ackley sighed. "Impossible. She can't find it without a human to show her the way."

"Why's that?" asked Owen.

"Fairy magic," said Yoric. He shrugged, although it was more of a luxurious stirring of shoulders than a simple raising and lowering.

"Don't lead her there," said Ackley, "and don't disassemble

the protective ward at the entryway. The consequences to you would be …"

"Blah, blah, blah," roared Coach, interrupting the dark elf mid-warning. "I've heard enough out of you two." She turned and strode from the clearing, with no looking back, no second thoughts, no apparent interest in what she was leaving behind.

Jeff and Owen exchanged a questioning look as the trees swallowed her up.

"I'm tired, let's go," she shouted. They followed her, unsure what else they could do.

"You'll be sorry," called Yoric. "Certain death waits within those doors, and Ivy will lead you straight to it."

That sounded ominous. Jeff, as a rule, was inclined to heed ominous warnings. Or at the very least to hear them out, so as to weigh their benefits and give them the sniff test for truth.

"Shouldn't we listen to whatever they have to say?" he asked, while rushing to catch up with Coach.

"Nah, they're a couple of liars. It's in their blood, lying and tricking humans. Anyways, they're trapped, harmless. There'll be no trouble tonight."

On the walk back to the Subaru, Jeff wanted to believe Coach. He really did. Yet, the trees pressing in on them felt no less menacing than they had on the way in. Perhaps G12 was a safer place than it had been an hour ago, but it didn't feel that way.

21 AN OAK TREE

Sector G12 was home to many forest giants. The large trees huddled together, resisting intrusions from the outside world while seeking to secure their treasures and conceal the travesties occurring within their confines.

Yet within G12, there stood a towering presence out of scale with its surrounds. Among giants, it was a true titan.

It was an oak tree, but it was a most unusual oak tree.

The tree hunkered, a hulking presence, dark and foreboding, not far from where the two elves were spending the night confined within the mystical clutches of a bear trap.

The oak was of colossal proportions, with limbs far thicker than telephone poles and a trunk whose cross section would easily span a cabin.

Many of its thick dark branches reached for the sky, even as others intertwined with the thinner arms of its lesser neighbors or groped downward towards the soil. The oak produced a twisted canopy of leaves, each appearing light gray under the moon's limpid light.

It was the sort of tree that belonged either alongside a haunted mansion or guarding an ancient graveyard.

The oak was positioned atop a hill, within which its root base stretched far and wide, as well as deep. But the roots weren't content to simply grow into the ground. Many burst forth around the tree's base before delving into the soil, reaching far down into the earth below.

Between the size of the tree and the hill it sat upon, the oak should have been visible for miles. Yet it wasn't. Curiously, from some angles it appeared as a normal oak, lacking gargantuan scale.

Under the moon's curious gaze, a door embedded in the oak's hill slowly yawned open. It was a strange door. Circular like a great porthole, it was set into the soil with no hinges to be seen. Overgrown with lichen and shrubs, it was near invisible to the naked eye, until one saw it, then it became blatantly apparent.

Through the opened portal, a stir of shadows moved. Dark matted hair and sharp edges aligned along a giant humanoid frame that emerged from the hill, stepping into the night. It should never have fit through the door, yet it did.

After snuffling about a berry bush, it pulled its head back and bellowed, shaking the forest with its inhuman screech.

With no one or nothing there to hinder it, the thing set off, blundering through the trees, jagged antlers scraping branches.

Through the forest it stomped, glorying in its freedom.

Finding its companion amongst the pines, the monster's heart swelled.

They adventured through the woods that night, leaving a pair of bloody deaths in their wake. One was a camper, communing with nature. The other was walking their dog on the outskirts of the town of Cayuga. Despite brutally killing the person, the monster and its soulmate let the dog run free, for they had boundaries. More importantly, they were getting tired and the dog, a greyhound mix, was very fast.

At daybreak the creature returned to the oak tree. It had no choice. Its hunger sated, it slept.

22 WIDDERSHINS

In blissful ignorance of the murders, Jeff and company set out the next morning in search of fairy gold. Or silver, or jewels, or whatever treasure the elves were stocked up on.

The night before, Coach had crafted a new divining rod, specially designed for locating the elves' home. The process had required the careful perusal of several exotic tomes she'd swiped from a library years ago that she kept hidden in the spare tire compartment of her Subara. Also, a painstaking search for the perfect stick, y-shaped and sturdy. Then lots of practice doodling. And finally, she'd meticulously transcribed the appropriate runes into the perfect stick, carving them with a silver blade she kept for just that purpose, and no other.

Bumping along in Coach's Subaru, listening to Jimmy Buffett sing of a man who went to Paris, Jeff felt less trepidation than his standard recent levels and more of a sense of adventure. It was a pleasant change.

But when he, Coach, Owen, and Ivy stepped into G12, all lighthearted happy feelings ended, swept away by the area's pervasive gloom.

Immediately, the trees pressed in. Their presence was stifling; their weight felt with every step. They loomed over the party, as if trying to listen in on their discussions.

Ivy, however, was untroubled by the imposing woods.

She looked as though she hadn't slept. That wasn't unusual—she was a night owl and day sleeper. Despite that, she was overjoyed, dancing in place, walking on air, literally. Several times Jeff saw her actually in the air, her toes inches off the ground.

But underneath her excited outward demeanor, it was plain to see Ivy was anxious. No level of joy could mask the nerves she was feeling. As they moved through G12, her manic attention roamed the environs, darting from one tree to the next as if danger lurked around every corner. Even with the elves confined, these woods held dangers. If nothing else, the ghastly bunny Jellybiscuits lurked somewhere.

"Let's see how well this bad boy works," said Coach. She pulled the new divining rod from her backpack, handling it with love. "It oughta find this fairy house just fine."

"What a wonderful device," Ivy crooned, admiring the y-shaped stick while gushing levels of enthusiasm commensurate with a kid on Christmas morning.

Coach matched the pixie's enthusiasm, then amplified it. "Isn't it?" she effused, hefting the divining rod into the crisp forest air as though it were a sword she'd just triumphantly pulled from a stone.

Studying the focus of their admiration, Jeff saw nothing but a forked stick with symbols cut through the thin bark and into the soft wood beneath. By the standards of a stick, it was perfectly fine, and might have made fine kindling, or perhaps a weak slingshot.

"And we need it, since this place is hidden by fairy magic?" asked Owen. He was also admiring the stick, although with less fervor and awe than Coach or Ivy exhibited.

"Yup."

"Why can't you find it?" Owen asked, gesturing to Ivy. "You have fairy magic."

Ivy lowered her voice and spoke with great gravitas. "It is cursed with unfindable-ness, a sort of undiscoverable-osity. Only a human can locate it, and then only with the help of great magic."

Owen shrugged, satisfied with the vague answer. He thrust his hands into the pockets of his ratty cardigan sweater, its color somewhere in that listless region spanning gray, brown, and tan. Wearing it, he appeared as a male model who sidelined as an eccentric artist, or vice versa. Jeff had borrowed it once, hoping for the same effect, but had looked like nothing more than a dowdy librarian, aged far past his actual years, beaten down by the grind of reshelving steamy romances and hefty reference volumes.

"Those aren't real words," Jeff said accusingly. Stress and panic deadened his sense of humor in situations such as this.

Ivy sprang at Jeff and kissed his cheek in a flutter of crimson hair and wildflower scents, wiping his mind clear of anything but her soft lips and the smell of honeysuckle. "Do you have a better name for it?" she asked.

As Jeff blushed and stammered, Ivy continued, "They were hiding it from pixie folk like me." She bathed him in a mischievous smile, focusing her lovely kaleidoscope eyes on his dull brown ones. It was incredibly distracting. "They think we're pesky. So, I need a human to show me the way."

As Jeff failed to formulate a sensible response, Coach said, "And we humans need magic." She shook her new divining rod, a forked stick with wee symbols whittled into the shaft. "Otherwise only the elves can find it, most likely. I've included our names in the rune magic, so Jeff, Owen, and I should be able to find it again after the first time. Without the further assistance of magic devices, that is." She paused, looking uncertain. "You know, in theory, anyway."

Ivy nodded in delight. She softly clapped the palms of her hands together in silent encouragement.

Emboldened by the pixie's support, Coach wrapped her hands about the two shorter arms of the divining rod, held it up, and set off into the dense trees.

Shuffling through a carpet of fallen pine needles, they followed its unspoken directions, leading them deeper into G12.

It led them on a direct route, lacking the twists and turns that had marked their earlier quest. No, this rune-fueled stick was a true magical compass, leading them unerringly towards their goal.

Before long, the rod had led them to within shouting distance of the elves. When Jeff hiked himself up onto a branch and looked between a pair of pines at just the right angle he could see them.

Yoric was sitting upon an oak stump crafted into a throne. The throne, obviously, had not been there the previous day. Jeff wondered if it was truly there now. Unsettlingly, the light-skinned elf was staring back at him balefully, as if he'd known where and when Jeff would look into the clearing.

On the other side of the snug clearing, just across the bear trap from the throne, Ackley was swinging his obsidian blade back and forth, the jagged edge slicing a double loop through the air, like an infinity symbol.

Hopping down from the branch, Jeff backed away, feeling guilty that he'd been caught peeking. Even through the dozens of trees between them, he could feel Yoric's eyes tracking him.

They continued on.

The rod led them to a tree. It wasn't far away from the elves, although it was hard to judge with the tangled trees and dense undergrowth snarling them up, making them take a circuitous route that was far longer than the route as a crow flies.

Coach insisted the tree was a black cherry. Jeff could imagine eating burnt potato chips while looking at the bark, so he supposed she was correct.

The divining rod pulled them around the tree once in a counterclockwise direction, which Jeff now knew to call widdershins.

It then dragged them around the black cherry a second time, also counterclockwise.

And then, again, a third time, also widdershins.

Frowning at the rod as though it were being willfully disagreeable, Coach followed it a fourth time counterclockwise around the black cherry. Ivy, Jeff, and Owen followed, like little ducklings.

On that fourth time around the view changed, revealing a monstrous tree of epic proportions looming before them. Beyond contestation, it was an oak. Even Jeff could see that. It was nestled atop a hill. More of a massive mound, really, its soil dark brown and deep red. The sight stopped them in their tracks, for none of it had been there a moment ago. And, of course, the hidden existence of such a titanic tree was completely impossible.

Jellybiscuits was there, squatting on one of the enormous tree limbs like a gargoyle atop a cathedral. It was faced away from them, staring at the hill beneath the mighty oak. Seemingly lost in its own thoughts, if it had any, the ragged bunny did not move. It might have been a poorly made puppet propped up in a crook in the branch.

"Abra-freakin-cadabra," Coach mumbled, her wide eyes drinking in the wonder before them.

23 A DISCONCERTING INKY BUZZKILL

The scope of the tree was beyond the conceivable. None of them had ever witnessed the fabled giant sequoias of California firsthand, but this oak had to be their match, if not their older, burlier cousin.

Craning his head back, Jeff looked up and up and up, his awestruck gaze scaling the tree from one fat limb to the next. His visual ascent was eventually blocked, as the tree's crown was out of sight, its unlikely heights shrouded in low-level clouds, so far overhead as to make him dizzy. The individual leaves far above were indistinguishable, appearing tiny and insignificant, swaying in a breeze that didn't exist at ground level.

While his gaze was a helium balloon set adrift, floating upwards, Ivy's was a boulder, unable to rise above the lowest tier of branches. Her attention was firmly anchored to Jellybiscuits.

"Oh," she whispered, with an anxious awe permeating her voice. "That's the bunny you were talking about."

"Yup," said Owen as he started forward, his brow set in heroic resolve, as if he meant to scale the giant before them.

But before he could take a second step, Ivy threw her arms up, barricading the approach to the titanic oak.

Her jolly mood was gone, scoured away by the sight of Jellybiscuits. Although the horrid bunny was oblivious to their presence, studiously minding its own business, it had deflated her high spirits. It was a prominent spot of misery in her joy, a disconcerting inky buzzkill of mighty proportions.

"Problem?" Coach asked. She'd attempted a whisper, but her enthusiasm amplified her hushed voice, causing it to carry. The dark bunny's bony shoulders stirred, but the peculiar beast didn't turn. Rather, its gaze remained steadfast, affixed to a round portal in the earthen mound. It was an apparent entryway, fashioned from crude, weatherworn boards and set between two mighty roots. The portal looked shoddy, and its location set into the mound was not encouraging. Nothing could be on its far side but a cramped underground bunker, full of shadows, spiders, and filth.

"That thing freaks me out," Ivy said. She leaned forward and delicately sniffed the air. Intrigued by what she smelled, the sniffing quickly amplified into an intense snuffling.

"It's like a meat puppet," offered Owen, speaking up to be heard over Ivy's intense inhalations. He shrugged. "Or something."

Ivy stopped her impassioned assessment of the scent landscape and backed into the woods. She was practically slinking, like an animal with its tail between its legs. Jeff took a few whiffs, but he didn't detect anything out of the ordinary. Mostly just pine sap.

"I can't get near that thing," Ivy said. "Why don't you all go ahead? I'll kill time out here for a bit." She stretched and yawned, although it was completely forced, an act for their benefit. "Maybe I'll take a nap in a tree. Just scream if you find anything interesting." Manic glee in her eyes, she chuckled. Ivy was always easy with a laugh.

"You don't mind missing what's inside?" Coach asked. She lovingly placed the divining rod, its job complete, into her backpack.

"Oh, if you find anything interesting, I'm sure I'll hear about it," Ivy replied, followed by a giggle. "Besides, I imagine there's curses and incantations and enchantments and such to keep pixie folk out. But that's fine, you go in and look for treasures."

Her every sense attuned to Jellybiscuits, Ivy backed farther away, merging into a scattered sea of pines and lindens. Within seconds, she'd disappeared, which might have been pixie magic or simple camouflage.

"Whatever you say," Coach replied enthusiastically, with all the boundless joy of a soldier's long-awaited homecoming. "Jumpy pixies," she added vaguely under her breath, as she inspected the oak tree, ruminating on its architecture, stature, and very existence.

Owen did a quick circuit of the elves' home, discerning that the only apparent entrance was the round portal that Jellybiscuits was sitting above. Beyond a flick of one scroungy ear, the bunny didn't move. It simply stared at the door.

"Should we look for another way in?" asked Jeff warily. It felt silly to ask, since the only shortcoming with the door before them was that Jellybiscuits was there. They'd have to pass just under the bunny to enter. He didn't want to do that. Although unable to articulate why, entering its immediate vicinity filled him with a visceral dread. Hopefully the others felt the same way.

They did not.

"Nah," snorted Coach. "It's just a bunny, even if it is an ugly one. What's it going to do?"

Several steps away, the ebony bunny fidgeted, its stringy muscles rippling beneath its ratty fur. The smell of rot emanated from it.

"It's an elf bunny, so who knows?" replied Jeff. It could be that the grim little beast was a trained watch-rabbit and would spring down and chew their fingers like carrots if they attempted entry. He preferred his fingers to remain unchewed.

"Horsefeathers," crowed Coach. She shot them a look of supreme confidence, accentuated by a frantic fervor dancing across her eyes and mouth. "It's a spy for the elves, and they already know we're here. Plus, they're trapped and can't do diddly. Let's go."

With Owen at her side, Coach strode confidently towards the behemoth tree and its guardian bunny. Less confidently, Jeff followed, feet dragging through the pine needles.

24 AN UNSETTLING FEELING

As the trio approached the mighty oak, the ratty black bunny's head slowly swiveled, bringing its dead green eyes to bear on them.

Jellybiscuits watched them, not judging, not acting, just observing. The wind gusted, stirring its matted fur, making the quill-like protrusions dance.

Now that Jeff's mind was open to the possibility of fairies and magical doings, he felt differently about Jellybiscuits. Before, he'd assumed it to be a mange-ridden, rabid, inbred, freaky rabbit. Seeing the creature up close, he pitied it. The poor thing was probably enslaved by the evil elves, torn away from its expansive bunny family and career in carrot picking, and subsequently forced into service as a spy. It deserved better.

Although he pitied it, he was also completely unsettled by it. The bunny moved oddly, in a disjointed manner, as if it were sleepwalking, or not in full control of its faculties. Or even as if it were unaccustomed to the movements its body made. That, he supposed, could be a consequence of being hypnotized into service to the elves.

On the other hand, Jellybiscuits radiated bad vibes, plain and simple, so it might not be so innocent. It could perhaps be a zombie bunny. A simulacrum of life, innervated by fairy magic into movement, if not full sentience. In that case, he'd want to end its misery. Better yet, to have someone else put an end to its misery. He didn't have the heart for it.

Just below the bunny, the wooden portal set into the mound had a metal ring dangling from it. The metal looked to be bronze, or perhaps copper. Jeff's online searches had educated him enough on fairies to tell him they didn't like iron.

Passing beneath Jellybiscuits, who might be a helpless

victim or perhaps an undead monstrosity, Owen barely spared it a glance. He jiggled the bronze, or copper, ring, which was clearly meant to serve as a handle.

When Owen gave it a tug, the door sprang open. "Not locked," he observed.

Owen and Coach seemed pleased by the lack of a lock. Jeff took it as an ominous sign. His wary paranoia whispered that someone only leaves a door unlocked if there are significant security measures, like a hulking maniacal rottweiler thirsty for blood. Or, more optimistically, it might be unprotected by a lock since magic was required to find the door in the first place, so it didn't require the safeguard of a lock.

Before Jeff could voice his reservations, which would have gone unheeded, Owen pulled the door wide open and stepped into the darkness. Coach followed. Reluctantly, Jeff did as well.

The inside was utter darkness, the sort of complete absence of light that is disorienting, since there isn't so much as a spare photon available to reveal your surroundings or orient yourself.

A lurch shook them, much like the beginning of a hastily assembled carnival ride.

Despite his disorientation, Jeff kept one hand behind him, preventing the door from shutting. Leaving the door open was critical, that much he knew. Anyway, the feel of the door kept him grounded, otherwise he might have lost his footing and tumbled into whatever dark oblivion they'd stumbled into.

They felt a squishing, akin to a pressure crushing them from all sides at once. Then a feeling of floating that lasted an eternal second. The air was densely liquid, like a gel, somewhat like the thick fluid in a sensory deprivation tank.

When the feeling of being encased in dense gel dissipated, Jeff's eyes opened upon a snug room. It had a bench on each side, as well as lockers to hang up coats, and cubbyholes to put boots into. Indeed, there were cloaks, jackets, and boots occupying many of the spaces. It was a room designed to allow entry into a home without tracking mud and water inside, which he immediately labelled as the mudroom. That was what his late mother had called them anyway. She'd always wanted one, but they'd never had a house big enough. The passing thought of his dead mother tugged at his heartstrings, but he shoved it aside.

He was holding open the entrance behind them, which now appeared to be a tall double door. Yet it also looked like the simple round portal they'd walked through. Looking at the conflicting visions hurt Jeff's head, the consideration of the superimposed doors pinching his cranial capillaries, summoning the beginnings of a migraine.

With his inherent sense of always knowing the exact right thing to do, or at least perceiving that he always knew the exact right thing to do, Owen dragged a bench over to prop the door open. It was heavy and squealed across the wooden floor, protesting every inch. Yet, once the bench was in place and Jeff removed his hand, the door settled, becoming only the double door, shedding its appearance of also being the round portal.

Coach nodded. "Step one, the outer door stays open. Very important."

Producing a notepad from her backpack, she said, "Step two is to draw maps. Don't wanna get lost in here." Patting at her pockets, she located a stubby pencil, its eraser worn away from hiding her paperbound mistakes.

"It's a tree house. How are we gonna get lost?" Owen's tone was dismissive. Amongst his few faults was overconfidence, which had often led him into trouble, whensoever Jeff's more cautious nature had not been sufficient to rein him in. Today was a prime example. Owen perceived their current activity as full of wonder and excitement, partaking in an experience completely new to them. Jeff, however, saw it as attempting to loot a house inhabited by lunatic magical dirtbags.

"Trust me," said Coach. She stepped forward and opened the door opposite the entrance, revealing the utterly impossible. "Step three."

Beyond the door was a truly grand foyer. Ridiculously expansive, it stretched before them with a dozen doors along each side. At the far end, a pair of sweeping staircases rose up to a landing holding an entry to a dimly lit corridor. Below the staircases, a hallway marched into infinity.

Everything was constructed of dark wood, intricately carved, crafted by a true master. Upon inspection, the structure's components appeared to be sculpted from a single piece of wood. All of them, the floors, door frames, walls, bannisters, each of them part of a contiguous whole.

Along the walls were tapestries of fierce huntsmen, bright flower gardens, thundering horsemen, inviting meadows, looming giants stomping medieval towns, a basket of leering kittens, and armored soldiers fighting a dragon.

Chandeliers dangled from the high cathedral ceiling, each holding dozens of candles, all of them lit. Yet, the candlelight was superfluous, for sunlight poured in through windows set high in the walls. The windows should have faced out into tree innards, but it was better not to think of that.

In spite of being under a tree, or certainly now within that tree, the air was fresh and crisp.

Jeff teetered on the brink of disbelief but then tipped over into the side of acceptance. Where they were was impossible, but they were there, nonetheless.

The atmosphere was bright, clean, and perfectly pleasant, yet also completely alien. Something felt wrong. Rather, everything felt wrong.

An unsettling feeling had taken residence in Jeff's gut,

quickly spreading to his spine, heart, and brain before gradually radiating out to his extremities. Part of it was associated with entering someone else's home without their consent. Intruding upon another's space and seeing how they lived without an invitation was completely against his nature. It was only fair to give warning before you visited, so your host could hide their dirty underwear, stow their trash, and cover up anything embarrassing. That was how society worked.

But it wasn't just going into someone's home unannounced that was upsetting him. That sour feeling was amplified by the inherent danger present in being in the home of monsters. Such a place could have traps anywhere. Poisons, spikes, razor wire nets dropping from the ceiling. Yet, it was also the nagging certainty that they didn't belong here. And the obvious ridiculous impossibility of the dimensions of the home within the tree, couldn't forget that.

Coach paused to feverishly sketch in her notepad, the same one she used to practice drawing runes. She was deep in concentration, the tip of her tongue thrust out and clamped between her teeth.

There was utter silence, broken occasionally by the scraping of leaves, as if they were in a house and the wind was bashing branches against the aluminum siding.

They went straight through the foyer and into the corridor under the far stairs. Each footstep was muted by the lavish carpet, every utterance a yell against the silent backdrop.

The hallway they entered was unbearably long, each side having door after door after door, although no two doors matched. Between the doors were portraits, potted plants, busts carved from marble, and the occasional piece of taxidermy. The taxidermy was of high quality, each animal looking more alive than Jellybiscuits. There were, however, many animals they didn't recognize, which made Coach speculate they were perhaps from Australia.

Through the first door on the left was a ballroom, painted a deep maroon, with golden chandeliers, a highly polished parquet floor, and vast windows partially covered by somber yellow curtains. The windows looked out upon a grass field, extending out to the far horizon, dappled with stands of wildflowers. The grand ballroom felt like the sort of place where a powdered wig might be required and a butler would loudly announce your arrival.

A peek into the first door on the right revealed a massive library, with shelf after shelf of ancient tomes alongside modern-day thrillers, romances, and horror. There were several tables at which to read and a lit fireplace, its flames crackling happily. The windows looked out upon a tundra, a full moon just rising in the night. There was an elevated walkway to reach a second tier of bookshelves stretching to the ceiling.

As with the corridors and ballroom, the physical space of the library was entirely inconceivable. Even beyond the impossibility of it being set in a tree and the windows looking out on a different landscape, there was the impossibility of the inner dimensions. The next door along the hallway was less than twenty feet away, but both the ballroom and library spanned three times that distance, at least.

The incomprehensible spacing intensified Jeff's unease. Danger prickled his ears and phantom spiders danced along his spine.

They continued on, peeking into rooms as they went, hoping to find a pile of treasure. Gold, diamonds, a magic sword, jewel-encrusted doodads, anything.

When hallways intersected, sometimes the trio turned and other times they went straight. Each new corridor stretched as far as they could see. At every room and every turn, Coach added to her map.

There were countless bedrooms, each very different than its neighbors. Some were small and others large. Some bright and some bleak. Their environments varied, most of them warm, but a few icy cold, like a meat locker.

One dark room held a pair of worn leather recliners, their fabric fraying at the edges, springs sagging, cushions grooved with the pronounced indentations of relaxing elf rumps. They were pointed towards a large television upon a stand fashioned from the same contiguous piece of wood as the wall it jutted out from. The stand's shelves were packed with disks. Based on a quick scan, it appeared that elves enjoyed a wide array of movies and shows, from action to romance to comedy to science fiction.

As they examined room after room, it became obvious the dwelling within the tree was far more than a home. It was an expansive mansion. No, it was a base, built for dozens, or hundreds even. Entire platoons of elves could have called it home, as well as dozens of sprites and gnomes, along with a surly minotaur and its manticore sidekick.

They saw many wonders and oddities amongst the rooms. But what they did not see was equipment or other paraphernalia for cooking meth. No scales, no beakers, no flasks, no hoses, and no baggies. No miniature magical men in yellow biohazard suits cooking chemicals. The possibility that Ivy was completely mistaken dropped a seed into the soil of Jeff's thoughts, even if it did not fully take root.

Dozens of rooms and a few corridors into their exploration, they came upon a hiccup in the well-appointed serenity that was the elves' home. It was a door. Yet, unlike many of its fellows, it was a simple wood door, unpainted, unadorned by any intricate carvings. Aesthetically, it was decidedly mundane.

An unusual feature of the door was that it had locks on the

outside. Fat metal bolts, thick as a thumb, meant to partner with solid steel housings set into the wall. Placed as they were, they were meant to hold something within, away from the hallway.

Another atypical aspect of this particular door was that it had been battered down, from the inside, and was in splintery tatters in the hallway. The burly metal hinges leaned crookedly out of the door frame. What remained of the door was thick, four inches of dense, hard wood.

Peeking in, they saw a staircase leading downward. Several steps in, darkness swallowed the treads. Jeff's unease amplified again, his heart rattling his ribcage.

Stepping away from the door, Coach said, "Seems like someone, or something, broke out of here." Knocking on a bent hinge with a knuckle, she added, "Something with some real oomph."

Drifting from the open doorway were the musky smells of a large animal. The sour emanations crawled into the back of their nostrils and clung there like a foul epoxy.

Waving a hand before his face, Owen shrugged. He had one reckless foot down the staircase and was leaning in, peering curiously. "It stinks down there. Maybe it's a moose or something. That could knock through this door. Might be a whole grassy field down there for all we know. Regular rules don't apply here."

An echo came from below. Something was stirring.

"Let's go," said Jeff. He grabbed Coach's elbow and gave it a tug, back towards the way they had come from.

"Let me think," mumbled Coach, yanking her elbow away. She consulted her hand-drawn maps as if they were a world-class atlas.

A long low scraping noise rose from the dark space below. It sounded like wood on wood and was moving slowly, but unmistakably, closer.

It was all Jeff could do to not turn tail and sprint. Even Owen found the noise ominous, as evidenced by his stepping carefully out of the staircase.

"What do we do?" asked Jeff. The scraping continued, low and slow. A heavy huffing filtered up from below, although whether real or imagined was not yet certain.

Coach didn't answer.

Owen paced restlessly, eager to do something. Jeff touched the pistol in his pocket, hoping to do nothing. If fate forced the gun into his hand, it would be a dark day.

Something crashed below them, within the dark abyss that was the lower portions of the stairs. And then it bellowed, much like a dozen grizzly bears screaming in unison. A spurt of urine escaped Jeff, soaking his zipper. He barely noticed.

Heavy footsteps escaped the darkness. The house shook, as if in warning.

The scraping sound intensified, like irate nails on a dusty chalkboard.

Coach held up her scribbled map. She turned it upside down, then frowned. She turned it sideways and winced.

"What's the matter?" asked Owen. He was less concerned than seemed reasonable, considering that Jeff was witnessing his life flashing before his eyes while lamenting the fact he would die a virgin.

"Oh, nothing," said Coach in a reassuring voice, of the sort a mom uses on her young kids when something's wrong but she doesn't want to admit it. She tilted the map to be parallel to the floor and rotated herself about, looking at the doorways. Finally, after turning it completely around again, she smiled. "Got it."

The scraping grew closer. The stairs were shaking, slowly and gradually, one by one, as if something large were climbing but had to wedge itself into the space.

Jeff squeaked.

As evidence he possessed at least some sense of self-preservation, Owen looked mildly concerned, if not actually nervous. His apprehension was akin to what Jeff might exhibit if he saw a wasp nearby.

"Okay, here's what I'm thinking," said Coach conversationally. "We should go now. Maybe the big thingy crawling up these stairs is guarding some awesome treasure down there. We could maybe check with the elves on that."

Already hurrying back along the way they'd come from, Jeff yelled, "Great idea!"

Owen and Coach followed him, but with less vigor, since terror and adrenaline weren't fueling them. She held the scrawled map before her as she walked, studying it constantly. It was the classic tourist gait, consulting the map every few steps, desperately afraid of missing anything interesting, like a t-shirt shop or ice cream parlor.

Owen said, "Ask the elves? But you said they lie."

Coach waved a dismissive hand. With the enthusiasm of a carnival barker, she said, "Yeah, but we can't stay here. That thing tore this door down, and it's coming our way. Can't hurt to at least ask those two pricks what sort of critters they keep in the basement."

25 CURSED

Standing in front of the elves once again, Jeff felt a chill. Its origins were partially in the weather, for it was approaching dusk and the temperature had dropped while they'd been inside the weird tree fort. The chill also had roots in the residual fear zigzagging through his central nervous system. The spiteful glares from the elves didn't help either. Also, Jellybiscuits was watching them from beneath a prickly bush, which amplified the chill.

"What the heck manner of beast is stomping around your house?" asked Coach. Her tone and expression were incredulous. She shrugged and threw her hands up helplessly, as if asking to be let in on an inside joke she didn't quite get.

"In the basement," Jeff clarified, through teeth chattering with fear and the chill. It was best to be clear, since who knew how many other beasties were wandering the vast expanses within the huge oak tree.

"Oh, did you meet the Spookum?" asked Yoric, his bright eyes dancing in mean-spirited delight. Despite the translucent magical cage separating them, his words were clear as a bell.

"He dwells in the basement, when he isn't outside," said Ackley.

Yoric squinted, a thoughtful expression knitting his brows. "But he should be locked in the basement, unable to access the rest of the house. I can't believe you went down there." He sounded impressed, which made Jeff wonder what horrors resided in that basement.

Owen's hands were in his pockets as he scuffled his feet through the fallen leaves and yellowing pine needles underfoot. "We didn't, but he's battered the basement door down. You know, the one with the big fat locks?"

Ackley grimaced. Yoric smirked. The pair exchanged a

look, unspoken messages zinging back and forth as a silent conversation played itself out.

"Tell us what you know," demanded Coach, waggling an accusatory finger at the imposing duo.

Their reply was several seconds of silence, until Yoric eventually said, "Figure it out for yourself."

"It probably can't hurt to share," Ackley said, his voice resigned. "Perhaps they can be useful."

"That would be a first," Yoric replied, countering his partner's resigned tone with a dismissive one.

Ackley turned to the humans. He visibly gathered his thoughts, assembling them into a cohesive whole. "Let me tell you a story."

"A sweet love story," interjected Yoric, a smug smile playing across his pink lips. His brown hair blew in the nonexistent breeze.

"Of sorts," Ackley allowed, crossing his indigo arms with their patchwork scars across his chest, with its own sea of scarred flesh.

Seemingly in no mood for a story, Jellybiscuits scurried awkwardly away, its gait containing all the fluid coordination of a rockslide.

The dark canopy of leafy branches and needle-laden limbs loomed close overhead, as if intending to eavesdrop.

"Centuries ago," said Ackley, while staring into the middle distance, his dark focus lost amongst the arboreal denizens surrounding them. "When these lands were still pure and not yet despoiled by your technologies, a native lad was just beginning to find his way in his tribe. Still learning the ways of the world, he'd recently come to manhood, and was to be a hunter. A comely fellow, he showed promise, as do so many of your kind at that age, before life batters them into mediocrity. Yet, one fateful day when he was hunting in this very area, a woman emerged from amongst the oaks. She was breathtakingly beautiful, with shimmering eyes and hair flashing red such as he'd never seen nor heard of. He was immediately taken with her, as she was with him. But she wasn't human. Rather, she was of the fair folk. A pixie."

"She lavished him with her attentions and he became entranced, bound by his carnal lust," muttered Yoric scornfully.

Ackley nodded. "Initially it was lust, no doubt, but he quickly grew to love her. He was young and innocent, so he was a fool. What the lad hadn't yet learned was that beauty is often only on the outside. A fair face and tempting veneer can conceal a rotten core. It is a matter of truth that not all pixies are sweet."

Determined to interrupt with whatever tidbits he deemed important, Yoric said, "And in truth, she wasn't simply a pixie. Her lineage was unclear but certainly more complex than that. There was probably an ogre or wood witch or changeling amongst her grandparents. It's difficult to say exactly, since not all monsters resulting from such couplings can be easily categorized."

Coach nodded. "Like if a bigfoot were to marry a selkie," she mused, as if she made a habit of considering such esoteric couplings in her spare time. The level of deep intellectual conjecture infused into her nonsensical statement again made both Owen and Jeff question her sanity.

"A majestic creature such as a selkie would never deign to couple with a grubby, hairy sasquatch," sneered Yoric incredulously, as if personally affronted.

Before Jeff could ask what a selkie was, Ackley resumed his story. "The lad and the pixie began a torrid love affair amongst the pines. But before long, she wanted more, the irksome creature that she was. She made him earn her lascivious attentions, setting him tasks that slowly but surely grew more adventuresome. During that time, she stoked his inner darkness."

"All humans have a spark of evil. She fanned his into a flame, fueled by his lust," said Yoric. The lighter-skinned elf visibly savored the words as they rolled from his tongue.

Ackley said, "At first, she wanted him to kill animals. Which, as a hunter, he'd already done many times throughout his short life. Yet this was different. For it wasn't for meat or hides, it was simply for the sake of killing, the sheer pleasure of watching organs and entrails spilling out into the light of day."

With great enthusiasm, Yoric said, "They quickly moved to people, focusing on neighboring tribes where the youth wasn't known. First there were beatings, brutal assaults that were sometimes pure violence, but other times sexual." He revealed the last few words with gleeful flair, his gaze roaming from Coach to Owen to Jeff, gauging the impact of the notion on each of them. Jeff was horrified and Owen deeply offended. Coach didn't react, maintaining her concentrated fascination.

"Naturally they progressed to murders," said Ackley, who was enjoying the storytelling far less than his partner. "When that quickly became too mundane for the pixie, they proceeded to the use of torture as an appetizer to the murders. Many, many murders. It seemed the pixie strove to test the extent she could push her mortal lover past the boundaries of his innate humanity."

With a grin that stretched his shark-toothed mouth from one pointed ear to the other, Yoric said, "Eventually they arrived at cannibalism, as the pixie led the native youth down all the sordid pathways humans aren't meant to tread." He frantically rubbed his hands together, spidery fingers rasping against one another. "Some of their escapades were especially lively.

Towards the end, some episodes began with carnality, rutting like animals, then progressing into murder and gobbling up fleshy bits, finally culminating in lusty exertions atop the torn bloody remains."

As their storytelling progressed, Ackley remained calm, delivering his parts much as an academic would, albeit one who had delivered this lesson many times before and had no passion for the subject. Yoric, however, grew increasingly more agitated. Fantasizing, perhaps, of the horrid, lurid details of the narrative.

Nervously, Jeff fidgeted, wilting under Yoric's occasional scornful glare. He wanted nothing more than to leave these woods and never return. His aspirations to become a medical doctor, or perhaps a veterinarian, now felt as if they were worth any amount of work. Certainly, neither of those professions brought one into the company of murderous fairies.

His attention lazily tracking a butterfly, Ackley continued in a bored tone. "The explicit details of their crimes are unimportant. Let us just say they went too far, and due to his egregious actions, the youth became cursed. It was all simply too much, and the fairy folk came to police the issue and mete out punishment, since unsupervised cursed creatures can upset the balance."

Yoric sneered. "And balance is important, a truism humans have never learned and never will."

Ackley said, "The duo were tracked and eventually found in the midst of a bloodbath. It was a small village, as many were back then. Men, women, children, the elderly, all of them brutalized and murdered. The area was painted red with gore, the two villains writhing in a pool of it, satisfying their beastly urges with one another."

Now pacing restlessly about within the confines of the translucent globe cast by the enchanted bear trap and seashell,

Yoric said, "Coming upon that scene, a sprite duke named Conall was horrified and cursed the boy in a most annoying way, the ridiculous fool. Even beyond his original curse, the blood-dappled lad was now further cursed to walk the earth for centuries as the monstrosity that he truly was, his body transformed to match his twisted soul."

"Which was rash and incredibly ill-conceived on Conall's part, since a hasty death was the appropriate solution," said Ackley in a conciliatory tone. The topic was one they had doubtless argued over many a time. "Conall was prone to be overly dramatic, while not considering the consequences of his actions."

Yoric halted his pacing. He said, "There was only punishment for the boy, though. No repercussions for his lady friend, who was the true villain. She was untouched, for her family had standing in the fairy court at the time, although they've since fallen from grace."

"Regardless," said Ackley slowly and deliberately, hitting each syllable with the resounding note of an iron bell, attempting to preempt any disagreement. "Mistakes were made but lingering on them is pointless. The cursed creature was imprisoned here, with martial supervision, while the pixie was sent away, enchanted to prevent her finding her way back to her accursed lover."

"That was the beginning of the fall of her family's standing in the court. Sad really," mused Yoric.

Itching at the sleeve of scars embedded in his arm, Ackley sighed. "Yes, but these fools don't care about fairy court intrigues." He swept his hand to include the trio of human listeners.

Their story told, the elves grew quiet. The lull in conversation grew, becoming prolonged as Jeff and company processed what they had heard.

It had grown darker, although not yet to the point where flashlights were required, even if the light would have been reassuring.

The wind had picked up, shaking loose noises from the rattling trees and stirring bushes. Each of those understated sounds whispered to Jeff of monsters creeping stealthily on tiptoed claws through the forest.

"So, this thing in your basement is a wendigo then, right?" asked Coach. She sounded perfectly content, perhaps even mildly exuberant, as she sought the point of clarification. "Human eats a human, gets cursed. That's a wendigo."

Ackley scrunched up his face, his pointed ears tipping back as his lips parted to reveal jagged pointed teeth. Although the elves' faces were decidedly inhuman, they displayed emotions exactly as humans do. His current expression bespoke irritation, but also resignation, as of a snobby tenured professor of string theory being forced to explain gravity to a high school physics class who hadn't done their homework.

After a pause, he said, "It's not so straightforward. It's a bit of skookum, a bit of a wendigo, a bit of cursed human, all combining into a twice-cursed, enchanted monster that can't die. So, it's hard to say exactly what it is. Much like the pixie temptress, monsters are not categorized so easily. We call it a Spookum."

Coach nodded, as if that were exactly what she had expected. "Um, so you two are actually like prison guards, keeping this Spookum confined and guarding these woods to keep humans safe?"

"We aren't guards," spat Yoric, affronted as only a noble being such as an elf can be. "We're simply here to keep the beast in check. Many of us rotate through this duty, taking a year or two at a time."

Ackley said, "Human safety is not our true concern, we

simply seek balance. Our orders are to contain the beast as well as we can, limiting its murderous urges."

"Yes, down to acceptable levels," offered Yoric cheerfully.

"What are acceptable levels?" asked Jeff, somewhat dreading the answer. He imagined catapulting the elves past the far horizon, forgetting they'd ever existed, walking out of G12, and moving back to the city, any city.

"Well, it gets out rather often. The basement isn't a true prison. And one doesn't limit such a creature to zero casualties. Some will inevitably occur, but one mustn't get all worked up over them," said Ackley. He pressed at the hazy orb imprisoning them, perhaps conjecturing on the irony of being so well confined, even though they themselves were meant to be the jailers.

Yoric had resumed pacing. Every few laps he kicked at the hazy orb imprisoning him. When he did so, it shimmered and flickered, the vibrations salvaging its scant visibility otherwise lost in the diminishing light. He said, "Well, we could fully contain the beast, but it would be a lot of work."

"Oh, certainly," agreed Ackley. "It would be tiresome. And they don't reward us sufficiently for that level of effort."

"But containing this Spookum better would save lives," protested Owen. He himself could not imagine a greater reward.

The elves shrugged, nearly in unison, each of them unimpressed, unable to convince themselves of any benefits to the preservation of human life.

A subtle notion had been nuzzling its way into the forefront of Jeff's mind, slowly but surely. When it finally revealed itself in its entirety, he was shocked by how much it surprised him. "Wait, wait, wait," he said. "Ivy isn't the other half of this story, is she? It's her grandmother or something, right? It isn't her."

Coach snorted, gave her head a quick shake, and mumbled, "Good grief."

Incredulous, Ackley said, "It should be blindingly obvious it was Ivy, even to a clod such as you."

"You are rather dull-witted," Yoric said, pointing at Jeff.

"Slow on the uptake," Ackley added, as an aside to his partner. "That is a thing they say nowadays. Or dumb as a rock. That would also work."

Rubbing her chin, thoughtfully probing the errant dark hairs found there, Coach said, "I see. Hadn't anticipated that." With a pointed look at Jeff, she added, "Although I got the gist of it right at the beginning of the story."

"Yeah dude," mumbled Owen, sounding embarrassed.

"She is a villain, a temptress, a monster swaddled in a charming guise," said Yoric.

Ackley replied, "She dearly loves the Spookum though, which is a redeeming quality. There's a certain nobility to be found in true love, even when it exists among the absolutely wretched."

Jeff let the revelation roll around in his head. The notion that Ivy was a monster had the ring of impossibility. They'd drunk together, laughed together, eaten cookies together, and watched TV together. And Jeff had lusted after her, urgently and often. His tall and hairy Uncle Bob, who he only ever saw at Thanksgiving, might as well have been a bigfoot and it would have made just as much sense. And yet, thinking back on the night when she'd danced with Snakebite and spun him into the emergency room, it was hard to deny the notion. Much like your own death, as farfetched and impossible as it might seem, its inevitability couldn't be ignored. Although he didn't like it, he believed the elves' story.

Initially, Yoric had made a sour face at the prospect of true love's nobility. A dire sadness swept the sourness away but was quickly replaced by his usual visage of subdued hostility, tinged with lunacy. He said, "She wasn't ever supposed to find her way back to this area. However, the magic constraining her has grown thin over the centuries, enabling her return."

"She seeks her lost love," said Ackley. His monstrous ebony blade had materialized in his hand, and he stared wistfully into its obsidian depths. "And for his part, although now a complete monster, the Spookum will do anything for her. Their love, it seems, endures."

"The Spookum escapes some nights and roams the woods. When that occurs, the lovers find one another and have a night together, but eventually the Spookum must return to our base, where she cannot follow," said Yoric. Somewhere above them, an owl hooted, as if in agreement.

"Our home is enchanted to keep Ivy away," muttered Ackley. "She can't find it without a human guide. Although that enchantment, as well as the one to force the Spookum's return, requires constant upkeep and reinforcement."

"By us," Yoric added pointedly. "Which we can't do from inside this ridiculous confinement. The protections keeping the lovers apart is fading rapidly even as we speak, deteriorating every second."

"Tick tock, tick tock," said Ackley, as Yoric hummed the theme to *Jeopardy*. Jeff pictured the two elves in their tattered armchairs watching the quiz show. It made them seem more human.

"But we already led her right to your place. Your home. Your base, whatever," said Coach. "Is that bad?"

"She needs a guide each time," said Ackley, with a dismissive wave of his scarred hand.

"But she didn't even want to go in," said Owen. "If she was looking for your place all this time and finally found it, she'd want to go in and find this Spookum thingy, right?"

"There are magical countermeasures against her entry. She would sense them. I'd imagine she thought you would lead the Spookum out," said Ackley.

"After it killed one or two of you," added Yoric merrily.

"Yes, certainly," agreed Ackley. "Then, with us trapped here and the magic weakened, they could doubtless get away. Elope, as it were, to murder and pillage as they wish."

"Oh my, yes," said Yoric, his delighted eyes twinkling in the gloom. "There'd be assaults, rapes, murders, regicides, enslavements." He smiled, shark teeth gleaming. "Various depravities of all types. Whatever their wickedness demands of them."

"Cannibalism, certainly," Ackley speculated. He then winced, and turned to Yoric, expecting an argument.

Yoric obliged him, responding in a combative tone. "We've discussed this. It would no longer be cannibalism, since he isn't human and she never was."

"Very well, the consumption of humans. Which in such a case, would not be cannibalism," conceded Ackley. He sounded tired, beaten down.

Supremely satisfied and triumphant, Yoric nodded. "Exactly."

The weight of the darkening forest was suddenly pressing on Jeff's back. The prospect of a thousand creatures staring at them from the darkness poked at him like tiny needles. One of those staring set of eyes could be Ivy's. "Ivy could be out there right now, listening to us."

Yoric's backhand wave dismissed Jeff's fears. "Jellybiscuits has an eye out for her at all times. It would alert us to her presence."

That didn't make Jeff feel any better, to know the horrid rabbit was on the case. It did raise the question of what Jellybiscuits was exactly.

Before Jeff could ask, Owen said, "And you can't just kill this Spookum?"

Visibly sagging under the weight of his responsibilities, Ackley sighed. He said, "Would that we could. But that dolt Conall's curse has rendered the Spookum unkillable. So, we simply monitor and contain the beast."

"Like a vacation from actual meaningful work," Yoric offered. "While we watch the Spookum, we also seek the pixie. But she eludes us. Pixies are hard to track, very difficult to find."

"Alrighty, now that we understand this whole mess, what can we do to fix it?" asked Coach. Her demeanor was that of a mother standing before a sobbing child who'd just broken their favorite toy, and she was trying to make it all better. Yet, at the same time, the mother was delighted by the broken toy clutched in the child's little hand and was intensely excited by the opportunity to fix it. In fact, the mother might even have broken it on purpose, crushing it under her heel when the child's attention was elsewhere.

"Setting us free seems the obvious course of action," replied Yoric. The words "you stupid idiots" were strongly implied at the end of the statement, even if not spoken.

Ackley gestured towards the rune-scribbled bear trap and seashell. "Yes, there is little we can do to contain the Spookum from within this ridiculous cage."

"Can't be too ridiculous if it's holding you two supposed bigshots," Coach replied. She infused those several words with voluminous amounts of a taunting, told-you-so attitude, savoring the power trip of having bested the elves. It was a moment of triumph for her, most certainly, but Jeff felt she had rubbed the elves' pointed noses in her victory a bit more than was wise.

The elves bridled, but didn't deign to respond, beyond

furious glares burrowing into Coach's skull.

"But anyhow," she continued, "I can't just snap my fingers and make this awesome, brilliant snare go away. Runes don't work like that." Coach rubbed her jaw and studied the bear trap within the smoky orb. The trap had a few cracks in the dark steel, wee fractures wending their way through the hardened metal. Cracks that hadn't been there the day before. The seashell looked aged as well, on the verge of crumbling. "It's already deteriorating, but I should be able to speed the process up. It'll take some research to do that."

Coach stepped back and set her hands on her hips resolutely. "Until we can release you, you'll need to layer us in protective spells, something to keep Ivy away from us, since she's obviously going to notice the Spookum didn't come out with us."

"Ooh, that sounds good," said Jeff. A few protective spells from the elves would go a long ways towards soothing his frayed nerves. He was relieved Coach was in charge. She had great ideas sometimes. He wouldn't have even known that was something worth asking for.

"Great idea," said Owen, giving Coach a friendly nudge with his elbow.

Apparently, it wasn't worth asking for. Ackley rolled his charcoal eyes. "You hear that? They think we can enchant them." He sighed. "It doesn't work that way."

"Sheer ignorance," Yoric observed, overtly amused by the request.

"This is what will happen," said Ackley in an authoritative voice. As a commander of soldiers, a general, he was accustomed to being listened to. Battalions had stoically rushed off to their bloody deaths at his remorseless command.

"You free us," he said, pointing at Coach.

He pointed a finger like an icepick at Jeff. "You try to help

216

her, although I have doubts as to your capacity."

"At very least, don't get in her way," Yoric added, which he seemed to envision as helpful additional advice.

Turning to speak to Owen, Ackley's voice lowered, becoming conspiratorial. The indigo-hued elf leaned forward, whispering his battle plans. "Ivy and the Spookum must stay separated. She can't find the base without the help of a human, so the primary danger becomes the Spookum escaping the tree and finding her. With the containment magic weakened, they might then be able to get away, creating an entire inconvenience of murders and a trail of gutted humans. That must be avoided. So, the beast must be kept within the tree. Luckily, the Spookum has a one-track mind. It won't leave the imprisoning sanctuary of the oak tree if it has prey to chase within the tree. You simply have to avoid it for a time. It can't fit through many of the doors, although that isn't a perfect means of evasion since there are circuitous routes for it to bypass any such chokepoints. You would need to avoid becoming trapped in a room without an exit, since it can batter down any portal if given time."

Listening to the elf's speech, Jeff grew more confused. What did this have to do with Owen? Yet, Owen looked energized, in a way he rarely did, like a swashbuckling adventurer in a stereotypical librarian's cardigan.

"Understood?" asked Ackley.

Owen nodded. He clapped Jeff on the shoulder and flashed a movie star smile. That was when Jeff understood what was happening. If Owen had a fault, and that was a big if, it was that he could be rash. And too selfless for his own good.

"I'm on it," Owen said. He raced off, cardigan flapping behind him like a superhero's cape.

Full realization dawning, Jeff chased his friend through the darkened woods. He heard Coach behind him, blundering through the trees. Farther back, Ackley, or perhaps Yoric, yelled, "Off you go."

Jeff was faster than Coach, although not as much as he would have guessed. Owen, however, was far faster than either of them.

They found the titanic oak with no problem. Since Coach's rune magic had led them there once already, finding it again was simplicity itself.

By the time Jeff reached the oak, Owen had plunged inside and slammed the door shut.

Behind Jeff, Coach bent forward, setting her hands on her knees as she huffed, tired from the short sprint. "Step one was don't close the door," she said. "Anything can happen with the door closed."

"What do we do now?" asked Jeff. His immediate impulse was driven by his conscience, which told him to follow Owen, to help his friend. But, that frantic notion was quickly wiped from the whiteboard of his mind by the eraser known as logic. Logically, and without contestation, Owen had a greater chance of keeping the beast preoccupied if he didn't have the slower, weaker Jeff to look out for.

"We do exactly what the big-eared goofy elf said. I'll figure out a way to spring them ahead of schedule. It's tricky, but I can do it. Probably take a few hours, maybe overnight. Owen just has to stay away from the Spookum for that long," said Coach. Seeing the angst on Jeff's face, she added, "In such a big place it should be easy for a guy like him. Don't worry about it, he'll be fine."

26 CHOCOLATES

Jeff and Coach were triple-checking the correct direction to go along the darkened trail to return to the Subaru when they heard the honeyed voice.

"Hi guys. Where's Owen?" asked Ivy. Without so much as the flutter of a single leaf, she'd emerged from the forest inches from Jeff. Her breath, infused with peppermint, warmly caressed his cheek. Heat poured off her.

Close proximity to the beautiful crimson-haired pixie, which had so aroused Jeff's lust over the last few months, now only aroused fear. His heart was thundering, his nervous system stomping ruthlessly on whatever internal button activated the fight-or-flight response. Despite what he now knew of Ivy, or thought he knew, seeing the creamy skin of her smooth cheeks up close made it hard to conceive that she was centuries old.

"Oh, uh, he had to pee," said Jeff. He gestured vaguely into the woods, towards a line of pine trees perfect for peeing privacy.

Ivy sniffed delicately, sampling the air. She peered closely at Jeff, who was an awful liar and could practically feel the fearful anxiety rolling off his own skin.

"Uh huh," she said suspiciously. "So, were you chatting up those elves?" The spotlight of her wide eyes shifted, resetting on Coach.

"Some," said Coach, as she and Ivy entered into a staring contest, drab brown versus shimmering green, each attempting to delve into the other's thoughts and discern their motives. Jeff used the opportunity to edge away from the pixie.

After a moment, Coach calmly said, "They were very credible." She studiously maintained eye contact with the pixie, as if the fate of the universe rested on who broke first.

Meanwhile, Jeff's eyes roamed the darkness, like a caged animal seeking a means of escape.

"Good liars always are," responded Ivy, breaking eye contact. She hadn't been as invested in the starting contest as Coach. "But anyway, what did you find in the fancy tree house?"

Nearby branches shifted and animals scrabbled along them, the denizens of the forest going about their nocturnal business of either hunting for food or avoiding being food.

"The house was empty," said Coach. Jamming her flashlight into her armpit to free her hands, she rooted around in a fanny pack. "Spacious and fancy but nobody was home. We'll have to try again."

"We didn't find any meth cooking stuff," said Jeff, but then regretted it. Had that sounded accusatory?

"That's a shame," said the pixie absentmindedly. Her focus was on what Coach had produced from the fanny pack. Her button nose wriggled adorably, the tip of her pink tongue exploring her top lip.

"Want some chocolates?" asked Coach. She held out a Ziploc bag stuffed with her homemade sweets.

"Always," said Ivy, greedily shoving her hand into the bag.

Terror had turned Jeff's stomach into an acid pit. "No thanks." This didn't seem like the time for candy.

Shoveling candy into her drooling mouth, Ivy barely chewed the first several pieces. When she slowed, she looked confused. "These are crunchy. Are there nuts or something?"

"Something like that," Coach said, directing her flashlight at Ivy, spotlighting the pixie in a cone of light to separate her from the descending gloom of night. She studied the pixie closely, as if eager to hear her verdict on the quality of the candies.

"Spicy," Ivy observed, flapping a hand at her open mouth.

She scrunched her face. "Chili peppers?" she asked, with a hint of trepidation. A single bead of sweat trekked down her porcelain forehead.

"Nope," said Coach, reaching back over her shoulder, grasping to retrieve something from her backpack.

In cartoons, when the illustrators want something to be adorable, such as a kitten, they make the eyes overly large. Normally, Ivy had just such eyes. They were enchanting. But right then, they widened and bulged obscenely, which was decidedly less attractive. These were the eyes of a cave monster, raised in the dark, and therefore designed to gather every photon of light possible.

Ivy's mouth expanded, yawning open like one of those Christmas soldier nutcrackers. Within that maw, her teeth were polished pearls but also yellowed fangs.

With a sound like a thunderous gack, she spat a bloody glob onto the forest floor. In the splattered red slobber, Jeff could see a silver earring. Where it wasn't still encased in chocolate, the silver was smoking.

"Old silver jewelry inside the candies," Coach said. The exuberant self-satisfaction in those words gave her a congratulatory pat on the back. "Silver is toxic to pixies, particularly if ingested. Burns in the old stomach doesn't it, sweetheart?"

"Bitch," Ivy hissed, between great hacking coughs like a cat trying to bring up a hairball. She bent over, hands on knees, and coughed mightily, great wet sounds, foretelling of vomit. Peeking up through the scarlet locks dangling before her face, she gave Coach a look of direst hatred.

Finding what she'd been groping for in her backpack, Coach produced a sawed-off double-barreled shotgun. With no hesitation, she leveled the barrels on the pixie, drew back both hammers and fired. Twin roars melded into one as cones of fire leapt from the shotgun and crashed into Ivy, cascading over her torso.

The blast threw her slender frame back, slamming her into a tree trunk. She crumpled to the ground, but by the time she hit the fallen leaves she was different than she had been. The impact had jostled her from the shape she'd been wearing into another—one that was perhaps her true, natural form.

Coach's flashlight revealed a monster on the forest floor. It was still distinctly Ivy, or parts of it were, at least. The face, for instance, was mostly the same. Her clothes were unchanged, although her sundress was tearing at the seams over this new form, not to mention the holes from the shotgun pellets. She'd reverted to what, if Jeff were to describe it, was a large humanoid weasel. It was longer than a tiger, if nowhere near as thick. The hair atop her head was still red, but it was now a mangy crimson tangle sprouting in a line from her head to her buttocks like a dingy cascade of fire. Her body was partly pink flesh and partly fur, with some patches of the matted pelt brown, and other areas red. At the ends of her hands and feet, now somewhat akin to huge paws, were wicked claws, inches long and razor sharp.

Ears ringing, Jeff felt the world spinning, the trees dancing around him in some chaotic samba. With a detached clarity, he realized he was going to pass out. This turn of events was finally, indubitably, more than he could process. His only hope was that his sanity was not irretrievably broken, but rather might return to normal sometime in the near future, should he be fortunate enough to live that long.

Through his fading consciousness, his senses continued to function. Distantly, he smelled sulfur and something like rotten eggs, which was perhaps from the shotgun. Or perhaps the giant weasel monster that had so recently been a beautiful woman.

And his vision still worked. His eyes remained focused on Ivy's snarling face, even as her monstrous body writhed on the forest floor. Eons of evolution have taught mankind to fear and avoid that which goes bump in the night, and Ivy's rancorous visage represented just such a sight, raising the hairs on Jeff's arm to stand at attention, chilling his guts, voiding his bladder.

His sense of hearing was also intact, despite the ringing from the shotgun blasts. Through the incessant ringing, he heard Coach speaking. "The shells were filled with straight, pure iron, shaped like jagged little chunks and shavings and filings and scraps and whatnot. I've got a guy that makes them for me. A real artist. Gotta use pure, uncut iron, since it can actually hurt fairies, just like silver. Especially, of course, when you blast it into their bodies. Burns them something fierce."

As Coach rambled in amped excitement, the pixie weasel squirmed, screeched, and hissed. Like a horrific car wreck, Jeff couldn't look away.

He felt a pluck on his sleeve. Coach was gently pulling him up the trail. "We've gotta get moving, pronto," she said merrily.

Somehow retaining his consciousness, and hopefully his sanity, Jeff went up the trail, tugged along by Coach, and pursued by Ivy's anguished howls.

27 SCAMPERING

Scampering, it must be said, is inherently adorable. Particularly when it involves a chase.

Fuzzy creatures scampering though the woods, making fervent, disjointed haste as their sweet little paws patter atop the pine needles, their sniffers delicately testing the air as they pursue friends, or food. Charming.

A puppy scampering quickly, romping after its littermates, clumsily tumbling over the top of them, before they all collapse together into a ball of fluff. Priceless.

A cat playing with a stuffed toy mouse, slapping it across the hardwood floor and scampering after it in chase. Entirely adorable.

Strictly speaking, according to the term's generally accepted meaning, what Ivy was doing was scampering. She was moving with haste on all fours, her scuttling strides short and disorderly, her paws slapping the forest floor as she chased Jeff and Coach. That is scampering. Yet, there was nothing remotely adorable about it. Not the way she did it.

Detracting from the adorableness was her vicious snarling, throaty and threatening, as of a titanic rabid wolf. Those dire growls were intermittently interrupted by hacking coughs that rattled her frame as she paused to spit up steaming bloody gobs of chocolate, silver, and slobber.

Retching completed, she would return to dragging herself after them, albeit slowed by the silver in her belly and shotgun wounds peppering her mid-section.

One such time when she paused to gag, Jeff craned his neck back and got a good look at her, providing a mental snapshot he'd always remember, should he be torn to pieces in the next minute or pass away peacefully in a nursing home after several decades.

With frantic clarity, he decided she perhaps looked more specifically like a tayra rather than a standard weasel, although he wouldn't have been able to explain exactly why. Perhaps since he'd seen a tayra at the last zoo he'd visited, and the slinky creature had lodged itself in his mental repository.

Her face was twisted in animal fury, yet still recognizably hers, despite the jaw hinging unnaturally wide and flashing fangs the length and thickness of pinkies. She was simultaneously beautiful and hideous.

A snarled mass of red hair ran along her back, poking out through the torn remains of the sundress she still wore.

Her hands and feet were huge, and mostly bare skin, but furry along the backs with elongated, clawed digits, making them look like giant tarantulas with fleshy legs.

It hadn't registered with him before, but sprouting from her back were wings, dragging along the ground like wet sails unable to grab the air. They were weighty, not airy, possibly vestigial, and wouldn't be fueling any liftoffs in the near future.

Finally, she had a tail, thick as her limbs, trailing her, being towed along like a red, furry snake. Fat and puffy as it was, it might have been adorable, if not on the hind end of a nightmare.

Snapshot firmly rooted in his mental scrapbook, he returned to his headlong flight. Within ten steps, he'd bounced off a tree trunk, nearly blinded himself on a pine bough, and tripped over a grasping maple root, but he continued on, hounded by the pixie's hungry snarls.

A moment later, he again heard Ivy retching. The sounds, and the temporary respite they promised, spurred him into action.

As he'd been sprinting for his life, grazing away his flesh bit by bit on the rough surfaces of the forest, a heaviness in his pocket had been chafing his thigh and tugging at his pants. That heaviness might be the solution. The Glock. He'd forgotten it.

"Hold up," he called to Coach, who was just ahead, at the border of his perception through the deep gloom.

With inspired, uncharacteristic, heroic resolve flooding his veins, Jeff pulled the pistol from his jeans, somehow managing not to fumble it away into the night, which was miraculous in and of itself.

He turned, held the Glock out, and aimed in a squinting, cringing sort of way that he envisioned as true action-hero style. Ivy had paused to gag far enough away that she was hazy. Yet her green eyes glittered, collecting moonlight and throwing it back in a rainbow assortment. He aimed for those kaleidoscope eyes, his own eyes pinching closed as he yanked the trigger.

Six booms tore through the night, the compact pistol leaping in his hands with each shot. It was louder than he would have guessed, amplified as it was by the surreal stillness of G12. And it had far more kick than he'd surmised it would. Also, there was the smell, a rancorous odor, as if a noxious gunpowder Hell had settled nearby.

Ivy didn't flinch, didn't even blink, her baleful gaze boring into him as he fired. Not that he could know that, with his eyes clamped shut as they were.

Magazine empty, Jeff pried open his eyes, only to see that Ivy hadn't moved. If he'd struck her, it'd done nothing. Although, between his closed eyes, adrenaline-fueled shaking hands, and inexpert marksmanship, he hadn't the vaguest clue where any of the bullets had struck. Most likely, none had come within ten meters of the giant amalgam of weasel and pixie.

Hacking fit complete, Ivy reached out her front paws, grabbed the soil, and flung herself forward, resuming her pursuit.

Coach's voice drifted back from up the trail. "Nice shooting, Tex." She'd paused as he'd fired but now resumed her charge up the spotty, uneven path.

His heroic resolve depleted, Jeff followed Coach, the Glock squeezed tight in his sweaty grip. There was one other loaded magazine tucked away in his back pocket, should the opportunity arise to use it before the pixie ripped him to bloody shreds. That fact gave him little reassurance.

Ducking boughs, hurdling roots, and dodging trunks, he and Coach achieved a groove in their flight through the forest. They could see just far enough ahead in the fading light to perceive obstacles an instant before slamming into them.

Ivy grew more distant, her growls and the sounds of her claws tearing the earth fading away. She wasn't moving well, slowed as she was by shotgun and candy injuries, although unfazed by Jeff's errant barrage of lead.

Wounded as the pixie was, the humans pulled away, distancing themselves. Despite their heaving lungs and burning legs, they continued running, one of Hell's own monsters on their heels.

It was immediately obvious when they emerged from Sector G12. The oppressive canopy eased, revealing the stars above. The air was fresher, the moonlight stronger.

Flinging themselves into Coach's Subaru, they were away before the pixie burst from the woods.

28 CATFIGHT

Jeff paced the apartment, his nerves fraying further with every lap. He was scared for Owen, who was locked away in the elves' tree house, seeking to distract the Spookum from exiting. But also frightened of Ivy waltzing in the door as a human, then dropping down on all fours and morphing into a humanoid weasel monster who would rip him to shreds.

The apartment wasn't a very big space to pace in, although Owen's absence made it feel woefully large and empty. Even so, every twenty seconds Jeff passed by Coach. She was studiously working on her newest rune project, a means to free the elves from the trap she'd built.

After passing by Coach, he would next walk by Carla, who was sitting on the loveseat, her feet up on the worn coffee table. She wasn't impressed by their story of monsters and expansive tree forts but had come over, nonetheless, even if she was disappointed Owen wasn't there.

With each lap, he checked the windows and doors. Each entry and exit point had sugar sprinkled across the base. The doors and windows also had a protective symbol hastily scratched into their wood. That would come out of his deposit for sure. Coach had gouged them into the surfaces first thing when they'd returned. They would provide protection against the pixie's entry, or at least slow her down.

Coach was deep into her work, planning appropriate runes, practicing them on paper, then scratching them into the surface of a pink pencil eraser she'd produced from her backpack. It was a big, rectangular block eraser of the sort he hadn't seen since elementary school.

Carla tore her attention from the television for a moment to cast a quizzical look at Coach, who was hunched over the table exerting the focus of a brain surgeon as she etched runes into one slanted side of the pink rubbery block.

"Is it important that you're using an eraser? Couldn't you doodle your nonsense on a bookmark or a popsicle stick?" Carla's questions cast doubts onto Coach's task, but not as much as her tone did, which left no doubt she found the entire thing ludicrous.

Coach looked up, tongue poking out the right side of her mouth, clamped in concentration. After a thoughtful pause, she replied with utmost sincerity, "No, the symbolism of the eraser is important."

"Sure, sure," said Carla, in a tone normally reserved for humoring your elderly grandmother who thought Nixon was still president. She slurped her drink. It was Owen's gin. Jeff hated gin. It smelled like rotten berries and funky citrus were dueling for olfactory supremacy.

Carla poked a finger at the sugar barrier along the base of the sliding balcony door. "Why the sugar? Aren't the doodles enough?"

"Generally, pixies and similar fairy folk have to stop and count sugar granules, so it will slow her down if she comes. Runes and sigils are nice, but every little bit helps." Coach spoke as if mesmerized and surprised by her own words.

Shrugging, Carla returned to channel surfing.

Jeff continued pacing, stopping to stare out the sliding balcony door. No monsters in the parking lot. Not yet anyway.

Several laps later, the doorknob jiggled. The door was, of course, locked. At the knob and also with the deadbolt.

Pausing his pacing, Jeff stared at the doorknob, assuming he'd imagined the jiggle.

A faint scratching sounded at the door, just at the edge of his perception. Fingernails trailed down the wood, pressed ever so lightly, making the faintest of whispers.

"Um," Jeff whispered quietly. Eyes glued to the door, he

waved his hands for attention, but didn't know if anyone saw him. With all the psychic power at his disposal, he willed the furtive noises to be nothing but his overactive imagination.

Proving his lack of psychic abilities, a light knocking started. "Can I come in?" asked Ivy.

"No," barked Jeff, his voice somehow managing to crack in the middle of such a short word.

He risked a peek through the peephole. Mercifully, Ivy was human, although disheveled, still wearing the torn dress and looking more exquisitely attractive than any human possibly could. She was twirling a lock of crimson hair, batting her ridiculously large eyes. Jeff's gaze met those eyes and he fell right in, leaning forward to bump his forehead against the door.

"Ignore her," said Coach. She often sounded bewildered and awestruck when she spoke, but these two words had the feel of a command. Even if that command seemed to come from a thousand miles away, since Jeff had felt the world narrow to just he and Ivy as he stared into her glimmering eyes.

"Please," Ivy purred. "I need you Jeff. Don't you want to see me? Don't you want to touch me?" She fluttered her eyelashes and pouted, her pink lips forming a puffy heart shape. Ivy tilted forward, staring intently at the peephole, almost as if she could see him.

His thoughts cloudy and indistinct, Jeff was lost in the green-tinted rainbow of her eyes. Those weren't the eyes of a monster. If anything, they were the windows into the soul of a unicorn—lovely, trustworthy, virtuous. He put his hand on the doorknob, not wanting to keep her waiting. With his other hand he wiped away the thin stream of drool pouring from the corner of his mouth. He didn't want Ivy to see it. It was unsightly.

Coach ripped his hand away from the doorknob. At the same time, she pushed him away from the peephole. Her finishing move was a cuff upside his head, which cleared away the cobwebs.

"You shouldn't look at her. Pixie magic can easily befuddle the weak-willed," said Coach. With a wince, she added, "No offense."

"Boob magic, you mean," said Carla.

"Go away," Coach yelled at the door, returning to her work of carving what looked like a crooked snowman into the pink eraser. "Scat," she added, with a snicker.

"Oh my God, just let her in. Who cares?" said Carla from the loveseat, where she was idly scrolling through Netflix menus with ever expanding boredom. She preferred to read, but neither Owen nor Jeff had any books to her tastes, which primarily involved either romantic vampires or crime-solving forensic pathologists.

"Yeah, let me in," Ivy whined. Her fingernails were again scratching at the door. They were less tentative now, more insistent. Jeff could imagine gouges being dug into the wood.

"Go away," he commanded, in a firm voice that brooked no disagreement, although some would describe it as panicked pleading, if not a whimper.

"Fine," the pixie huffed.

There was a bit of shuffling in the hallway. It was light-footed but had a scraping quality to it. As if from clawed feet. The shuffling quietly receded, giving Jeff hope that she'd left. Silent seconds passed, each laden with reassurance.

As is often the case, the hope was premature. The door shuddered in its frame as a great weight struck it from the hallway. The wood squealed as the hinges made a sickly popping noise.

The door shook a second time, accompanied by a growling bark. The wood splintered, sending pointy fragments flying from a vertical crack running from floor to ceiling.

A third crash tore the deadbolt's receiver loose from the

jamb. The door sagged, splitting away from the frame. With the frenzied confusion unique to deathly peril, Jeff didn't move. Nor did he think. He simply existed, mind washed clear of any productivity beyond reinforcing its certainty he was about to die. Eventually, he summoned a vague thought, which was to wonder what Owen would do. The answer was to grab the gun and defend them. Yet Jeff couldn't imagine where he'd left the polymer gadget of death.

The door was just beginning its slow collapse to the floor, and Jeff was pondering whether or not to pray when the miracle happened. The runes Coach had carved into the door and frame glowed, spun like pinwheels, jumped away from the surface, and then rebounded back with great force. When they slammed back into place, the door was returned to its original state. Unbroken, unbent. Relatively flimsy in a physical sense yet reinforced with ancient rune power.

The magic was fascinating to behold. A delight for the senses. Although, not as delightful to Jeff as the fact that he was still alive. That was both a delight and a surprise.

In the hallway, the monster growled its annoyance. The primeval snarl rumbled aggressively.

"See, we're fine," said Coach. She'd been watching the buckling door but returned to her work, drenched in self-satisfaction.

"That was a weird optical illusion," Carla remarked. The eternal cynic, she returned to Netflix, considering whether to start watching *Squid Game* yet again. Swirling her gin, she gave it a gulp.

"That silliness earlier was just a little misunderstanding," whispered Ivy, barely loud enough to be heard through the door. "Plus, you guys started it, feeding me poison. I just got carried away. Let me in, Jeff." She was using her wheedling tone, which was hard to resist, pixie magic or no. Hard, that is, until you knew she was a monster trying to kill you.

Somewhere in the hallway, a door opened. A muffled male voice asked, "What was that noise?" He sounded irritated.

It was Larry, the guy across the hall. Most of what Jeff knew about Larry was that he was into tennis and worked as an assistant manager at the bank up the street. And sometimes he played video games and had drinks with Jeff and Owen. Like every heterosexual male Jeff had met in the last few months, Larry adored Ivy.

Irritation dropping away, Larry assumed the butt-kissing demeanor he always wore in Ivy's presence. "Hey there! Are you okay? What can I do?" Although he couldn't see, Jeff could easily imagine Larry puffing his chest out.

"Hi handsome, can you let me into Jeff's apartment?"

"I would, but I don't have a key," Larry said quietly. Raising his voice, he pounded the door. Thump, thump, thump. "Dude, Ivy's here. Open up."

At a loss, Jeff turned to his companions, seeking guidance. Having Larry involved infused a dose of reality into the situation. The juxtaposition of a fantastical world populated with pixies and monsters with an everyday world where your banker neighbor knocked on your door was disorienting.

Carla shrugged, her indifference failing to hide her fresh surge of annoyance. She'd witnessed Larry's ardent admiration of Ivy on several occasions, and each time it rubbed her the wrong way. Although he was no Owen, Larry was a catch. Yet, it hadn't ever registered with Ivy that Larry adored her. Carla wanted to be adored, so seeing adoration flung at the redheaded beauty only to be rebuffed with oblivious indifference was intensely irritating.

Without looking up from the pink eraser, Coach flicked her hand dismissively. "Tell him to go back into his apartment and mind his business."

Getting as close to the door as he dared, Jeff's lips were inches away from the runes, which had returned to looking like ridiculous hen scratch as opposed to sigils imbued with powerful magic. "Tell her to go away," he yelled.

"But, it's Ivy," Larry called back, incredulous that someone would want her to go away.

"Just go back to your apartment. Get away from her." Jeff considered spilling the truth that beneath the beautiful nymph-like wrapper she wore, Ivy was actually a squalid, hairy monster with slash-y claws and a puffy tail. Except, obviously, that would be pointless since Larry wouldn't believe it.

Larry chuckled. "You wanna come in?"

"You're so sweet," said Ivy.

"I really am," Larry replied, probably with a wink. And perhaps with a pat on her elbow, trying to break down the culturally required social distance separating them, getting her used to his hands. Jeff had seen Larry in action before. He was a quick mover with the ladies.

But before Larry could make any progress in his wooing, he gasped. That rapid intake of breath quickly transformed into a gargle, then became a groan.

In rapid succession, there came a hiss, a slam, a sob, a wet tearing, and then a muffled scream.

After that were several gruesome seconds of what sounded like chewing. Then some giggles.

Appalled, Jeff backed away from the door, driven by the horrid sounds of chuckles and slurps. Carla didn't seem to notice them. Coach shook her head as if trying to clear it, then renewed her focus on the pink eraser, which was rapidly filling with tiny symbols.

Larry's door clicked closed.

Cowering, Jeff didn't move. Like a gazelle in the African veld that senses a lion, he froze up, making no noise and stirring no muscles. He strained his ears for any scrap of sound, any indication of what was going on. Seconds passed, perhaps a minute.

The door across the hall opened, then softly closed.

Almost immediately, there was once again a soft scratching at the door. "Jeff, let me in."

He ignored her. She kept talking.

"Did Coach cut some nasty symbols into the door? You should scratch those out."

He ignored that as well.

"Jeff, I really want to see you. If you help me, I'll help you. I can get money. Do you like money?"

Jeff continued his campaign of ignoring her.

"Or would you rather have me? You can have me if you want. I'll do anything you like."

Picturing the giant weasel that had chased them through G12, that was extra easy to ignore.

Eventually Ivy stopped talking. Shortly after that, she ceased her scratching. Jeff risked a glimpse through the peephole and was rewarded with the sight of an empty hallway. Perhaps the pixie hadn't left, but she'd at least moved farther away. He resumed his pacing.

Coach worked on her runes. Carla became bored of the TV and her phone. She began pacing, her circuit including Owen's room.

Two people pacing seemed like too many, so Jeff sat and watched Coach. In her notebook, she sketched a symbol that looked like a squished spider in a top hat. After intently studying it, she redrew it. Shaking her head, she did it again. Muttering, she tried again. And again. Each one looked about the same, but none satisfied her enough to copy it over to the pink eraser of power she was constructing.

A bit later, with a guilty look and an extravagant yawn,

Carla exited Owen's room. She hustled the first few steps down the short hallway until she reached the bathroom door, as if pretending she'd been there instead of snooping through Owen's things.

"I'm tired," she declared.

"Go to sleep in Owen's bed if you want," Jeff said. He was so wired from worry he didn't think he'd sleep for days. Carla's droopy eyes illustrated she didn't understand the gravity of the situation.

"Thought about it," she said, "but the sheets are stinky."

"We haven't done laundry lately," said Jeff. That was true, but not all the truth. As young men with nonexistent sex lives, clean sheets weren't a priority, and wouldn't have been included in any loads of laundry. Sheets finding their way into the washing machine was more of a once or twice a year exercise.

"I want to sleep in my own bed," Carla said. Looking in the fridge, she found nothing interesting, so slammed it closed. Sulking, she returned to the loveseat.

"You can't leave. It isn't safe." Jeff peeked through the vertical blinds covering the balcony door and was pleasantly surprised to find no monsters lurking outside.

"Why?" demanded Carla, confirming that she didn't believe a word of their story. Which, Jeff reasoned, wasn't surprising, given that you really had to see a person turn into a weasel monster to believe it.

"Ivy could be out there," Jeff said.

"Is definitely out there," said Coach solemnly, verbally underlining the first word.

Rolling her eyes, Carla spun her finger in the air and said, "Whoop-de-doo." She slumped back further into the loveseat, draining her glass and cocooning herself in moody silence.

She typed on her phone. Seconds later, it dinged with a text.

She smirked and replied. The text conversation continued, punctuated by giggles and sly peeks at Jeff. He ignored her.

Abruptly, Carla asked, "Can you get me a blanket?"

"There's one there." Jeff pointed at the fleece throw wadded up on the floor.

Indignant, Carla said, "That one smells. I want a clean one."

"Owen might have one in his closet," Jeff said. He set off to find a clean blanket, or at least one that didn't smell too much or possess Rorschach blots of pizza sauce stains. It occurred to him that he and Owen might be slobs. Him more than Owen.

A moment later, he returned with a fleece blanket that vaguely smelled of dust but was not outright offensive. Carla was gone.

"Where's Carla?"

Coach looked around, then shrugged. "Must have left."

"You didn't stop her?"

Holding up the eraser as though it were a trophy, Coach replied, "Sorta busy here."

Jeff took a resolute step towards the door, determined to race outside and retrieve Carla. But, by the second step, doubts had set in. And the third step became a half step, covering a measly pair of inches. Should he go? Should he not? Again, he desperately wished Owen was there.

"Catfight!" yelled a slurred, drunken voice, with all the fevered excitement of announcing a bingo win. It came from outside.

Jeff rushed to the sliding balcony door and peeked into the parking lot below.

The first thing he saw was a group of several people, mostly guys, a few of whom looked familiar. His apartment complex was largely occupied by young adults, past high school or college but not yet settled down with kids. Part of the social scene included regular community jaunts to the local bars, with the returns being late-night, noisy affairs. This was just such a gathering.

The group was laughing and yelling, pointing to the far end of the parking lot. As a group, they were slowly making their way in that direction.

Following their pointing, Jeff saw Ivy. She was spotlighted by a pole-mounted lamp, still human, and still in the torn dress, which amplified the hoots from the drunk crowd.

Her hand was clamped firmly in Carla's hair. Carla was screaming and thrashing, but to little effect, her fists rebounding from the pixie like raindrops from a windshield.

The pixie was staring forlornly up towards Jeff's balcony. She yelled with a resonance that shook the world, sending queasy ripples into Jeff's gut. "I'm going to my sweetie's place," she roared. "I need your help to find it. Just do this for me, and I'll let her go. You know where I'm going, so meet me there."

Ivy sauntered away, dragging Carla along in her wake. For her part, Carla put up a good fight, kicking, screaming, and struggling. Regardless, she was remorselessly pulled along like a kitten by a bulldog. They disappeared, merging into the darkness at the far end of the parking lot.

"Well, crap," said Coach, who'd appeared at Jeff's side. "I guess this is gonna have to be good enough," she added, inspecting the eraser, covered with sloppy rows of marks like crop circles, each etched in with a small knife and colored in by a Sharpie.

And so, they gathered what they needed and charged out to face their destinies, ignoring Larry's blood splattered on the door across the hall.

29 LITTLE MISTER

Less than an hour later, whether he liked it or not, Jeff had returned to Sector G12, and was watching a disheveled, scuzzy black bunny kicking a bear trap.

The LED lantern at their feet illuminated Jellybiscuits standing on its lanky hind legs, battering Coach's elf trap with robotic determination. Blow after blow, kick after kick, the dark bunny's mangy paws banged into the bear trap and seashell.

The display was reminiscent of Jeff's dad kicking their rusty Ford Bronco when it had broken down on the interstate during their one and only attempted trip to a water park. There was no swearing this time though. Nor did Jellybiscuits exhibit any evidence of rage, just mechanized calm.

But the trap gave only the barest of trembles, as if it was stapled in place and time by Coach's runes and sigils. Or as if it truly existed in a separate plane of reality, and what they saw was simply a placeholder in this one. Or perhaps that was true of Jellybiscuits instead.

Although, on close examination, the battered trap now looked noticeably crumbled, as if it were a confection that had been drying in the sun. But still the hazy shield persisted, holding the elves in place, even if not as solidly as it might have the day before. Despite the bunny's best efforts, Jeff suspected it was the passage of time, rather than the roundhouse kicks, that weakened the trap.

"Try biting it," suggested Yoric. He gave the seashell a desultory kick of his own, but it achieved nothing, similar to the bunny's strident punting. Despite having been trapped for days, his long brown hair was entirely clean, and the alluring smell of flowers and berries wafted from his pristine body.

Without pause, Jellybiscuits leapt atop the steel trap and

began nibbling voraciously, its overgrown teeth like jagged chisels. As with the kicking, the gnawing achieved little, beyond perhaps shaving away the scantest iota of metal, peeled away in a whisper, disappearing into the grass below. The combined integrities of the foul bunny's teeth and claws were truly impressive.

"Wow, look at him go," said Coach with admiration. Pumping her fist, she yelled, "You give it hell, little mister." Between her gleeful face and electrified demeanor, she was the very picture of sincere encouragement.

Ackley's coal eyes rose from the raging rabbit and swept over Jeff before landing on Coach. The dark elf said, "This might take quite some time. I assume you have a plan of some sort. As you can see, our method to hasten our exit lacks a certain elegance."

Coach proffered the eraser. Bringing it into the lamplight, she handled it with the reverence normally reserved for a prized artifact at a museum. "Use this to rub those symbols off. The shield will drop away, lickety-split."

She tossed it through the night air, into the translucent orb. Without looking, Ackley snatched it from the air with a speed that made his hand blur. After examining the symbols upon the pink rubber block, his eyes drifted towards the heavens in an eye roll that wept tired dignity.

Somewhat sheepishly, Coach said, "One caveat though, I was a bit rushed, so it might not work completely perfectly. Could take a few minutes."

Ackley raised a sleek white eyebrow as he slowly rolled the enchanted eraser around in his wide hand. He handled it with disdain, as if he might fling it off into the woods at any second. Jeff imagined a millionaire fallen on hard times accepting spare change from a stranger. "Very well," the elf said.

"Great!" yelped Coach. She did a little jig of unfettered high spirits before turning to face Jeff. "You go stall Ivy while we crack these two out of here."

Eyeing their dark surroundings, Jeff felt the bottom drop out of the glimmer of confidence he'd been starting to experience. Even if the elves were sketchy jerks, they were powerful sketchy jerks, and they were mostly on his side, so leaving them seemed ill-conceived. Before fear could sink its greedy hooks into him, he strode away. "Right," he said, with every ounce of bravado he could pretend to have.

After two steps into the shroud of trees, he halted, looked around, and returned to the comfort of the lamplight. "Uh, which way?" He had no idea.

One of Ackley's indigo forefingers was already thrust into the air, pointing in an entirely separate direction than Jeff had walked.

"Cool," Jeff mumbled. Looking in that direction, he was able to see through a gap in the canopy, where he beheld a field of stars. As much as G12 was a creepy place full of unpleasant misgivings and ominous phantoms looming in the shadows, at least its sky held a million stars, each a brilliant diamond on a sable tapestry.

Gaze roving the sky, he found a distinct absence of stars that painted the spectral shape of a treetop. The titanic oak towered over its neighbors, the skyscraper of the forest, blotting out the heavens.

He set off, as quickly as his trepidation would allow.

At points the canopy closed over him and the tree-shaped absence of stars was lost. At those times it was difficult since there was no trail, and the trees all looked the same, beyond some having leaves and the others pine needles. No doubt they were each as unique as snowflakes, but the night and his ignorance blinded him. Yet he stumbled along, guided by hazy instinct, guesswork, and occasional glimpses into the night sky.

The location of both the tree and the pixie became obvious in short order. Carla's screams beckoned him. And her sobs, as well as Ivy's guttural cackles.

Abruptly, the intervening forest fell away, and he saw them. Ivy was in her human form, a bruised and battered Carla at her feet. The gigantic oak loomed behind them, impossible for him to miss but cloaked in magical invisibility to them.

With no plan, for he had no time nor capacity for levelheaded thinking at that moment, Jeff stepped into the clearing, feeling himself every inch the hero. Immediately, he felt Ivy's glare, her eyes cold as ice, freezing him, even as her snarling mouth contained the heated fury of a volcano, burning away his feigned heroism.

He didn't know what to do. What would Owen say? What would Owen do? Jeff couldn't imagine.

Stepping slowly forward, he tripped over his own feet, sprawling onto the forest floor. Picking himself up and valiantly dusting himself off, he said, "Uh, so … uh." It wasn't eloquent, but he liked to think there was steel in his voice, shining through the anxious trembling.

30 AN UNVEILING

"Where is it?" Ivy screeched. She flailed an arm wildly, almost hitting one of the fat low-hanging branches of the titanic oak squatting behind her like a shadowy stalker.

Jeff's vocal cords failed to respond with a witty heroic response, so he settled for gesturing vaguely.

"Come show me," she commanded. "Do it now." Ivy whipped her head around, searching her surroundings for a glimpse of the tree she knew to be close. Her crimson hair flew. He would have found that mesmerizing days ago, but now saw just a monster's overgrown, raggedy coat.

Jeff lurched forward slowly, burdened with guilt for Carla's peril, hampered by fear for her and himself. He moved slowly, since he didn't have the vaguest idea what was the best thing to do in this situation. It had never come up before in his life. No college course had covered it. All he could do was drag his feet and hope the cavalry swooped in.

"Faster," barked the pixie. Although Ivy was in human form, her fingertips were capped by wicked claws. With a manic smile that split her face from ear to ear, beyond the bounds of human anatomy, she dragged a handful of those claws down Carla's abdomen, shredding blouse and skin alike. Red, wet streaks spread along the tattered fabric.

Blood splattered onto the forest floor, lost in the moonlight.

Carla's screams were deafening, accelerating Jeff's halting stroll towards the towering oak.

Coming closer, he got a better look at Carla. She wore a bib of vomit from chin to chest. The reek of the gin assaulted his nose, mixing with the vomit and blood. She was distraught and in great pain, but also livid.

He passed by them and circled around the base of the mighty tree to the door set into its base.

Ivy followed, dragging Carla like a sack of potatoes, if such sacks could sob, scream, and kick while oozing blood.

The Glock in his pocket called to him, for he was now close enough to be certain of hitting his target. Yet Carla was there as well, and the possibility of hitting her loomed large. The pistol was a card that would have to wait and be played at just the right moment.

"It's right here," he said.

"Open it," the pixie replied. Her body was energized, shaking with triumphant glee at being so close to her goal, a reunion with her beloved.

Just then, Carla rotated herself around on the ground, braced herself with her butt and hands as a stable tripod in the dirt, and shot her legs out like pistons, directly into Ivy's knee. It was a crippling move, executed perfectly. The sort of strike she likely learned in a self-defense class. Jeff was awestruck.

However, the powerful strike barely registered with the pixie. Her leg didn't so much as buckle. With an air of casual distraction, as if she'd entered an elevator and initially forgot to hit the button for her floor but was now rectifying that situation, Ivy slammed her knee forcefully into Carla's face. The crunch of breaking cartilage was sickening. Blood flowed and Carla sagged. Ivy released her hold on her captive, letting her collapse onto the soil.

"Open it," the pixie repeated, her tone implying he was next.

He saw no option but to open it. He reached for the handle, his hand traveling at the speed of stall.

There was no set plan in his head, but rather more of a hope for how the next few moments would play out. That hope was simple and straightforward. It was that he would open the door and Owen would leap out to do something fabulous. Something heroic. That hopeful presumption had the weight of experience behind it. Owen had never let him down before.

Heroes appeared when needed. Sidekicks, however, simply stalled and set the stage.

He turned the handle and pulled.

The door opened, revealing nothing but disappointment and the crushing realization that it was up to him, and him alone. The next few moments doubtless held his pending devastating failure. That presumption was also based on historical past performance.

A second after the door opened, Ivy gasped and craned her neck up. Her bright green eyes sparkled with delight as the mighty oak flickered into existence for her.

Carla, however, didn't seem to notice the appearance of the impossible tree, for she was scrabbling away, huffing loudly and trailing blood.

Ivy yelled, "Sweetie, are you there?" Her voice projected well, reaching stentorian levels.

A bellow answered from deep within the confines of the elven fortress. The ground shook with its power.

Now uninterested in Jeff or Carla, Ivy quivered in ecstasy. She yelled, "I'm right outside." She leaned forward, thrusting her head through the simple wooden door.

The portal flared, a charged blue shield sizzling across the opening. It flung the pixie back with an electric shock, sparking and fizzing. Runes flared along the rim of the door.

By the time she hit the forest floor, the pixie had reverted to her weasel form. Tail slashing, claws gouging the earth, she writhed in pain but still seemed thrilled.

"As expected, can't go in there," she announced in a chipper tone. The beast shakily stood, then shook like a dog just in from the rain.

For this one time in his life, to Jeff's astonishment, he didn't freeze. Rather, his legs took the initiative, powering him the several steps towards Carla. With what felt like heroic aplomb, he scooped her off the ground and carried her away, awkwardly but effectively, a hero at last. Perhaps he didn't need Owen after all.

A hero, that is, until the root tripped him on his third step.

Collapsing to his knees, he spilled Carla onto a mattress of pine needles and fallen oak leaves. But, with a ferocious growl, Carla sprung up and grabbed him, forcefully towing him off into the night. Like most everyone, she was better suited to the heroic role than he was. As a good sidekick does, he followed as best he could, tugged along in her mighty wake.

31 ON TOP

With Carla's sweaty, bloody hand in his, pulling him through the night, away from the terror of the pixie, Jeff felt resurgent hope.

Any minute now, the elves would arrive, and all would be well. Or Owen would swoop in. Or maybe Coach. Whoever it was that saved the day, he'd done his part, rescuing Carla. Or perhaps she'd rescued him. Whatever, the point was that he'd done something, and now they were both safe. He was a success, even if he'd stumbled into it, leaning heavily on luck. Even a blind dog pees on the hydrant sometimes, as his dad liked to say.

His balloon was burst by a beautiful face, and not for the first time. Beautiful faces often convey bad news. Their attractiveness softens the blow.

In this case, it was Ivy's face emerging from the dark woods, and them not yet sixty steps into their flight to freedom.

The pixie materialized from the trees, her weasel monster body following after. The limp wings caught on the dense branches of her cover, breaking some loose and dragging them with her.

Her lovely countenance was lit from above by moonlight. She was smiling, happy.

As Jeff sluggishly processed the pixie blocking their path, and what might be done about it, Carla acted. She juked right, then flung herself left, speeding up in an attempt to blast past the pixie.

Jeff tried to follow but was thrown off by the feint to the right and tripped over his own feet, sprawling on the ground.

Carla paused, trying to put on the brakes so she could turn and gather him up again, and that was her downfall. In that momentary fateful pause where Carla's momentum was forward but she was attempting to reverse course, Ivy lashed out with one of her horrid paws. The smack battered Carla with gut-wrenching force, sending her flying into a tree trunk. Her body wrapped around the trunk with crunching impact, then sagged to the ground amongst roots and a patch of dark mushrooms, where she lay unmoving.

Dropping to all fours, Ivy slunk like a Komodo dragon onto Jeff's prone body, pinning him with her weight. They were face to face, although her chimeric pixie and giant weasel body extended far past his, even without considering her tail, which twitched excitedly, like a cat watching a squirrel through a window.

Flicking her head to send the greasy scarlet tumble of her hair to the side, she pressed her face up close to his. The hot gusts from her malevolent smiling maw tickled his cheek. The puffs carried an unsettling combination of peppermint and rotting meat. Her grin grew wider, revealing pointed teeth like a meat saw meant for elephants.

He struggled and thrashed, but she was far stronger than him. All he could hope for was to earn some latitude for his right hand, for that was where his salvation was held.

Ivy gyrated her lower body against his and dragged a slimy tongue along his chin, over his cheeks, and up to his eyebrows. Jeff whimpered, a high-pitched noise he wasn't proud of.

Her face, lovely and malicious in equal measure, became a melodramatic veil of shock and wounded feelings. "What's the matter, Jeff? You always wanted me on top of you, didn't you? Or don't you like being on the bottom?" Pressing her torso harder into his, she jutted her lower lip out in a pout that had been far more endearing a few days ago.

It was now or never, so he frantically began pulling the Glock's trigger. The weapon was in his right hand, clenched in a death grip. The pixie's left paw was pinning his forearm down but he aimed the best he could.

She hadn't noticed the weapon, but the instant he began firing, Ivy tightened her grip on his arm, pressing it hard into the pine needles and soil, reacting with a speed a human could only dream of.

With hateful roars, deadly slugs flew through the forest. Each were wasted, for they struck nothing but dirt and trees, neither of which meant Jeff any harm.

Readjusting and angling the weapon as far to the front as his wrist would allow, he fired on the pixie again. At that angle, the recoil threw the weapon from his hand. It landed a foot away but might as well have been a mile. If that final bullet hit the pixie, Jeff didn't know it.

The smell of gunpowder drifting away, Ivy frowned, looking disappointed. "That was rude."

The monster climbed off him and began slithering back towards the titanic oak, dragging Jeff behind her. Her claws were dug into his calf, rooting themselves deep in the flesh, ensuring a strong grip.

As the back of his head banged off roots and scraped through pine needles and leaves, Jeff saw a snatch of stars above. Perhaps they would be the last he ever saw. Scrabbling for purchase, he could find nothing to grab that might slow them or be used as a club. The few kicks he was able to land on the pixie's furry limbs were ineffective, like slapping a mountain gorilla on the wrist.

Ivy's voice slid through the darkness, seeming to come from everywhere, cutting across the sounds of him being towed through the detritus of the forest. "Sorry, but I just couldn't let you leave. My sweetie is going to want a snack. He gets so hungry."

32 BACK AT THE BEAR TRAP

The snug clearing acting as the elves' prison was dreadfully dark.

Coach had turned off the LED lantern, since she wanted to preserve and build her night vision for whatever came next. Previously, she'd approached similar situations pirate-style, wearing an eyepatch to build night vision in just one eye. However, she'd found the resulting disparity in vision between eyes to be disorienting, so she'd abandoned the eyepatch, beyond an occasional flourish for social outings.

In the absence of the lantern's artificial light, sparse luminance remained.

The green canopy of the forest leaned in, as if curious to see what was happening, choking off the moonlight to nearly nothing.

The hazy orb surrounding the elves was faintly visible but provided no illumination to anything except itself.

It was very little light for humans to see by, but an abundance for the elves.

"Keep rubbing." Coach's voice sounded unusually loud, amplified by the intrinsic stillness of G12. Through that hushed silence, frantic sounds carried from the direction of the colossal oak tree the elves called home. Plus, the gunshots, which were thunderous cracks in the muted landscape.

Eraser in hand, Ackley was scrubbing at the runes on the bear trap. Slowly but surely, the symbols on the trap were fading, becoming inexact, imprecise. And precision was key in such matters. A magical rune that's only 99% accurate is equally effective as a doodle of a cat chasing a parakeet, which is to say not at all.

The runes on the eraser were nearly worn away, but still the shield stood, even if not as stoutly as it once had.

Jellybiscuits sat off to the side, watching intently. The creature was but a bleak smear in the darkness, visible primarily by the green fluorescence of its eyes.

Near the rabbit, Yoric was stretched out, lying on the ground with his hands behind his head, feet rocking back and forth to a melody only he could hear. He looked like an idling cloud gazer, seeking dragons or turtles in the puffy white pillows lazily floating by in an afternoon sky.

"This is used up." There was a crisp plop as the eraser was dropped into a pile of dead leaves.

The steel of the bear trap was noticeably withered, cracks running along its dark surface. The seashell, as well, was visibly deteriorating.

"I think it's weakened enough that you two should be able to push through, if you want it bad enough. It'll probably sting quite a bit."

With a dramatic sigh, Yoric rose from the ground. The imprisonment troubled him less than his companion. Their duty did not call to him in the same way, since preserving human lives was not a topic of any interest to him. Truthfully, it barely was for Ackley, but the indigo elf's sense of honor demanded he put forth some level of effort.

Motivated or not, the elves set to pressing their bodies against the globe encircling them, trying to thrust themselves through.

It was an unpleasant and painful process, lasting minutes, placing great strain upon the magical beings. Their efforts might have gone quicker, but it could fairly be said that Ackley was trying far harder than his lackadaisical companion.

Finally, there was a crack, which made no physical noise but thrummed through their souls. A wave of pressure rolled away from the shattered trap, knocking Coach to her knees.

The bear trap lay in pieces, shards of steaming metal in a

heap. Fragments of the seashell littered the clearing, the smallest ones falling away to dust.

"That did more than sting." The lighter elf sagged to the ground after speaking.

"Payment is due," said the other. His vast black blade flashed.

A gasp of pain followed. A spray of blood. The leaves crunched as something fell into their midst, followed immediately by something much larger crumpling to the forest floor.

A sob, growing into an incoherent wail that quickly trailed into complete silence.

"I would suggest the other as well."

"One is sufficient."

"Two would be more fitting, considering her audacity."

A long-suffering sigh. "One is enough."

"We'll need a moment to recover before we set off."

"Yes, pushing through there gave me the wobbles."

"Shall we send it ahead?"

"An excellent notion. Jellybiscuits, off you go."

The ugly bunny jetted into the night, a guided missile of grim intent.

33 FREIGHT TRAIN

Jeff was on his back, a few yards away from the portal into the elven mansion. Ivy was hunkered atop him, her paw pressing him flat, holding him in place as surely as any manacles might.

The pixie gazed expectantly into the portal, waiting patiently.

There was not yet anything to see through the portal, nor could anything truly be made out on the other side. Its surface was cloudy, a staticky, shifting aura blocking the view within. Mercifully, that aura emitted a light that cast the surroundings in a dim glow, augmenting the moonlight enough so that Jeff could see.

Captured and weaponless, Jeff had no concept of a proper escape plan, nor the energy or bravado to enact one. His best hope was for Owen to pop out of the door. Or some help from the elves, or Coach, or maybe even Jellybiscuits.

The only upside was that Ivy hadn't grabbed Carla. Hopefully she'd gotten away, assuming that the trauma of being flung into the tree hadn't broken her. It probably hadn't. She was far scrappier than he'd ever given her credit for. Far scrappier than he, certainly.

A thunderous howl erupted from the confines of the sprawling home beyond the hazy portal. It shook the leaves, and the trunk, and Jeff's scant nerves. The Spookum's call was an earthquake, and it was coming nearer.

"Ooh, he's close," Ivy said, quivering in glee at the prospect of a lasting reunion with her lost love. "Hurry, sweetie," she yelled into the door. A bellow came a second later, answering her summons.

Stomach clenching, Jeff faced the reality that he had to do something or end up as a monster's meal. There were no more opportunities to drag his feet or hope for someone else to save the day. It was now or never. He wasn't ready, but then again, he never would be, even if given a year to prepare.

Hoping for the silence of a ninja, but actually grunting loudly with the effort, Jeff grabbed the paw pinning him down. The fur, or perhaps it was hair, was greasier and wirier than the silkiness he would have imagined that Ivy would have as a monster. Not that he'd ever imagined her as a monster before recent events.

Gritting his teeth, he twisted the paw, while simultaneously kicking upwards, driving the toes of his hiking boot cruelly into her soft underbelly. He kicked again, and again, as he tried to squirm out from beneath the beast.

"Cut it out," Ivy whispered absentmindedly. Her attention primarily remained focused on the door, giddily excited for her mate's return.

Her tail, thicker than Jeff's arm, swung around and whacked him on the head. Ears ringing and world spinning drunkenly, Jeff stopped struggling. The top of his skull throbbed and ached, as if caught in a vise.

"Settle down, snack" Ivy said. She chuckled to herself, pleased by what seemed to be her own personal inside joke.

Hands clamped to his head, Jeff gave it a shake to try to clear it, but that only made the pain worse. His vision swam, casting the world in a blurry canvas of streaky afterimages and dancing multicolored dots.

It was the blurred vision that made him discount the shifting darkness beyond Ivy. But very quickly, it became apparent it was no hallucination. Jeff's imagination could not conjure up such a sight.

It materialized from the dark background, visible only because of the light from the doorway. Jellybiscuits was trampling towards them, a soundless ebony blur.

The creature unfolded before Jeff's blurry eyes, unspooling and spilling forth. The remains of a desiccated rabbit pelt split and fell away, discarded like an old carapace. The thing that emerged was impossibly dark, as if glimpsing the heart of a black hole. It was a void scraped from the ordinary, a peek into someplace else, a realm that was dark and foreboding.

The lime-green eyes remained yet grew into a multitude spread across the beast. Jellybiscuits maintained the general shape of a bunny, in that it was a long-eared creature on four legs. Yet this was a predator, of that there was no doubt.

Inflating into an inky elephant-sized horror, Jellybiscuits shot towards Ivy in absolute silence, as inexorable as a freight train. It lunged, mouth yawning open like the back end of a garbage truck ready to compact whatever was fed into it.

The jaws clamped down, sealing her in their grim embrace. Trapped, the pixie tilted her head back to behold the beast. When she saw what held her, she shrieked in purest terror.

It hoisted her as if she weighed nothing and pulled her straight backwards. Although it had the rough dimensions of a natural animal, Jellybiscuits did not shake its prey or chew it as a wolf or great cat might. Rather, it coldly and mechanically hauled her, deaf to her screams. Conversely, those screams were pure nightmare fuel for Jeff.

Backing away, the shadowy beast receded into a leafy tree, merging into the trunk as it went.

Ivy, clamped in the shadowy midnight jaws, was slowly pulled in with it, magically merging with the tree, inch by inch. She clawed at the ground, frantic to pull herself away, but it was impossible to resist the bleak entity that held her.

When just her face was left, thrust forth from the tree, her eyes met Jeff's. They were pleading, desolate, terrified. Those perfect green eyes then flicked to the elves' tree and she yelled, "Sweetie, help me!" Her final word extended into a wail, abruptly falling into dead silence as the tree swallowed her mouth and face.

Just like that, she was gone, save for a crimson curl dangling from the bark of the tree's trunk.

The curl waggled, since the world shook as her sweetie, the Spookum, emerged from its prison.

34 THE SPOOKUM

It crawled from the portal, wedging its bloated mass through the small opening, violently birthing itself into the forest.

Once free from its confines, the beast stood, drawing itself up to its full height, towering over nine feet tall, without even considering the gnarled and twisted dark antlers that reached from its skull towards the heavens. It was an abomination, a Frankenstein's monster of animals. Its construction defied logic, an amalgam of disparate pieces haphazardly fused together, patches of scales, feathers, fur of all colors, and wrinkled gray skin covering its humanoid body. The Spookum's face was that of an elk, save for its coal black eyes and the ragged fangs thrusting from its snout.

Unlike what Jellybiscuits had revealed itself to be, the Spookum appeared to be entirely tangible and of this world, even if it belonged in a primordial forest of nightmares.

A bellow of anger and hunger tore loose from its slick lips, the trumpeting noise rolling across the dense forest. Sector G12 grew still; every animal, whether magical or mundane, freezing in their tracks in hopes of avoiding the beast's notice.

In mortal terror, Jeff watched the Spookum lumber towards the tree that had swallowed its beloved. It sniffed the single lock of hair protruding from the trunk and wildly clawed the bark. It bellowed again, a howl with Ivy's name buried somewhere within. The tree screamed as well, its voice that of the lost pixie. Confused, the beast stumbled backwards, then turned, looking for a target for its ire.

Its cold blank eyes fell onto Jeff. Sitting in the foul regard of the nightmare monster fueled his instinct for survival, spinning him around and exhorting him into flight, even as his brain struggled to process what was happening.

In a blind rage, it chased him, its heavy footfalls pounding the soil.

It moved ponderously, a battleship of a beast. Yet, its legs were long, swallowing yards with every stride.

Jeff swerved to run towards where he suspected Carla to be. In an ideal world, he could gather her up and carry her away. He had to try. He owed her that much for getting her into this mess.

The passage of the longest twenty seconds of his life brought him to his destination.

But she was gone, disappeared into the night.

That was just as well, since he felt his death closing in. The monster had narrowed the gap between them with surprising swiftness, fast in that way of slashers in movies, walking behind runners but catching them all the same.

The Spookum reached out and slammed him from behind. Barely within reach of the beast, it was hardly a nudge by the standards of its might, yet it was more than enough to send him spinning to the ground.

Desperate and despairing, he scrambled forward, dragging himself between two trees. They had grown close together, leaving too little room for the Spookum's antlered head to thrust far enough into the space to snare him in its snapping jaws. Undaunted, it reached a clawed paw in and grabbed his kicking foot, drawing him out from his short-lived sanctuary.

Mesmerized, he gazed upon its dripping fangs. Staring horrid death in the face, he sobbed, for this was truly the end.

A single shot ripped the overwhelming stillness of the night, tearing loose an explosion of fur along the Spookum's long, thick neck. It staggered back, roaring in pain, or anger, or both.

Over to Jeff's right, Carla was propped against the trunk of a maple, pulling the Glock's trigger. But it was for naught, since there were no more bullets.

35 AN INTERLUDE OF ELVES

Yoric fingered the red curl bursting from the tree, twirling the lock around his pale index finger. Sniffing it, he observed, "Smells like coconut." Touching the silky tress, he felt true regret, which was not an emotion he was inclined towards. However, he had lusted after the pixie, and now that would never be.

Above the curl, claw marks were gouged into the bark, scoring the underlying wood. A red oozy discharge seeped from the torn bark.

Ackley leaned close, placing his pointed ear against the tree. Morose sobs and bitter screams poured from the wood in equal measure. Somewhere within, Ivy was supernaturally entombed. He nodded thoughtfully, satisfied at a job well done. The pixie would no longer be a bother. Unlike Yoric, he had no regrets.

They gazed speculatively at the tree, their majestic faces displaying a range of emotions, although what they were was difficult to decipher. If anything, the most certain might be satisfaction. Of pity, there was no sign. Their pace of consideration was leisurely. They were in no hurry.

Despite the pain and trauma involved, they had fully recovered from their forced passage through the remnants of the orb. Elves are a hardy bunch.

"Jellybiscuits did good work," observed Yoric.

"Their kind always does," agreed Ackley. His massive obsidian blade flickered in his hand, first solidly there and then gone. It shimmered, fading in and out of reality, as if it couldn't decide if it was needed.

A single bang echoed through the foliage. Somewhere, wings fluttered as a bird took to the sky. Or perhaps a bat. Or, considering that it occurred within the eerie confines of G12, it might have been something far darker, more cryptic in nature.

"We could leave them," suggested Yoric, letting his hand drop away from the curl that was the sole remaining physical evidence of Ivy's existence. "Let the Spookum finish them off." He gazed into the surrounding forest, his attention purposefully directed towards the exact opposite compass point from where the shot had originated. His brows were intently furrowed, as if watching the best scene from his favorite movie. "Now that we're free again, the sanctuary will draw the beast back into its prison soon enough. We need not intervene."

"I suppose," answered Ackley, his voice trailing off. The indigo elf's sharp inhuman visage held a very human emotion, that of doubt. His gaze lost focus, lids lowering, as he viewed the forest through the eyes of its animals. For a moment, he watched the Spookum through the eyes of a terrified shrew.

"Then we wouldn't have to deal with the humans anymore," offered Yoric, in the manner of someone suggesting restaurant options to an old friend, knowing they probably wouldn't be interested.

Ackley drew himself up straight. His centuries of soldiering had crafted him into a being who chose duty over convenience, without fail. That's just what a general does. "Our duty is to contain the beast."

Yoric shrugged, quickly becoming indifferent to whatever they did next. "That's true, but we could contain the Spookum after it finishes them. Feels like less pointless hassle for us."

"We could, I suppose. Our directives are somewhat loose in regard to the value of a few humans here and there," said Ackley. Again, the vast obsidian broadsword was in his hand, having materialized of its own will from the ether. It quivered in the night air, eager to be hefted, to be swung, to bite. Its name was Banderhaunt. It was a cursed blade, and thirsty.

What conscience or intellect it could be said to have, if any, tired of this forest sentry work, and yearned for war. Its hold over Ackley was strong, perhaps stronger than the grip duty held on him.

"I'd have to find the paperwork assigning us to this tiresome mortal station and peruse the various subordinate clauses," said Yoric. He waved an elegant hand, its fingernails sharp as razors. "I honestly don't care either way."

Although the way forward was clear as crystal in his mind, Ackley feigned intense thought, as if their next move was truly a coin flip, at the whims of random chance.

After a moment, he said, "Come," and marched into the forest, Banderhaunt leading the way.

Rolling his eyes majestically, Yoric strolled behind, hands in his pockets, eager to be done with this tedious business.

36 JUST ANOTHER DAY AT THE OFFICE

The bright moon, gathering clouds, and the reaching branches aligned just so, bathing Carla in moonlight. It was as if the night and the forest had collaborated to shed a spotlight upon her.

From his nearby vantage point, Jeff could see her clearly, which was an awful thing.

He received a completely clear view of the horrid moment the Spookum lowered itself and took an exploratory bite from her right thigh. Its teeth, like razor chisels, sliced through the meat, fat, and skin like a spoon through soft serve ice cream.

An inarticulate cry of horror sprang from her throat as Carla battered her fists against the Spookum's head, mashing her knuckles on its jagged antlers. Her hands careened off the monster's thick skull, doing nothing to pause its languid chewing. The massive jaw bobbed up and down, the monster savoring its snack.

Better you than me, Jeff thought, although he was mortified by the notion, and instantly dismissed it, denying its inherent truth while recasting it into a poor attempt at gallows humor.

While mentally kicking himself for cowardice, Jeff's body surprised him by grabbing up a fallen knobby branch from the underbrush. Hefting the yard-long gnarled bough, thick as his upper arm, he again felt the call to heroism. Without further thought, and with no plan in mind, he charged the beast.

Swinging it like a baseball bat, he brought the thick limb around in a wide arc and struck the monster's head, connecting near the base of its antlers. The impact ran up his arms and shook his shoulders, letting him know he made solid contact.

The Spookum stood, its head rising higher and higher above the forest floor, impossibly massive. Antlers scraping the canopy, it slowly turned, directing itself towards him.

Black eyes, shiny like polished coal, locked onto Jeff's own. For the barest moment he could see the young man the Spookum had once been, before the pixie had led him astray. Before the curse twisted him into the monster he now was. There was guileless innocence there, a yearning for love, a prayer for release. But a dreadful veil quickly dropped over its horrid face, wiping away the past, leaving only bloodlust as the remains.

Its bloody maw, which was so like that of an elk, although crammed with a predator's sharpened teeth, yawned wide. Through the shreds of meat clinging to the gaps between its fangs, it bellowed. The enraged roar might have come from a Tyrannosaurus in a summer blockbuster, but was instead inches from Jeff's face, carried on an outpouring of rancid breath.

His sympathetic nervous system pushed to the limit, Jeff's body raced to produce and disseminate every molecule of adrenaline it possibly could. Heart racing and blood freezing in his veins, he nearly dropped his makeshift weapon. Yet, miraculously, he didn't drop it. Rather, he reached up and struck the monster again, jamming the knobby branch into its grotesque face.

There was a satisfying crunch, but no apparent harm done. The Spookum gave its head a quick shake, and by the time it had refocused, Jeff had scuttled off, into the snug hollow between the broad trunks of a multi-stem tree several yards away.

Crammed into the tight space, he felt a shred of hope. There was only one gap between the trunks sufficiently wide for the Spookum to reach its thick arm through. And with only that one avenue to defend, it seemed possible to fend it off until help arrived. It had worked in the movie *300*, anyway.

The Spookum appeared at the gap in the trunks, peering

hungrily inside. Its shoulders were a yard wider than the opening. Between that and its crown of antlers, the Spookum's ability to invade Jeff's snug sanctuary was limited, as the monster's vast size worked against it.

Pressing his back against the rough bark to gain every inch of reprieve possible, Jeff held the branch out, hoping to batter the creature's grasping paws away.

The monster studied the tree, its dark gaze traveling over every inch of bark and branch before returning to Jeff. It snuffled, greedily inhaling his panic sweat, tasting his fear. A long tongue, coated with blood and ichor, dangled from its panting mouth.

It then planted its massive paws upon the two trunks framing the opening and pushed with a casual, unrelenting strength not found in a standard earthly being. The tree trembled, the branches and leaves overhead rustling as if murmuring their concerns.

With a sickening crack, one of the trunks split and tipped drunkenly to the side, allowing space enough to admit the Spookum.

Knobby branch in hand and battling a wave of nausea that threatened to empty his stomach onto his boots, Jeff steadied himself.

He frantically searched the several interconnected trunks, hoping for a gap that might allow him to get out. He intended to run, fast and far, without looking back. While that might seem to be running for his life, it would actually be heroically leading the Spookum away from Carla. That would be the way he would remember it, anyway, should he survive.

Alas, there was no other exit. He was trapped.

Carla's blood on its chin, the Spookum drew an arm back, its claws gleaming in the moonlight. It intended to impale Jeff to pull him out, like using a fork to get the last olive from the jar.

As the Spookum cocked its hairy arm, Jeff jabbed it with the branch, as if it were a lance and he were a knight. He was going out swinging. His dad would be proud. More importantly, Owen would be proud.

From there, it all happened so quickly, faster than he could process.

The Spookum screamed. Not a challenging bellow or roar of fury, but rather a wail of surprised irritation. The howl changed quickly, expressing pain and frustration.

The cry was not because of Jeff's timid pokes with the knobby branch. That was an insignificance to a monster of accursed brawn and wretched claws such as this.

The elves had arrived, a magnificent fairy cavalry. They were hacking at the beast. The indigo elf swung a sword of jagged midnight, while the lighter elf wielded a blade that gleamed, and could only have been carved from a fallen star. They moved in an incomprehensible flurry that Jeff could only partially decipher later, recalling flashes in bits and pieces that lived in his dreams and nightmares.

The Spookum flailed at them with mighty swipes of butcher-knife claws that could disembowel a bear. Each of its roundhouse swings crawled through the air, pitifully slow compared to the speed of the elves as they darted about. The duo moved at the speed of harmful desire, sliding under swipes, severing chunks from the beast with their fearsome blades.

As they chopped away at the raging monster, the elves looked almost bored. This creature that was a mortal terror to Jeff was just another day at the office for them. The cursed abomination was simply too slow to present a challenge to their inhuman reflexes.

The battle raged for an eternity of a few dozen seconds,

concluding before a hundred panicked heartbeats had rattled Jeff's chest. The Spookum wailed in pain and fury, crashing to the forest floor. The elves chopped some more, flinging gore and meat everywhere. Eventually, the monster ceased moving. The elves stood over it, not even breathing heavily.

A moment passed as the elves serenely reflected over the Spookum's tattered remains, and Jeff sought to control his panting and slow his thundering heart.

"Is it dead?" Jeff asked, slowly creeping out of the cover of the protective tree trunks. He craned his neck to view the mangled pile of fur, scales, and flesh, yet was careful to keep the elves as a barrier between him and the beast. If movies were to be believed, such creatures always popped up one last time, right before the ending credits.

Ackley's attention moved away from the Spookum and towards the haunted blade in his hands. He did not answer.

"It can't die," said Yoric, sparing a single disdainful look for Jeff before returning his baleful regard to the Spookum.

That wasn't reassuring.

With idle cruelty, Yoric poked the Spookum with his shining sword. The wicked tip sank several inches in. The elf twisted the blade, but the monster didn't respond. "As we said, it is cursed. It will heal. It will always heal."

Silent as a tomb, Jellybiscuits coalesced from the darkness. The creature was a scrap of bleakest midnight, once again wearing its bunny suit. That costume was now even less convincing, the ragged hide torn along the belly, flapping loose to reveal the black eternity within.

A grim automaton, the black bunny grabbed the Spookum by its massive ankle and towed it away. In their wake, stray bloody bits and ragged black smears decorated the grass, reminders of the night's gory escapades.

Mottled blood and scraps of meat clung to Ackley's black

broadsword. Fascinated, he tipped the sword to and fro, watching the remains crawl along the blade. A grim smile rode his face, although present more in his eyes and cheeks than upon his lips.

Shining sword disappearing into the gauzy moonlight, Yoric thrust his hands back into his pants pockets. With a cold, world-weary amusement stemming from centuries of misadventures, he watched the Spookum's insensate removal as it was hauled away by whatever form of being Jellybiscuits was.

Silence reigned until the two monstrous creatures were out of sight, swallowed by Sector G12.

Timidly, as if breaking the prevailing silence might shatter the peace, Jeff said, "So I guess you're really the good guys after all."

Ackley ignored the comment, enraptured as he was by Banderhaunt's coating of gore.

Yoric's face, unbearably handsome but undeniably inhuman, held a scornful look poking out from between the splatters of the Spookum's blood.

Being on the receiving end of that look, Jeff understood that even as they had saved his and Carla's lives, the elves were indifferent to that fact. They had simply been doing their jobs.

The mocking glare from Yoric was all the answer Jeff would receive at that moment, so he checked on Carla.

Although woozy and in great pain, she was conscious, even if it might have been a mercy if she were unconscious. The bite in her thigh was deep, revealing a disturbing flash of splintered pinkish-white bone. Blood gushed in a torrent from the ragged gap in her flesh, its jagged edges marking it as a horrendous bite wound.

During his first glance at the gruesome sight, Jeff feared he might faint, or perhaps vomit. But to his pleasant surprise, the dizziness and nausea passed, and he managed to not even gag. Perhaps he was made of sterner stuff than he had suspected. Indeed, sterner than anyone had suspected.

37 BEHOLD

"I don't completely love the way this turned out," said Coach from the darkness. Her voice was exuberant as always, yet weak, barely above a whisper.

She staggered into view, gingerly holding her left arm with her right hand. Or rather, holding the portion of her left arm that remained attached to her. The arm was a stump, cleaved just below the elbow, the forearm and hand shorn away. A length of paracord was clumsily tied around her bicep as a tourniquet. But that precaution was unnecessary, since the wound was already sealed. The arm ended in a cap of fresh and smooth pink flesh, as if it had been healing for months.

The sight of Coach roused Ackley from his prolonged reverie. As he looked away from his ebony broadsword Banderhaunt, it faded into nonexistence. "Oh yes," he said, "I meant to tidy that up a bit more."

With a dismissive toss of his hand indicating they had more important considerations, Yoric murmured, "You've done enough. There should always be a price to pay for insolence."

Gaping at the wound, Jeff asked, "Was it some sort of magical sacrifice? Like, to undo the trap, or something?"

Furrowing his brow, Ackley replied, "No, I lopped it off," as if the answer was obvious.

"For inconveniencing us with that ridiculous trap," added Yoric helpfully.

"But I also healed it some." Ackley sounded almost defensive.

"Yeah, some. But it still hurts like heck," answered Coach, waving her newly shortened appendage in Ackley's face. Oddly, she'd apparently accepted the necessity of the wound and was more affronted by the nagging discomfort than the crippling. She was very much the sort of person to always roll with the punches.

If Ackley had felt any fleeting wisp of guilt over the maiming, it was already gone, replaced by cold indifference. "There will be phantom pains. Ignore them. I asked Banderhaunt to close the wound as it sliced. You were fortunate it agreed to do so. It would have preferred to make a wound that weeps and cries forevermore, drowning the rest of your days in misery."

"Well, I guess this is better than that. Maybe I'll get a hook," Coach replied, grinning gleefully at Jeff in an unspoken request to share her misplaced merriment. Mouth hanging open in horrified wonder, he looked at her as if she were a six-legged cat. Her characteristic enthusiasm was beyond his comprehension.

Coach poked her stump at Carla. "Will she be okay?"

Glancing at the wounded barista as if he'd never noticed her before, Yoric said, "Whyever do you think I would care?"

Coach shrugged, wincing at the unaccustomed pain it triggered in her newly shortened limb. "Maybe you could heal it some? Just enough to stabilize her until we get her to a hospital." Her appeal had a we're-all-buddies-here quality to it, but Jeff wasn't sure that was actually the case. If the elves had any particular affection for them, he'd missed it so far.

Yoric flapped his hand contemptuously. "I don't even know her."

Sympathy was not amongst Yoric's most pronounced character traits. Nor was it for Ackley, but his senses of duty and fair play were strong.

"I'll help a bit. She's earned it. Within her chest beats a warrior's heart," said Ackley, emphasizing the feminine pronoun. As he spoke, the elf pointedly cast a look of disappointment towards Jeff that made him want to wither away and disappear into the woods.

The indigo elf crouched over Carla, laying his hands upon her wound. She grimaced in pain but quickly calmed. A moment passed, a gauzy aura dancing between his hands and the bite wound. When the elf rose, the bleeding was staunched, although the wound remained raw.

In complete silence, Jellybiscuits reappeared, drifting from the surrounding trees like an ebony fog. It took up a position by Yoric, sitting on its haunches and settling into complete stillness.

"What is that thing, exactly?" asked Jeff, gesturing at the black bunny.

"That is not your concern," answered Yoric, as if offended at the audacity of the question.

"A demon," replied Coach. She might have been completely convinced, or simply taking a shot in the dark. It was impossible to say.

"Perhaps," said Ackley vaguely. He dusted his hands off, sending drops of blood flying. They might have belonged to Carla or the Spookum.

"Where's Ivy?" asked Coach. With childlike glee, she was poking at her nub of an arm, delighted by the magical healing that had sealed the wound, although wincing with every poke.

"She is handled and no longer your concern," said Ackley.

"Indeed," agreed Yoric. He spit on a slim pile of bloody remnants at his feet, an act that felt oddly elegant when he did it. "And you're out of questions. Let's return your comrade Owen, and you'll leave these woods forevermore."

"I don't have to warn you to stay away from here, do I?" asked Ackley. His black eyes bored into Jeff, although not malevolently, but more like a concerned father ensuring his daughter knew not to take rides from strangers.

Jeff rapidly shook his head. "No sir." Once he and Owen left G12, he did not intend to return. Ever.

With Carla slowly limping along, supported by Coach and Jeff, they trekked back to the giant oak tree to collect Owen from wherever he was within its boundless confines.

Cloud cover had moved in, blocking the moon and casting the forest into pitch blackness.

It was the shortest of journeys before the colossal oak was in sight. The tree towered over its neighbors, impossible to miss, even in the darkness of the witching hour.

As they approached, they heard a shuffling, as of a wounded beast stumbling weakly through a tangled mass of fallen leafy branches.

"Ooh, interesting," crooned Yoric. His tone was excited, but there was something else there as well, something that sent shivers down Jeff's spine.

Ackley clucked his tongue in disappointment. "That's unfortunate."

"Let's give them some light, so they can see better," said Yoric. He chuckled, obscene little huffs lost in the night. With a graceful wave of his hand, a soft glow flooded the woods. "Behold," he said, with perverse satisfaction.

38 TAINTED MEAT

A creature stood in the center of the magical fairy light, framed as though it were the star of a Broadway play. Draped in conventional clothes that did not befit a monster, the creature was bereft of color, painted in naught but shades of whites and grays, as if faded by time.

Blinking in the light, it shook its head ponderously. Long white hair stood out from its withered skull.

It was emaciated, a ragged being of bone and tendon. A revenant, hewn from dust and wasted mortal materials.

Although it had been wandering aimlessly, the sight of them gave it purpose. It shambled towards them, drawn like a putrid moth to a flame.

Lurching towards them, the revenant's gait and mannerisms were that of a movie zombie, reaching its gray hands out before it. Its right sleeve was rolled up to the elbow, revealing a desiccated forearm. Both bones, radius and ulna, were clearly visible, accentuated by the scarce, pallid flesh encasing them. The skin was sunken away, a hairless furrow between the bones. The abomination was an anatomy chart in motion.

Although it shambled along with erratic, fitful movements, there was power within its frame. It was plain to see that beneath the withered sheath, great strength flowed.

It wore a cardigan. Although tattered by misadventures, the sweater's fabric was fairly new, not aged and decrepit as the wearer was.

Despite the rest of the revenant being bleached of color, its eyes were a bright blue.

Slowly wobbling towards them, it screeched, "Jeffff, you left me." Its warbling cry was terribly high pitched and horrible to hear, not something meant for this world.

Without doubt, Jeff knew it to be Owen, a realization that

stole his breath, froze his heart, upended his world. His mind shut down, productive thinking paused, brain naught but a maelstrom of terror, dread, and remorse. All he could manage was a ragged gasp of a single word. "Owen."

Ackley pointed an accusing finger at Yoric. "He was clearly in your pantry," said the dark elf.

"It seems so," Yoric observed. He swiveled to face the humans, a look of bemused delight upon his pointed countenance. "Your friend was in the larder, nibbling away at whatever he could find. That seems likely, anyway."

Coach nodded knowingly. After a hesitation, she reversed course and shrugged. "No idea what that means."

"He ate tainted meat," elaborated Ackley. Behind him, the colorless phantom drew closer. Its mouth snapped frantically, the sharp clicking sounds unpleasant to the ear, like nails on a chalkboard.

"No, it's clean meat. Simply from a source you don't personally care for," said Yoric. He patted his lean stomach. Turning a sinister gaze towards the humans, he wiggled his perfect eyebrows. "Hikers taste best. Nice and lean. They usually aren't smokers and tend to be well hydrated."

Coach shook her head to clear it. "Wait, are you cannibals?" she asked, in the same tone she might use to query if they'd attended the same college as her.

The revenant continued its slow shuffle towards them. Jeff's brain remained frozen with horror.

Yoric sneered, which was an expression his face wore naturally, as if he'd been born that way. "It isn't cannibalism, since we aren't human. We're as different from you as you're different from a fawn. And you would eat a fawn wouldn't you?"

Coach refrained from answering, contenting herself with staring at the approaching revenant. Jeff couldn't find his voice to answer, so Carla did it for them. "No."

Yoric waved his hand impatiently. "Very well. What about a cow? You would eat cow."

"Yes," Carla said. She shook loose from Jeff and Coach and began backing slowly away. Within two steps, her injured leg crumpled, spilling her onto the carpet of leaves and twigs.

"There you go," the elf said with delight, as if he'd won an epic debate.

"Although for Owen, it is cannibalism to eat human flesh, obviously," Coach observed, if halfheartedly.

Jeff's stomach lurched dangerously, bile eating away at the top of his throat.

"Yes, of course," Yoric agreed. He thrust a triumphant finger into the air. "But, you see, it isn't cannibalism for me." He smiled, his mouth laden with miniature interlocking ivory daggers.

His world crashing down around him, Jeff watched Owen's slow approach. His best friend's hands were grasping, reaching eagerly towards them. The nails were terribly long, and ragged, as if the only trimming they'd received in years had been from scrabbling at the frame of the immutable exit portal, seeking an escape he obviously did not find. His eyes were wild, erratically bouncing from spot to spot, unable to focus. After every circuit, however, they returned to Jeff, who Owen was guided towards by animal instinct and diseased desire.

"Jefffff," Owen screeched, that single word trailing into infinity, holding all the pain a human soul can contain. Rather, more than it can contain, since this poor creature's agony overflowed. Its anguish had grown so great that it burst the vessel containing it, spilling out into the world.

Experiencing a lightbulb moment, Coach's brown eyes grew wide, electrified by a perceived epiphany. "Okay, wait, so he's a wendigo? Cannibalism turning someone into a monster, that's a wendigo." She couldn't hide the excitement in her voice, not that she really tried.

Ackley's head bobbed side to side in thought, his pale hair flopping. After a pensive pause, he resolutely said, "Not a wendigo."

"No, probably not," Yoric agreed, although he seemed less certain.

"Similar, but no," Ackley added, studying the wraith-like being shambling towards them. "They tend to be more agile, although perhaps he'll grow into it."

Jeff's head spun, his vision dimming around the edges, befuddled by the unreality of these monstrous elves discussing Owen's fate with detached academic interest. Didn't they know what a wonderful person he was? That he had singlehandedly carried Jeff through college? That he'd been his friend through thick and thin? Didn't they care? Of course, they didn't. Humans weren't their concern.

"Then what is he?" asked Coach. Her question was nearly drowned out by a shriek from the approaching abomination.

Ackley's cursed obsidian blade was again in his hand, although whether because he intended to use it on the horror creeping towards them or because he enjoyed holding it was unclear. He said, "As we've said, categorization in such instances is difficult. All circumstances are ultimately unique, and not amenable to your human preoccupation with labeling. That thing shambling towards us is some unique indefinable monstrosity, probably partially a result of the human meat. But also, based on its withered aspect, I'd hazard a guess that centuries probably passed for it within the elven magic of our fortress, even as mere hours passed out here."

With a curt nod, Yoric said, "Good point. Centuries by his perception, yet not for the Spookum, I'd wager."

The pale specter drew closer as the elves continued their

speculative debate. Tears rolled down Jeff's face.

Ackley said, "Yes, reality warps for humans within a fairy realm. Once enclosed, anything could happen if they aren't properly watched over. He probably spent what seemed an eternity, sometimes fleeing the Spookum and sometimes woefully alone."

"I'd imagine it caught him quite often and gobbled him up," said Yoric. He pinched his hands open and closed, thumbs striking fingers, emulating little mouths that he aggressively pushed towards Jeff.

"Certainly," said Ackley, "but then the warped reality resurrected him and the cycle began anew. He's quite mad now, obviously. Cursed and insane. It's a shame, since he was the only one of them worth anything."

As they bantered, speculating on the generation of the wretched being before them, Jeff's world continued collapsing. Horrified and forlorn, he couldn't speak. Now who would be the best man at his wedding? For that matter, who would introduce him to his future wife? Who would he play pinochle with at the old folks' home someday? Owen deserved so much more than this. If he hadn't played the hero, this wouldn't have happened. Conversely, perhaps they'd all be dead and the Spookum and Ivy would be roaming the countryside, sowing carnage across the fertile soils of humanity.

Carla sobbed. As if that woeful sound had provided tacit permission, Jeff did as well, his breath hitching violently in his chest amidst his weeping.

Grimacing towards the thing that had been Owen, Coach simply said, "Yikes."

"Jeffffff, where were you?" Owen screeched, his voice an acute trill. Ever so slowly, it had drawn close to them, its clutching hands, like withered pincers, mere yards away.

Jellybiscuits stepped forward, unfolding to human size, a

bleak shade in the vague form of a humanoid rabbit. It intercepted Owen and steered him back towards the tree, ushering him along like an attendant helping a dementia patient back to their room.

The revenant that had been Owen resisted but feebly, craning its head almost completely backwards to stare at Jeff as it was led away, sometimes howling his name in a high-pitched shriek.

His hands now empty, accursed sword returned to wherever it dwelled when not in use, Ackley snapped his fingers before Jeff's face. Receiving no response beyond tears and woe, the elf spoke to Coach. "Leave now and stay away. Keep the loggers away from here forevermore, or we won't be responsible for the deaths. You've been warned."

"Not sure how to do that," said Coach. She was distracted, attention wrapped up in the retreating revenant.

"Have him say he's investigated the area and found the wood to be rotted," said Ackley, hiking a finger at Jeff.

"Perhaps a virus of some sort," offered Yoric. He was already moving away, all interest in the humans and their dramas completely expended.

Dire warning infused into the words, Ackley said, "Howsoever you do it, just have them stay away."

Finding his voice at last, Jeff croaked, "What about Owen?" There was so much he wanted to say, to explain how important his friend was, how they had to do something. But no further words came.

Yoric gave a gleeful shrug, basking in the human misery he was privileged to be witnessing.

With a tinge of sorrow and regret, if not pity, Ackley said, "He's forever lost to you. Best to forget him. He's our problem now." He was backing away, letting Jeff and company move into the rearview mirror of his long life.

"Don't make him live like that," Jeff begged. He found he'd sagged to his knees. Agonized, he choked on his next words. "If you can't fix him, would you end his life? Peacefully? Painlessly?"

Although only several yards away, the elves were receding from view. Ackley shrugged. "Hadn't considered it yet. We'll figure something out."

"Don't worry your ugly little head about it," Yoric said. He cackled, an ugly sentiment wrapped in mellifluous tones.

Then they were gone, dissipating in the blink of an eye. The mammoth oak tree remained, but the door was locked.

39 A YEAR LATER

Life can change a lot in a year, and it had. Quite a bit.

Jeff was out of the logging industry, having given his notice almost immediately after what he thought of as The Incident. The only legacy he left at Cayuga Logging and Reforestation was to convince his Uncle Chet to stay away from Sector G12.

He'd marched into Chet's office armed with fake reasons, including tree viruses and wood rot. Perhaps even a colony of endangered bald eagles. But they weren't necessary. Chet had gratefully accepted his Glock back and agreed to avoid the area. Uncle Chet was no genius, but he could tell something had happened. Something he didn't want any part of.

Jeff moved away from Cayuga and got a job selling cars. Much like trees, he didn't know anything about cars but selling them came fairly natural to him. Or as natural as anything did. At least he could tell a Honda from a Toyota better than he could discern an oak from a maple. It helped that the vehicles had shiny metal emblems announcing their lineage.

One night, he met a woman named Noelle. They began dating, and during a fateful weekend shortly thereafter, he finally lost his virginity. It was a burden happily discarded, even if rather anticlimactically. Anticlimactic for Noelle, that is. Not for Jeff. He had a great time.

Noelle was in dental school. She aspired to be an orthodontist, just as her mother was.

The notion of becoming a dentist struck Jeff as a good one, although he envisioned himself as more of a tooth cleaner and cavity filler than a fancy orthodontist. Noelle even had some administrative contacts at her dental school, so if he worked hard enough and aced his exams, he might even get in.

However, as the months passed and he saw how hard Noelle worked, he wasn't actually sure dentistry was for him. But maybe. Regardless, he and Noelle were happy together.

In the fall, they decided to take a road trip, spending a long weekend driving through the countryside, enjoying the fall foliage. Jeff proposed visiting Cayuga, so he could meet up with some old friends.

Friday morning, he left Noelle at the hotel and went into town. He promised not to be back for at least six hours, since she needed to study. Or, if he did come back, he was sworn to silence. That was fine, he had people to see, places to visit.

Driving through town, he reminisced about the fun times he'd had with Owen. And with Carla, and even with Ivy. Jabroni's Pizza wasn't open for lunch yet, or he would have gone in for a slice.

His first stop was Winterbottom's Coffee Shop. Carla was there, making lattes and pouring coffee, just as before. But unlike before, she moved with obvious pain, leaning on a cane to limp the few necessary steps behind the counter. She was forever wounded, and barely acknowledged him, despising him as the person responsible for the misadventures that led to her being flung against a tree and chewed on by a monster. After an uncomfortable moment of weathering her spiteful glares and sullen silence, Jeff slunk away, coffee in hand.

Despite the friction, he enjoyed seeing her. Even though it opened old wounds, they were wounds he wanted opened. He wasn't ready to move on yet. Seeing someone that had shared the bizarre experience confirmed that he wasn't insane. It was no figment of his imagination.

Sadly, he'd never seen Coach after that fateful day and perhaps never would again. After dropping Jeff and Carla off at the hospital, she'd driven off, mumbling about how difficult it was to steer with one hand.

Uncle Chet and Jeff's aunt were out of town. On one hand, that was good, since it spared him the awkward task of visiting and forcing everyone into pretending they'd missed one another. On the other hand, it was bad, since he would have liked to introduce them to Noelle, thereby proving he had an actual girlfriend, something that Chet had speculated might never happen.

After leaving the cafe, Jeff drove to his former company's newest worksite. It was a waste of time. No one cared he was there, not even Pinkie, the foreman whom he'd always thought he was sort of friends with. It seems he'd been wrong.

That only left one stop. He'd saved it for last, building his bravery even as he'd dragged his feet.

Stepping into Sector G12, Jeff got that same outlandish feeling, as if trodding on an alien world, even if one very visually similar to ours.

The reds, browns, yellows, and oranges of the fall leaves became less consistent at the border to G12, giving way to frequent patches of green or black leaves. This area knew no real passage of time through the regular churn of seasons, not in the conventional sense. It had its own rules.

As he walked, a haggard black fox followed him, monitoring his progress from the cover of the pines. It darted along through the undergrowth just off the trail, making no attempt at stealth.

Even when he couldn't fully see the fox, he could detect its lime-green eyes glaring at him. It looked like an escapee from the mange ward, coated as it was in matted black fur the consistency of an antique pelt from a trapper's cabin. Jellybiscuits wore a different coat these days, experimenting with the guise of a new animal.

This was the third time Jeff had been back. The first time, he'd been ignored. The second time, he'd been welcomed, if that's what you called a sullen, begrudging, dismissive greeting by a pair of new elves.

Based on their physical similarities, he judged them to be siblings, a brother and sister.

The pair were huge, tall and wide, with bright orange eyes, chalk skin, and shaggy black hair. Each was strikingly attractive but vaguely androgynous, just as their predecessors had been.

The male had hands like hams, shoulders so wide as to doubtless make it a struggle to fit through doorways, and a voice deep and powerful as an earthquake. He was thoroughly terrifying, although his sister was perhaps even more so. She was the more talkative of the duo, although her beauty, imposing build, and barely concealed irritation at Jeff's visits combined to make him feel intensely insecure in her presence.

Striding through the carpet of dead leaves, he passed the tree that served as Ivy's prison. It was easily distinguishable by the lock of red hair sprouting from its trunk.

As he walked by, Jeff could hear Ivy's voice calling to him from her wooden penitentiary, begging for his help. He quickened his pace, ignoring her. Her petitions faded with distance, but not before turning into maniacal gibberish.

Abruptly, the lady elf was at his side, keeping pace as he approached the massive oak. Neither she nor her presumptive sibling had ever offered a name. Jeff thought of her as Carol, which felt like a fun, ironic name for a towering supermodel who had ample capacity to end your life on a whim.

Carol said, "It does you no good to come here."

"I just want to see him."

When they were thirty yards from the elves' tree, Carol held up a hand, stopping Jeff in his tracks. "This is close enough," she said.

He didn't consider ignoring her command, not even for a millisecond. Just ahead, the portal into the base of the tree hung open. In the gloom within, a pair of bright blue eyes stared out, impaling Jeff on their cold glare.

"He can't come out when the sun is up," she said. In her hand was a spear, eight feet long, tipped with a shining silver point that looked as if it could pierce a tank. It had slid into existence when they halted.

Jeff said, "He's an evil monster now, I suppose." He was trying to talk himself out of ever returning. If he could convince himself Owen was truly gone, and these were just his monstrous animated remains, he could move on with a clear conscience. Not that emotions and feelings were that easy to orchestrate, but he could try.

"He's a being of pure hunger now. Is hunger evil? I think not. Many creatures crave human flesh, their hunger gnawing at them and driving them on. He is but one of millions," Carol replied. She sounded bored.

That was a fine point, Jeff thought. You don't begrudge a predator for following its natural inclination. Viewed from that angle, it was easier to envision the blue-eyed creature in the tree as something other than Owen, and therefore no longer his concern.

"Wouldn't it be better to end his life? Like, a mercy killing. You know, compassionately." He'd mentioned that the first time he'd met these new elves, but they'd shown little interest.

"That isn't for me to judge. The ineffable fates may have crafted him thusly for a reason. His future is for the fairy council to decide. But just between you and I, they take forever to make such decisions. Most such queries linger for decades, until they are no longer of interest. As for me, I simply guard." Carol checked her watch, the newest model smart watch from Apple.

"Well, I guess we helped capture Ivy, so there's that." Jeff was hoping for reassurance, confirmation of any kind that this wasn't all for nothing. That Owen's sacrifice had been worthwhile.

Carol shrugged. It was regal and lovely. Her midnight hair stirred in the breeze. It smelled of the ocean. "Yes, I suppose. Although, she wasn't causing much mayhem really, just another drunk harlot in the world, goading on the Spookum, her idiot boyfriend."

Mildly deflated, Jeff saw the sense in that. "I guess." The mention of the Spookum gave him chills. Presumably it was ensconced somewhere within the elven tree fortress, held firmly until the next time it escaped.

"Your bumbling misadventures gave us another abomination to look after, which was a job ill done." She gestured with her spear towards the door where the revenant that had been Owen lurked.

"So, you admit he's an abomination?"

With a hint of irritation, she replied, "A better word might be an annoyance. But, on the positive side, it helps my brother and I stay occupied during our time here."

Jeff nodded, interested to hear the confirmation they were siblings.

Second passed. They were not friendly seconds, spent at ease with a companion. These were seconds that were loudly ticking, marching towards the end of his visit. He had already worn out his welcome, Carol's minor irritation being a death knell to continued conversation.

Meanwhile, the frigid blue eyes remained affixed to Jeff, never wavering, never blinking.

Her tone and demeanor highlighting a clear intent to begin wrapping up this visit, Carol said, "Don't feel bad for Owen. Or do, I don't care either way." She scratched in the dirt with the butt of her spear. "I suppose you can take solace in the fact that he and the Spookum are companions. It's an apt pairing, actually. The Spookum is a being of instincts. It is reactive, and rarely does it seem to think in much detail, instead preferring to do what it is told. As such, it's an excellent minion. Your friend, though, is a thinker, a schemer, a leader. So, the Spookum once followed Ivy, but now follows Owen."

Carol nudged Jeff, her elbow striking his shoulder. It looked like the lightest of bumps, but he almost went flying. "It seems your friend has replaced you with a newer, better sidekick."

That was sad, obviously, but also somewhat reassuring. Owen had moved on and so should he. On the plus side, Jeff supposed he had become Noelle's sidekick, and that was something to be thankful for.

Jeff dared to hope the revenant that had once been Owen retained some vestige of his personality and would steer the Spookum away from trouble. He had been a hero, after all, not just a leader.

Yet, looking into those frigid blue eyes, he feared the opposite. Perhaps Owen truly was a monster now. And, with proper planning and reasoning, who knows what two such monsters were capable of?

He ruminated on that, trying to find the best way to voice these thoughts and concerns, and to do so quickly and succinctly before Carol ushered him away. But he took too long. When he turned back to the elf, she was already gone. It was too late. And, gazing back towards the door, he saw it had closed. There was nothing more he could do. Regardless, the wind blew, some branches rustled, and the Earth continued spinning.

As Jeff turned and trudged away, he was watched by the horrid inky-black fox, its lime-green eyes never blinking as they tracked his every step. He marched with a sense of finality, knowing he would never again return to these woods. This chapter of his life was closed. His best friend was forever lost to him, which made him profoundly sad, yet he drew a perverse comfort in the knowledge that his memories of Owen would never fade, since the hero-turned-monster would undoubtedly continue to visit his nightmares. If Jeff was very lucky, the fond memories would stay strong, outshining those nightmares. But he wasn't sure he would be so fortunate. Time would tell.

Jeff walked out of Sector G12 daring to hope for the best. That was all a human could do.

ABOUT THE AUTHOR

DS LaLonde is a pen name for Dave and Sara LaLonde, a married writing team who live in Northern Virginia with their child, cats, and dog. They completed graduate training in the biological sciences and have worked in biomedical research, veterinary diagnostics, and national security. DS enjoys reading, writing, and ruminating on the existence of cryptids.

Instagram: @ds.lalonde.author
Twitter: @glawackus
Bluesky: @glawackus.bsky.social
Email: DS.LaLonde.author@gmail.com